ALSO BY DARRYL BOLLINGER

TREATMENT
PLAN

A MEDICAL THRILLER

Darryl Bollinger

JNB
PRESS

Copyright © 2023 by Darryl Bollinger

JNB Press
Waynesville, NC

www.jnbpress.com

Printed in the United States of America

First Trade Edition: November 2023

ISBN 978-0-9989975-4-4

For those who fight fraud and corruption in health care.

TREATMENT
PLAN

True justice lies not in the power of the mighty, but in the compassion and strength of those who rise to defend the voiceless and shield the vulnerable from the shadows of injustice.

— Warren Thompson

1

It was quiet in Hank's Galley as Jon Cruz eased onto a stool at his usual spot near the end of the dingy bar. As always, he chuckled at the painting of an old man resembling Ernest Hemingway hanging behind the bar. Below the lit, gilded frame was a hand-lettered sign saying "Hank," the founder's name.

When Addie, the current owner and his boss spotted him from the other end of the bar, she turned and fiddled with the sound system. As he sat, it dawned on him that it had been quiet for too long in more ways than one. Soon, Eva Cassidy's sultry voice drifted out from the speakers in the far corners of the room, her rendition of "Nightbird" mesmerizing.

He watched as Addie drew a fresh beer from the tap, then headed toward him. She wore a Hank's Galley T-shirt tied up above her waist, displaying a flat, tanned midsection sporting a seahorse tattoo above her navel. Although one of Jon's many jobs at the bar and marina was maintaining order, Addie didn't suffer fools gladly. As a result, he seldom needed to don that hat. She brought the frosty mug over and set it in front of him with a slight nod, then turned to check on other customers.

Out of the corner of his eye, Jon noticed a pony-tailed stranger walk in. Like everyone in the bar, the visitor wore sandals, shorts, and a T-shirt. He looked around the room, then went to the other end of the bar to Ricky, a young, bearded regular wearing a Marlins ball cap. Ponytail didn't sit but stood next to Ricky as they chatted, his eyes continuing to scan the room.

Jon thought he seemed nervous, which unsettled him. He leaned back on his stool to get a better look and noticed the faint bulge in the stranger's waistband underneath his T-shirt. It was the unmistakable imprint of a pistol.

Automatically, Jon felt for his gun, then realized it was still on the boat. The stranger headed toward the front door, Ricky behind him. Jon caught Addie's attention and motioned her over. "Hold my dinner till I get back. Shouldn't be long."

Addie nodded and walked away. Jon waited till they were outside, then rose and trailed behind them.

Outside, he looked left toward the marina and momentarily debated going to the boat to get his pistol. Then, he heard voices to his right. They came from a vacant lot next to Hank's, unlit and in the opposite direction from his boat.

Quietly, he stepped toward the voices. As he got closer to the shadows beyond the bar, he could make out Ricky's voice.

"That's all I've got, man. You know I'm good for it."

A deeper voice with a Hispanic accent replied. "I'll be back tomorrow for the rest. You better have it."

Carefully, Jon peeked around the corner of the building. Ponytail, his back to Jon, held out a small baggie to Ricky.

Jon gauged the distance and thought he could surprise the stranger before he could draw and turn. He stepped around the corner and took two quick strides toward him.

When Ponytail saw Ricky's surprised expression, he reacted immediately. He pulled a gun, wheeled, and leveled it toward Jon. He was quicker than Jon figured.

"Hacer alto." Stop. "That's close enough."

Jon skidded to a halt, one step short of where he needed to be. He held his hands up. "A gusto." At ease.

Ponytail jerked his head back and seemed surprised that Jon answered in Spanish.

"You don't want to shoot an agente federal," Jon said.

Ponytail snorted. "I don't see no badge. No gun, neither."

Jon hesitated, buying a few seconds to calculate the remaining distance and time to the stranger. It would be close. He nodded toward the shadows. "The one over in the shadows behind your boy has both."

Ricky and Ponytail turned to confirm. Jon lunged and kicked out at the stranger's wrist, knocking the gun out of his hand. Jon spun sideways, hit him in the back, and knocked him to the ground, where Jon pounced and applied a wrist lock.

"Puto," Ponytail said, his face in the dirt. "You can't do this. I have my rights."

Jon applied additional pressure, which forced a grunt out of the stranger. "Yeah, then who's on the ground eating dirt?"

Jon spotted a length of electrical wire on the ground, then looked at Ricky. "Hand me that piece of wire." Ricky picked it up and gingerly handed it to him.

"You're fucked, man," Ponytail said to Ricky.

Jon tied the wire around Ponytail's wrists behind his back. Taking a deep breath, he stood and roughly pulled Ponytail up on his feet. Spying a utility pole, he pushed him over and tied him to it.

He turned to Ricky, frozen like his feet were nailed to the ground. "Go home. You were never here, understand? I'll talk to you tomorrow."

Ricky slinked away to the parking lot without answering. Jon pulled out his cell phone and placed a call.

"This is Jon Cruz over at Hank's Galley. You need to send a couple of uniforms over to pick up a dirtbag I caught dealing. He's not going anywhere. I'll be inside eating dinner."

He hung up, and Ponytail spat. "I'll be back on the streets before you finish eating."

"Probably," Jon said. "But I better not see you here again. If I do, you'll be hoping the police get to you before I do."

He walked over and picked up the stranger's gun, cleared it, and stuffed it in his pocket. He picked up the baggie containing four pills and held it up. He wasn't sure but guessed it was oxy—short for oxycodone, the street drug of choice in this area.

He stuffed the baggie into Ponytail's pocket. "You dropped these."

Ponytail's eyes widened. "That's not mine. Cops can't plant shit on people."

"You're right. But I'm not a cop."

Back inside, Jon returned to his stool.

"What was that about?" Addie said when she walked over.

Before he could answer, flashing blue lights appeared through the window. Addie looked at them, then back at Jon.

"I called them to pick up someone I left outside, tied to a utility pole." He stood to go out. "Give me fifteen minutes, then place my dinner order. I want to eat before I clock in."

Outside, he met with the two uniforms and gave them the gun he confiscated. He told them he'd interrupted an apparent drug sale. When Ponytail pulled a gun on him, Jon disarmed him and tied him up. During the scuffle, the other party ran, and Jon didn't get a good look at them.

After the cops left, Jon went back inside. Addie set the plate of food and a fresh beer in front of him. She drew another beer and put it on the bar next to Jon's. "Well?" she asked as she folded her arms.

Jon glanced over at the other beer, then shoved an onion ring into his mouth. Before he could say anything, Detective Beth Keller slid onto the empty stool next to him. The petite brunette wore her standard work outfit—tan slacks and a dark blazer.

"Get you anything to go with your beer, Detective?" Addie asked.

"No, thanks. I'll just have some of his." She reached over, took an onion ring off Jon's plate, and popped it into her mouth.

Addie didn't move. Beth turned to Jon. "I was on my way home when I overheard the call requesting uniforms here. What's going on?"

He pointed to his grouper sandwich. "You want some of this too?"

"No thanks," she said as she grabbed another onion ring.

He shook his head and took a bite of his sandwich. He finished chewing before speaking.

"A sketchy looking stranger came in, looked around, and left before sitting. I followed him outside and caught him in the middle of a drug deal in the vacant lot next door. He pulled a gun. I took him down and called it in."

"He claimed you said you were a federal agent," Beth said.

Jon shrugged, washing his food down with the beer. "I said there was one in the shadows. When he turned to see, I disarmed him."

"Who was his customer?"

Jon shook his head. "Don't know. He ran as soon as I came round the corner and confronted the dealer. I was kind of busy trying to disarm the guy pointing a gun at me."

Addie looked at Jon and cocked her head slightly but stayed silent while Beth continued.

"And a piece of wire just happened to be within reach?" Beth said.

"All sorts of junk in a vacant lot. What's going on with you?"

She took another onion ring, then stared at him. Finally, she shook her head. Addie mimicked her expression, then walked away.

"Someone dumped another overdose. I went by the hospital to interview him, but he was gone by the time I got there."

"Gone? He didn't make it?"

"No, he survived. Well enough to walk out on his own. No ID. A John Doe."

"Probably already back in rehab. Rinse and repeat." He knew that for most addicts, rehab was a revolving door, which suited the treatment centers. Typical of the U.S. health care system, you made money from doing things, not from fixing things.

Beth took a drink from her beer, then glared at him. "So, you don't know who the customer was?"

He shook his head, stuffing another onion ring in his mouth before she finished them "Nope," he mumbled.

She exhaled. "Why don't I believe you?" She paused, then continued. "Let's try another question. How are you doing, Jon?"

"I'm fine. Got a nice place to live. Do a little fishing, and work here as a security guard and handyman. Good food, cold beer. Life is good."

She stared at him with a jaundiced eye. "You're as full of shit as a Christmas turkey."

He had to admit his current position was a dramatic change. Two years ago, he was a federal agent chasing down bad guys for defrauding the government out of millions. He'd been through more in the last two years than most people dealt with in a lifetime.

"I think you're afraid to confront your feelings."

He started to answer, but what she said hit home. Maybe he was avoiding dealing with all that had happened. It was easier that way. Besides, there's nothing he could do to change things. It is what it is. "Thanks for the evaluation, Dr. Keller."

She finished her beer, reached into her purse, and fished out her wallet. He put his hand on her arm to stop her.

"Look. I appreciate what you're trying to do. But I'm fine." He straightened up and grinned. "This one's on me. One of my fringe benefits here is an employee discount."

Staring at him, she put her wallet back in her purse and slid off the bar stool. "You know, sometimes I could strangle you."

He chuckled. "You're one of the few people I know who could do that."

A thin smile cracked her stern facade. She shook her head and said, "You can't take care of others until you take care of yourself, Jon."

He watched her walk away. He wiped his mouth, put the napkin on the empty plate, and slid it forward, catching Addie's attention down the bar.

"Beth didn't stay long," she said as she cleaned the bar in front of him. "You piss her off? Again?"

He shrugged. "She did threaten to strangle me."

"I'd put my money on her. She's just worried about you. We all are. You're just too blind to see."

3

Jon finished his beer and walked back to *Trouble No More,* the Grand Banks 42 trawler that had served as his home for the past two years. It was a comfortable boat, stable on the open water. It was a lot for one person to handle, but it was such a good deal he couldn't resist, so he splurged.

He stopped at the gate to punch in the code, opened it, and walked out the dock, hearing the metal gate clang shut behind him. Ten feet past the gangway to his boat, the ginger cat sat, watching him. Jon stopped at the locker next to the gangway and looked down at the double pet food bowl, water on one side, the other empty.

"Waiting on me, huh, Felix? Let's see if I can find anything for you."

The big boat barely rocked when Jon stepped on board. Inside, he turned on some music. "Trouble No More" by Muddy Waters, the inspiration for his boat's name, soon filled the salon.

In the galley, he removed a can of cat food and walked back outside. Felix sat patiently at his dish, watching as Jon knelt and opened the can. He emptied the contents, then stood. "Okay, dinner's served."

The cat stared at him, waiting for Jon to leave.

"Really? After all this time, the least you could do is come over and thank me."

Felix refused to budge. Jon shook his head and walked back onto the boat. As soon as he stepped on board, he turned. The cat cautiously walked over to the food to eat, keeping a wary eye out.

Inside the cabin, Jon paused at the helm to look at the only picture in sight, a framed picture of him and his daughter Megan. It was a photo of happier times on the beach at St. Simons Island, GA. He remembered it as though it were yesterday, even though it had been two years ago.

At the bar, he picked up the nearly empty bottle of tequila, and poured a stiff shot into a small tumbler. He downed half of it, feeling the agave elixir slide down his throat, warming his insides. Booze and blues were his medications of choice.

He removed his pistol and holster from the safe and fastened it to his belt. Up on the flybridge, he placed his glass and phone on the small table and sat. It was a comfortable evening with a slight breeze blowing and the smell of salt air from the ocean only a few blocks away.

Although he could see most of the marina from this vantage point, he still made rounds every evening he worked. He'd met most of the locals and wanted to make his presence felt. It had worked. Those up to no good had learned to steer clear of Hank's, knowing he was watching.

He pulled the pistol out of the holster. It was his favorite, a SIG P229. He'd gotten lax over the last few months and didn't bother carrying it many nights. But, considering what happened a few hours ago, he wasn't going to get caught again without it. Out of habit, he checked the gun, laid it on the table, and picked up his phone for messages.

He kept the ringer turned off, much to the chagrin of those trying to call him. The device was for his convenience to make calls, not for those calling him. Anybody who needed to talk to him knew to leave a message or try to find him at Hank's.

There were several missed calls, including one from Beth. The last message got his attention. He replayed the voice mail on speaker.

"Hey, buddy. Trey here. You're a hard person to track down. Give me a call when you can."

Jon stared at the phone, thinking about Trey Stevens, his old service buddy from Marines Force RECON. They'd been ambushed while on a classified mission in Columbia. In the ensuing firefight, both of them had been wounded. The surviving guerrillas had scattered after the attack, leaving them stranded alone in the jungle. While a bullet had grazed Trey's shoulder, Jon's wound was more serious, ripping through his upper right leg. Trey packed the wound and using his belt, tied a makeshift tourniquet aound the leg. Against all odds, Trey had managed to carry Jon out to to a clearing where they were medevaced out. The medic on the chopper told Jon that he was lucky. Another hour, and they would've been carrying him out in a body bag.

When the two of them left the service, they returned to Cincinnati and lived in the same neighborhood. Jon had gone to work as a Special Agent with the Office of Inspector General in Health and Human Services, otherwise known as HHS-OIG. Trey went to work with a local bank. A few years ago, OIG transferred Jon to Jacksonville, marking the beginning of the end of Jon's career, and his life.

He punched Redial, and Trey answered on the second ring.

"It's been a while," Trey said. "You disappeared after the funeral. I called a few times but never heard back. Last time I tried, the number had been disconnected."

"Sorry. Got a new phone and a new number."

"I tracked Erika down, and she gave me your number. She told me the last she'd heard, you were living on a boat in South Florida. Delray Beach."

Jon stiffened at the mention of his ex-wife. "True."

"That's what I was hoping. I need your help."

4

After a long conversation, Jon and Trey said their goodbyes. Jon put the phone down, thinking about what Trey had told him.

Haley was Trey and Reece's only child, and she was missing. She'd been in a local drug treatment center, Delray-By-The-Sea, and checked herself out that morning.

Trey and Reece had not heard from her and were unable to reach her. They'd called her cell phone, but it went straight to voicemail, and her mailbox was full. Trey was flying into West Palm Beach tomorrow afternoon and wanted Jon's help to find Haley.

Jon didn't know how to help but couldn't refuse Trey. He told Trey he'd do what he could and gave him directions to Hank's Galley from the airport.

He picked up the pistol and stared at it. The gun felt good in his hand. He thought about how many times he'd pulled a trigger. Too many to count. Too many to remember. Some he wanted to forget. He tried to keep the dark thoughts away, but some days were tougher than others.

He held up his glass and said to himself, *May you never forget things best remembered and never remember things best forgotten.* He downed the remainder of the tequila and shoved the gun back into the holster. Time to go to work.

5

At Delray-By-The-Sea, Dr. Stuart Westbrook sat silently at his desk. He'd just got off the phone with the corporate office of Moren Health, the parent company that owned the treatment center, and his stomach was churning.

Every month, especially at the end of each quarter, corporate called each facility, pressuring the CEO to pump up numbers. They called it "dialing for dollars."

He popped two TUMS into his mouth from the emergency stash in his desk.

Two years ago, he'd been the medical director at Atlanta Recovery Haven, where he had developed and patented a customized treatment plan.

The clever secret to the treatment plan was that it was tailored to what the residents and their families could afford. If you could cover a year's worth of care, it became a twelve-month program. If all you could afford was thirty days (and they had an empty bed), the treatment plan was miraculously close to that number.

Families were delighted that it was customized to fit their individual needs and abilities to pay. For the treatment centers, it also turned out to be a great marketing ploy. When a family's insurance ran out, the treatment center could design an additional plan for further treatment, which was almost always required. This new plan corresponded to whatever funds a family could raise, perpetuating the endless cycle that made the treatment business so profitable.

Moren Health, a regional chain of treatment centers, took notice. Vowing to become a national leader in the field, they purchased Atlanta Recovery Haven to add to their growing stable of facilities. They promoted him to the CEO of their star facility in Delray Beach, Florida, where he'd been hugely successful. Through aggressive marketing in the Midwest, they had grown tremendously. Moren was about to go public, and he had stock options worth millions.

As the flagship, Delray-By-The-Sea was always under the spotlight. He ran a tight organization, and they usually bettered their forecast. But the last six months had been brutal. They were behind budget, and corporate was hammering them mercilessly to improve their bottom line. He'd learned the hard way: When you dance with the devil, the devil owns you.

The speakerphone on his desk buzzed. "Valerie's here, Dr. Westbrook."

"Send her in. Where's Kip?"

"I'm still trying—"

"Find him. I don't care what he's doing. Send him in here the minute he arrives."

Valerie Lee, his CFO, entered, closed his door, and sat at the conference table where Stuart joined her. "How did your call go?" she asked.

Not answering, he slid his handwritten list of corporate's demands across to her. He steepled his hands, waiting for her to read the one-page document.

Valerie's eyes widened as she scanned it. She looked up at Stuart, but they were interrupted by a light knock on his door before she could speak.

Kip Foster stepped in, shutting the door behind him. Wearing his trademark jeans, the bearded, young resident coordinator sported another T-shirt. SOAR, it read. Stuart shook his head, wondering how many motivational tees Foster owned.

"What's up?" Kip said as he walked over to the table and sat.

No one answered as Valerie slid the paper over to him. Kip quickly read the list. When finished, he looked up at Stuart with the same reaction as Valerie.

Stuart spoke in a measured tone with his hands still under his chin. "As you can see, we've got to be more aggressive in managing bad debts and past due accounts."

Moren Health had a strict policy of turning accounts over to their collection agency as soon as they reached thirty days past due, regardless of the amount. Days in accounts receivable were one of the company's primary metrics to judge management's performance. Delray already required a large deposit to partially cover the anticipated length of stay for private pay patients. But, as of this moment, they were on the wrong side of the ledger.

Valerie shook her head. "We are already pushing things—"

Stuart slammed his hands on the table, causing Kip and Valerie to jump.

"This is not a request." He paused and stared at each of them to drive home the point. "We've got thirty days to do this. Effective *immediately,* no payment, no service. Period. No exceptions. For patients without insurance, then *100% payment in advance*—not just a deposit. The treatment plan for patients with verified insurance is only as long as the coverage, not a day longer. To keep them here when their coverage ends, we get 100% payment *in advance*. If they're here and can't pay, they get discharged. Immediately."

Although Moren publicly used the term "residents," as a physician, Stuart still referred to them as "patients."

Kip shifted in his seat. "But we can't just arbitrarily discharge them. I mean, I know that we've occasionally encouraged residents to check themselves out, but that sometimes takes—"

Stuart leaned forward. "No more delays. Do whatever you have to do to get non-paying patients out of here. We've got a waiting list to get into our facility. We need to fill every bed with *paying* patients. Am I clear?"

They looked at one another, then nodded in unison.

Stuart swept his hand across the table, dismissing them. "Then get to work."

As they stood, Kip said, "Uh, one more thing. One of our previous residents uh ... discharged herself AMA yesterday morning. As soon as she left, I called her parents to let her know. She's missing, and her family's unable to get in touch with her."

Stuart raised an eyebrow. "So? It's not unusual for patients to relapse. We have no control over what happens when they leave here, especially if she left against medical advice."

"I know. But her father called back late yesterday afternoon. He's flying down today and wants to come by in the morning."

Stuart cocked his head. "I'm assuming everything's in order?"

Kip nodded. "I checked the paperwork. Everything's good."

"Then, what's the problem?" Stuart asked.

Kip and Val looked at each other. Val said, "She is one of our past-due accounts. Haley Stevens. $55,000, thirty-four days old. I was going to turn it over to collections—"

"What are you waiting for?" Stuart said. "Our policy was thirty days, not thirty-four. Now, it's zero."

Val opened her mouth to say something, then closed it and nodded. She turned and, along with Kip, walked out.

6

Only three other people were in Hank's as Jon ate breakfast at the bar. Addie opened for breakfast to accommodate the few liveaboards and any transients at the marina. He suspected she didn't make anything on the morning meal and had encouraged her to shut it down, but she refused. Hank's had always served breakfast, and she intended to keep it that way.

She approached him, pretending to wipe the spotless bar next to him. "What's going on with Ricky?"

He took a swallow of coffee and gave her a curious look.

Addie's eyes locked onto his. "The man you had arrested? I saw him talking to Ricky. They walked out together right before you went outside behind them. You told Beth you didn't see his customer. She didn't buy it, and neither do I." She folded her arms, waiting for his response.

He glanced around. The nearest customer was halfway across the room. He looked back at her. "Ricky's a good kid. He just needs a little guidance to help him get back on track before he ruins his life."

"You can't save everybody. When are you going to accept that?"

Jon finished his coffee and stood. "You're right. I can't. But there's a chance for Ricky. And where there's a chance, I will do all I can."

He left Hank's and walked to the gravel parking lot next to the dock where Lucille was parked.

Lucille was a plain four-door dark gray sedan that looked like grandpa's Dodge. Common enough in South Florida. Upon cursory inspection, the wide, low-profile tires and hood scoops might make someone shake their head, mistakenly concluding that it was for show only.

Jon cranked the car, and the deep-throated rumble from the dual exhausts echoed inside, dispelling any such thoughts. The 6.2L V8 in the Dodge Challenger SRT Hellcat produced over 700 horsepower, capable of rocketing from 0 to 60 in a mere 3.7 seconds. Straight off the assembly line, it could top 200 mph.

He was going to the boatyard, where Ricky worked as a mechanic. Then he had another idea.

He switched Lucille off, went back on *Trouble No More,* and prepared to leave. Onboard, he started the twin diesels to let them warm up before departing. All the gauges were normal, as usual, and the engines purred.

He pulled out his cell phone and called Ricky. "I'm on my way down to your place. Starboard engine's running rough, and I want you to take a look. We need to take a short run outside the Intracoastal where we can open her up and put her under load."

Jon was fabricating an excuse for Ricky to come fishing with him. Max, the marina owner, would bill Jon for Ricky's time, so Ricky was still on the clock and not at risk. What else did Jon have to spend his money on?

"I'll need to check with Max, but it shouldn't be a problem. I'll be waiting," Ricky said.

Jon went down to cast off the last dock line, then eased the boat into the Intracoastal and turned south. Thirty minutes and three drawbridges later, he turned into the Fish Tale Marina. Ricky was standing on the end of the dock, waiting.

Jon eased the boat up to the dock, where Ricky jumped aboard. Jon heard him bounding up the steps to the flybridge as he turned around and headed south toward Boca Raton Inlet.

Ricky joined him at the helm. He studied the gauges for a minute, then looked up at Jon. "What're you talking about the starboard engine running rough? There's nothing wrong with either one. They're perfect. I should know. I just serviced them a few weeks ago."

With a sly grin, Jon said, "I'd feel better if we went outside and got them up to cruising speed to make sure. And, if we're out on the open water, we might as well do a little fishing."

Ricky shook his head, laughing. "You know Max is going to bill you for at least four hours."

Jon shrugged. "So? Are you saying you don't want to fish while on the clock? Call the bridge and tell them we're coming through."

Boca Raton Inlet was the closest route to the open ocean. It could be tricky at low tide or in rough weather, but the tide was high this morning, and the winds were calm. Still, they had to raise the highway A1A bridge for *Trouble No More* to pass through.

Ricky picked up the VHF mic, hailed the Boca Raton Inlet Bridge, and requested an opening. Soon, they saw the bridge being raised. Minutes later, they cleared it and were in open water.

"Take the helm while I get us rigged," Jon said. Not only was Ricky the only one he ever took out, but he was also the only person he'd let drive. Ricky grew up in this area and, besides knowing boats, knew the waters as well as anyone.

Ricky used to protest at taking the helm, instead volunteering to act as a mate. But Jon squashed that, letting the younger man know he respected him as an equal on the water.

They soon reached one of their favorite spots, a reef seventy-five deep that had always been productive for them. That was one of the nice things about this area—you didn't have to ride for hours to find good fishing. Here, the Gulf Stream was typically only about five miles offshore.

As usual, they drifted across the spot, not bothering to lower the anchor. Ricky checked their position at the helm before joining Jon at the stern, where Jon already had his line in the water, holding the bait just off the bottom, rod level.

"Were you really a federal agent?" Ricky asked.

Jon stared at him, then nodded. "In a previous life."

"Like, an FBI agent or something?"

"Something. Not FBI. Lots of federal agents besides them."

Ricky waited for Jon to tell him more. When he didn't, Ricky said, "Thanks for covering for me last night."

"Believe it or not, I was once your age. And I probably did just as many or more stupid things as you."

Ricky chuckled, then immediately straightened up when Jon gave him a hard stare.

"I got into serious trouble once and faced a hard decision. I didn't know what to do. But, thanks to one of my teachers, I made the right choice. That's where you are today. I'm just trying to make it easier for you to pick the right option."

Jon let him digest that for a moment, then continued. "You've got a problem, Ricky. You're a smart kid with a bright future, but drugs are going to ruin your life." His voice caught. "They will. Take it from me."

Ricky started to protest, but Jon held his hand up to silence him.

"How much do you owe him?"

Ricky's eyes shifted away.

"Don't lie."

Ricky lowered his head. "Three hundred dollars."

"Look at me. That's all?"

Ricky looked him in the eye. "Probably four hundred by now."

"Tell me where to find him."

Panic crossed Ricky's face. "I can't—"

"I'll get his name from the cops."

"All I know is Carlos. I call a number and leave a message that I need to see him. He calls me back with a time and place, and we meet."

Jon nodded, not speaking, aware that something was checking his bait out at the end of his line in the water.

"Whoa," he said, cranking the reel as fast as possible, careful to keep the line taught but not jerking the rod tip up. The line went slack as suddenly as it got tight. "Dammit. Lost him." He wound the line in. When the hook broke the water, it was bare.

Ricky bent down to hand him a fresh bait.

"I'll get one in a minute," Jon said. "How'd you get hooked up with Carlos?"

"Hanging out with the wrong crowd."

"You need new friends. Two things. First, you'll never see Carlos again. If you do, next time, I'll tie you up for the cops, too. Clear?"

Ricky nodded, and he continued.

"Second, I'm making an appointment for you to see a counselor about your addiction. And you will do *whatever* they say."

"How am I going to pay for that?"

Jon started to tell him to *take the money he used to buy drugs,* but he bit his tongue. "No excuse. I'll cover it."

Ricky hung his head. "That's expensive. I can't possibly pay you back."

"Yes, you can. And you will."

Ricky cocked his head and opened his mouth to speak, but Jon held his hand up again.

"Staying clean and getting your life back on course is my payback." He reached into the bait bucket for another live cigar minnow. "You need anything, you know where to find me. I'll let you know when and where your appointment is."

7

After returning to Hank's and washing down *Trouble No More,* Jon cleaned his share of the fish he and Ricky had caught. He had a nice grouper along with three yellowtail snappers. Two of the snapper filets went to his fridge. The rest he'd put in Addie's freezer since Hank's Galley had more room.

Stowing the hose on the dock, Jon heard the crunch of gravel as a car pulled into the lot. He turned to see a gaunt, balding man climb out of a non-descript white sedan that appeared to be a rental. He wore khaki slacks, and the bright-green golf shirt appeared to be at least one size too large for his frame.

The man stretched as he looked around. When his gaze landed on Jon's boat, he looked over. Only then did Jon recognize him.

"You're in the right place," Jon said.

He was shocked at his old friend's appearance. The Trey Stevens that Jon knew was tanned and athletic with a head full of salt-and-pepper hair. The man standing before him was older and frail, with a complexion that hadn't seen sunshine in days if not weeks.

"So, this is home, huh? Not bad," Trey said. "You been out fishing?"

Jon stuck out his hand, which Trey took as they embraced in a man hug. "Yeah, got some fresh yellowtail in the cooler for tomorrow."

Trey licked his lips. "Can't wait."

Jon gestured to the open gunwale door. "Welcome aboard."

Trey stepped on board, his footing unsure.

They exchanged the usual chit-chat as Jon gave him a brief tour. He pointed to the forward berth. "Your quarters. Private shower, everything."

"I appreciate it, but I made reservations at the Courtyard."

Jon wrinkled his brow. "You didn't need to do that. Plenty of room here."

"I'm not sleeping well these days, and I didn't want to be a bother." He gave a weak laugh. "I'm so restless even Reece banishes me to a separate bedroom most nights. Thanks, but I'll be fine over there."

In the galley, Jon grabbed a couple of beers. Unsure that Trey could make it up the ladder to the flybridge, he led him out to the stern deck instead.

"How's Reece?" Jon asked.

"Fine, other than worrying about Haley. She sends her love."

"You look like you've lost some weight?" That was the best thing Jon could honestly say about his friend's appearance.

"A bit. You're looking good. Florida must be agreeing with you."

Jon shrugged. Wanting to avoid talking about himself, he cut straight to the reason for Trey's visit.

"So, what's going on with Haley?"

Trey dropped his chin, unable to meet Jon's eye. "I don't know where to start." He took a swallow of his beer before raising his head and continuing.

"Six weeks ago, we admitted her to a treatment program here. Delray-By-The-Sea. Opioids, mainly, but God knows what else."

Jon nodded, not surprised. The facility wasn't familiar, but he'd not kept up with the revolving door of treatment programs in this area. They came and went like the tides.

This area of Florida was Mecca for drug treatment programs. Some were legitimate, but many were not. All preyed on mid-western families with good insurance and a healthy bank account.

"This wasn't her first. Her first time here, but not her first program. This time, we thought she was going to make it. She was doing so well."

Jon remained expressionless, not letting on that he knew this story too well. Unfortunately, the odds were against Haley making it.

Trey told him about getting a call Monday from Delray-By-The-Sea. "They told me Haley checked herself out that morning."

"Checked herself out? Did they say why?" Jon asked. Recidivism was common in treatment programs. Most of the time, it was so patients could get back to the drugs that put them there.

Trey shook his head. "No. I'm not convinced she did. All they said was that she was of legal age, and without a court order, they couldn't keep her against her will."

Jon nodded. "That's true in Florida. Why do you say you're not convinced she wanted to leave?"

"Reece and I both thought it was different this time. She was so close. I know you've heard that story before, but remember, this wasn't our first rodeo. Our bullshit detectors are pretty good by now."

Jon was skeptical, recognizing the signs of denial from his own experience. "Any ideas as to where she might be?"

Trey shook his head. "I've tried calling her cell phone, but no answer. As far as I know, she doesn't know anyone in the area. The only time we've been to Delray Beach was when we admitted her to the program here."

"Maybe she made friends in the program."

Jon knew that people in rehab programs made friends—some were good influences, but most were not. Dealers would plant people in programs to recruit new customers and employees. Illegal, but programs would pay cash bounties for referrals. Contrary to Trey's comments, chances were good that Haley knew people in the area. Maybe she just wanted out.

"I'll ask," Trey said. "I've got an appointment first thing tomorrow." He slid a picture across the table. "This was her a year ago."

Jon studied the picture of an attractive young lady with short blonde hair and blue eyes. The last time he saw Haley was at Megan's funeral. He tried to slide it back over.

"Keep it. I've got plenty of copies." Trey looked at Jon with pleading eyes.

"Have you filed a missing person report with the police?" Jon asked.

"I thought a person had to be missing for 72 hours before—"

"You've been watching too many cop shows. When you leave here, go to the Delray Beach Police Department. It's over on Atlantic Avenue, not too far. Go in and file an MP—missing person report."

"Thanks. That's why I need your help. I'm a banker, for Christ's sake. I don't know what the hell to do."

"The police are your best bet. I know a detective there." Jon looked at his watch. "In fact, I'm supposed to meet her in thirty minutes for dinner." He paused, then continued. "You may not like where this leads, Trey. Chances are Haley's back on drugs."

When patients left a rehab program, the street vultures were there, waiting on them with the candy they craved. It didn't take much to persuade an addict to fall off the wagon. The lure of drugs was hard to resist, which he knew all too well.

Trey nodded. "I know. But we have to find her. One way or the other."

"We will." Jon stood to leave. "Sorry I have to leave you alone for dinner. Feel free to hang out here as long as you like. Mi casa es su casa. Don't worry about locking it when you leave. The gate code is 3938. The grilled grouper sandwich and onion rings here at Hank's Galley are fresh and reasonably priced, unlike everything else in this town. Stop by Delray PD on your way to the hotel. Come back in the morning after you go to Delray-By-The-Sea. We'll figure out a plan and have fresh yellowtail tomorrow night."

Jon walked away, then stopped and turned. "Do you have authorization for Haley's medical record?"

Trey nodded.

"Good. Be sure you ask them for a copy tomorrow."

8

Mediterraneo was a small, Italian restaurant on the Intracoastal that Beth liked. Simple, with checkered tablecloths and sparse décor, but the food was excellent. Jon had invited her to dinner there as an abject apology for his behavior the other night. The place was crowded, as usual, when he arrived. He weaved his way through the line to get to the hostess.

"I'm meeting someone," he said in passing as he pointed to the dining room. Beth was always on time, so he knew she was there somewhere. Then, in the middle of the larger dining room, he spied her outside at a table on the deck.

As he approached, she took a sip of her wine and glanced at her phone on the table.

"Sorry," he said as he sat. "An old friend who just got into town stopped by."

"You could've invited him. Or called."

Jon nodded. "I know, but I wanted to talk to you about why he's here."

When their server appeared, he pointed to Beth's glass. "A bottle of that and another glass."

He walked away, and she said, "I'm listening. By the way, I accept your apology for being an ass the other night."

"Mea culpa." Over dinner, he filled her in about Trey and Haley. He told her he sent Trey to Delray Beach PD to file an MP.

"I'm not hearing any reason to suspect foul play," she said. "What do you think?"

He shook his head. "Relapse. But he's worried they haven't heard from her."

"I'll check on it when I get back to the office. Based on what you've told me, it doesn't sound like a priority."

"I know. He's going by Delray-By-The-Sea in the morning. I told him to check the homeless shelters, hospitals—the usual."

Jon took a sip of his wine. "Who was the drug dealer I called in at Hank's?" He'd already gotten the name from Ricky, but he was hoping to get more information about him from Beth.

"Carlos. Small time dealer, trying to move up the food chain. He used to work for Ramon, one of the bigger fish in the area. Ramon's the one I'd like to nail."

"Now Carlos competes with Ramon?"

"Not really. Everybody here in the business fears Ramon. Even Carlos says the guy is crazy. But they seem to have an understanding. Carlos has a small territory that he had before he went in with Ramon, so apparently, Ramon lets him keep it if their paths don't cross."

She took a sip of her wine and studied him. "Carlos said the gun and drugs weren't his, and that you stuffed the drugs in his pocket the other night. He made bail since all we have is your word against his."

"My word doesn't count?"

"What would help is if we had a customer . . ." She let the words hang as she stared at Jon.

"Sorry."

"You know, but you're not going to tell me, are you?"

Addie was right. Beth didn't believe his story about him not knowing who the customer was. The server appeared with the wine, breaking the awkward silence.

After hr left, Jon asked, "You think Carlos might know something about Haley?"

Beth cocked her head. "Why do you ask?"

"Just curious."

"Bullshit. Don't even think about it."

He gave her his best innocent look. "I'm not going—"

"Save it. Don't go poking around in places you shouldn't. I'll put the word out at the station. We'll try to find her."

He held his hand up. "Any places you'd suggest that we could check?"

"Besides what you mentioned? Soup kitchens, food pantries. Public parks where people are panhandling." She gave him a stern look. "But stay away from drug dealers. And be careful about when and where you go. Delray Beach is a nice little town, but we have bad guys too."

"Five by five," he said, giving her the old telecommunications acknowledgment that a signal was received clearly.

9

The following morning, Jon thumbed through his well-worn book and flipped to the "A's." Under *Angel* was listed the number for D'Angelo Bowen.

D'Lo had been Jon's most reliable confidential informant in the area. Snitches were not always the most dependable sources, but D'Lo had been solid. He wasn't a dealer or a user, but his younger brother had been both.

The last time he had spoken with D'Lo, he was a CT tech at Delray Medical Center. That was when Jon was still a special agent with HHS-OIG. He punched in the number, wondering if it was still valid.

A deep, sleepy voice answered. "Hello. This D'Lo."

"D'Lo," Jon said, "This is J.C. How are—" Jon's greeting was interrupted by a "beep," and he realized he'd gotten D'Lo's voice mail.

"Shit," he said. "This is J.C. Call me back."

Thinking about the hospital, he recalled the emergency department manager there, a red-headed nurse he'd met when he was a federal agent. He grabbed his car keys and headed to Delray Medical Center.

When he got there, he parked near the Emergency Department and walked inside, stopping at the desk. A silver-haired lady wearing a volunteer vest was seated behind the counter.

She looked up at him and, in a pleasant voice, asked, "May I help you?"

"I need to talk to Nora Jenkins. Does she still work here?"

The lady sat up a little straighter, her expression indicating she knew the name but was conflicted about her response. "Uh, may I tell her who—"

He flashed the gatekeeper a big smile. "I'm sorry. I'm Jon Cruz." He dug out one of his old business cards that he kept for just such an occasion and handed it to her.

As he hoped, she seemed impressed by the information on the card identifying him as a Special Agent with HHS-OIG. Of course, Jon could be in trouble for passing himself off as a federal agent. But if cornered, he would claim that it was a mistake, and besides, he was careful not to say he was a federal agent.

"I'll try her office," the lady said, smiling at him.

"Thank you so much, Gladys," he said, noting her name on the volunteer badge. She beamed at the recognition and picked up the phone.

Jon stepped back a few paces to give her the impression of privacy. He overheard her telling the person on the other end his name as she held his card up with her free hand. Smiling, she nodded and hung up the phone.

"She'll be out in a few minutes," Gladys said, returning his card.

He took it and stuffed it back into his wallet. He thanked her for her help and strolled over to a seat next to the outside door, where he had a clear view of the double doors leading back to the emergency department.

Ten minutes later, an attractive redhead dressed in green scrubs strode through the doors, not missing a step as she pushed them open. She looked around the waiting area, and when she spied him, she smiled and walked over.

"Well, well. What a surprise. How long has it been?"

He stuck out his hand, and she froze, hands on hips, staring at his hand. "What's that?" she said.

He laughed and held his arms open. She stepped over and hugged him. "That's better," she said.

"Sorry, I wasn't sure you'd remember me."

She pulled back and looked at him. "How could I forget a handsome fellow like you?"

He shook his head. "You're just being nice to an old man. You don't look like you've aged a day."

"And you are still a silver-tongued devil. Good to see you, Jon."

"Great to see you, too. Listen, I know you're busy, but I'd like to buy you a cup of coffee if you've got a few minutes."

"I'll make time for you," she said. She nodded over her right shoulder. "There's a Starbucks down the hall."

After getting their coffee and sitting at the small table outside, Nora asked, "What could I do for you today?"

Jon hesitated. "I need a favor. But I'm no longer with OIG, so I'm asking unofficially."

She sat back and looked at him. "Okay, so who do you represent now?"

He took a deep breath. "It's a long story. The short version is that I'm doing this as a favor for an old Marine buddy. Trey Stevens."

He pulled Haley's picture out of his pocket and showed it to her. "She's his daughter. She was in rehab here in Delray Beach and checked herself out. But he hasn't been able to reach her since."

Nora folded her arms and leaned back in her chair. "You realize that with HIPAA and all of the privacy issues, not only could I lose my job, we both could go to jail."

He nodded. "I realize that. I just want to know if she's here or been admitted in the last week."

She thought for a moment, then held out her hand and took the photo.

"Haley Rae Stevens," he said. "Twenty-two. She disappeared after leaving Delray-By-The-Sea Monday morning after checking herself out. Her parents have tried calling her but no answer and she hasn't called them."

"Maybe she's a runaway."

He shook his head. "No. She was an only child and they were close. Trey said they'd chatted Saturday and everything seemed normal. Haley didn't mention anything about leaving."

Nora studied the photo and cocked her head. "Any distinguishing marks?"

"A butterfly tattoo on her left shoulder."

She wrinkled her brow and shook her head. "I don't recognize her, but I'll check with my supervisors and ask them." She held out the picture.

"Keep it," Jon said. "I can get more. Can you check your computer system, too?"

She shook her head. "You're pushing."

"Please?"

"For the record, no, I can't." She put air quotes around the *no* and winked.

"I understand," he said, smiling. "One more thing."

"Damn, do you think this is Christmas? What?"

"I've got a friend with a drug problem. Could you recommend a good place for him to get help?"

She nodded. "That I can do. I know the psychologist personally, and she's the best. I'll send you her contact information as soon as I get back to my office."

He wrote his number down on a napkin and handed it to her. "Thanks—for everything. I owe you."

Nora stood, her green eyes meeting his as she took the napkin. "You're welcome. And, yes, you do."

With that, she turned and walked away.

10

When Jon arrived home, Trey was sitting on the aft deck of *Trouble No More,* looking at his iPad.

"How'd it go?" Jon asked as he stepped aboard.

Trey shook his head. "Nada. Same story they'd already told me. Nothing new."

"Who'd you meet with?"

"Kip Foster, the resident counselor. He's the one who called."

Trey told him that Kip showed the documentation where Haley had signed the discharge form acknowledging that it was against medical advice. He also had the form showing she received her phone and personal items.

"He have any idea where she went?" Jon asked.

"Nope. According to him, she just walked out the front door. I asked for a copy of her medical record. He told me I could pick it up tomorrow."

"Good."

"I went by the police department last night and filed a missing person report."

Jon told him he'd had dinner with his detective friend, and she promised to follow up. He didn't mention that she said it wouldn't be a priority.

"This morning, I went by the hospital. I know the Emergency Department manager there. I showed her

Haley's pic. As far as she knew, Haley hadn't been there, but she was going to check with her staff."

Jon's phone dinged, indicating a text message. He saw it was the rehab information from Nora, then looked back at Trey.

"What now?" Trey asked.

He wasn't sure. And didn't know how to answer his friend. The good news was that Haley hadn't shown up at the hospital. But they didn't know if she was even still in the area. Somebody who didn't want to be found could be hard to find. They were going to have to talk with people in a position to know something.

Jon's phone buzzed. It was D'Lo. As if answering an unspoken prayer. "Cruz," he said, holding up his index finger to Trey.

"This is D'Lo." The voice was hesitant, but Jon recognized it.

"I need to see you. Where's a good spot to talk?"

"You got time for breakfast?" D'Lo's gravelly voice made him grin.

Jon looked at his watch. 11:10. Late for breakfast but he needed to talk to him in person. "I'm up for breakfast anytime."

"I'll be at the Waffle Hut." D'Lo disconnected.

"I need to meet someone," Jon said to Trey. "Might be some help. I'll explain later." He told him to go online and put together a list of homeless shelters, soup kitchens, etc. "We'll go check them out soon as I get back."

* * *

Fifteen minutes later, Jon walked into the Waffle Hut on 10th. A tall, black man with a shaved head sat alone in a booth with a cup of coffee. He wore slacks and a golf shirt.

D'Lo looked good, Jon thought, still in shape. He'd been a starting linebacker with the University of Miami Hurricanes. He was on his way to a promising NFL career until a knee injury threw him a curve. No dumb jock, D'Lo got his degree and was a CT tech at Delray Medical Center.

D'Lo had that amazing ability to connect with people of any social status. People innately trusted him, but his physical appearance showed that you did not want to get on his wrong side. Unlike many informants, all D'Lo ever asked for was an occasional breakfast and to look out for his brother, which is why Jon trusted him.

"D'Lo," Jon said as he approached. "How you doing? It's been a while."

D'Lo appraised his friend with a discerning eye as he stuck his fist out for a bump. Jon responded in kind as he sat.

"Too long," D'Lo said. "I'm good. Chief CT tech, still at the hospital. How bout you?"

Jon shrugged. "I don't work for the feds anymore. Retired a couple of years ago."

There was a long pause. "That's a good thing, right?"

"Sometimes. J.R. doing okay?"

D'Lo's younger brother J.R., who had also worked at the hospital, had been caught diverting drugs from the floor. Jon investigated the drug ring and won the successful conviction of three employees. J.R. got the minimum sentence in return for cooperating.

Drug diversion, or the illegal routing of prescription drugs to the black market, was a huge problem in health care everywhere, especially in South Florida. D'Lo repaid the favor by supplying Jon with information about this darker side of health care in the area.

"Yeah." D'Lo cocked his head and stared at Jon. "He's not in any trouble, is he?"

Jon chuckled and shook his head. "No, that's not why I'm here. And I'm glad he's doing well. You're a good influence."

D'Lo relaxed. "I appreciate what you did for him."

They ordered breakfast, and after the waitress left, D'Lo sipped his coffee. "So, what are you doing? Still on your boat?"

Jon nodded. "Little of this, little of that. Still on the boat over at Hank's, making do." They chatted a bit, then the food arrived.

The man loved his breakfast. Jon looked over at the overflowing plates of food in front of D'Lo. He always got the same thing for breakfast: Three eggs, bacon, hash browns, toast, and pancakes. And he never left a morsel.

"Do you ever miss it?" Jon asked. He was asking about D'Lo's once promising football career.

D'Lo paused after chewing his last bite and stroked his chin. "Have you ever been to Muck City?"

Jon shook his head. He thought he knew most of the small towns in the area, but this was a new one.

"It's what they call Pahokee and Belle Glade. The two towns together have less than 25,000 people. Only fifty-five miles from here. Still in Palm Beach County, like Delray Beach. Might as well be on another planet. You know what they produce in Muck City?"

Again, Jon shook his head.

"NFL players. Over sixty have come from there."

Sixty players? Jon thought. With 25,000 people. How?

As if reading his mind, D'Lo said, "There are two ways out of Muck City: Football and prison. I was one of the fortunate ones. J.R. wasn't."

He paused to eat another bite. When he finished, he said, "One of the good things about working at the hospital. Every day, whenever you start feeling sorry for yourself, you see someone in much worse shape than you.

Same thing with Muck City. Every time I go back, I see it. I may not be playing on Sundays, but I got an education, a family, and a good job. I try to remember that every morning when I wake up. That's why breakfast is my favorite meal."

After a few mouthfuls, Jon glanced around, confirming no one was nearby. He pulled out Haley's picture and slid it over to D'Lo. "I'm trying to find a friend's daughter."

D'Lo studied it for a moment and nodded once.

Jon continued. "Her name is Haley Stevens. Monday, she checked herself out of rehab at a local treatment center. Delray-By-The-Sea. Her parents can't reach her, and they're worried."

Processing the information, D'Lo took a few bites of his breakfast, then washed it down with some coffee. "What do you think?"

Jon looked away as he considered his answer. He'd always been upfront with D'Lo, and the man had always been straight with him. *And he understands the importance of family,* Jon thought as he turned back to D'Lo, still eating.

"My guess is she's on the streets, back into drugs and God knows what, embarrassed to face her parents. We both know how hard it is to kick the habit."

D'Lo nodded. "What's your connection?"

"Trey—her dad—and I were in the Marines together. We got in a jam once, and I owe him. So when he asked for help, I couldn't refuse."

"I'll see what I can find out. Anything else?"

"What do you know about a dealer named Carlos?"

"Carlos?" D'Lo snorted. "How do you know him?"

"I caught him dealing at the marina the other night. I had him picked up, but he's already back on the street. If she's back into drugs, there might be a connection."

"Possible. He's a wannabe. Used to work for Ramon, then decided to go out on his own."

"Competition?"

D'Lo chuckled. "Nobody goes up against Ramon. They parted amicably."

That squared with what Beth had told him. "Sounds like Ramon's the top dog in the business."

"He is. I'll ask around. Give me a couple of days."

"Thanks, D'Lo." Jon pulled out two twenties and laid them on the table and stood. "Good to see you. Talk soon."

11

On Jon's way back to the boat, Beth called.

"Where are you?" she asked when Jon answered.

"Almost back to the marina. Why?"

"Meet me at the Publix on Atlantic. Haley was here." She disconnected.

Shit. He called Trey.

"You still on the boat?" he asked as soon as Trey picked up.

"Yep, looking up places on the computer."

"We've got a lead on Haley. I'll meet you out front in five minutes." Minutes later, he wheeled into the parking lot at the marina, and braked to a stop in front of Trey. Before he could close his door, Jon started rolling.

"Where is she?" Trey asked as they accelerated toward the street, throwing gravel until the tires hit the pavement with a chirp.

"Beth—Detective Keller—called. Haley was spotted at a Publix supermarket here in Delray Beach."

Ten minutes later, they pulled into the parking lot. A patrol car and an unmarked that Jon recognized as Beth's were parked out front. Jon found a spot as close as possible, parked, and they ran into the store.

Beth and a couple of uniforms were over by the service desk. She was talking to the manager while the two uniforms were talking to an older woman a few steps away. Customers were rubbernecking as they walked past the commotion.

"Where is she?" Trey asked.

Beth looked at Trey, then at Jon.

"Beth, this is Trey Stevens, Haley's father. Trey, Detective Keller."

Beth shook her head. "She's not here. This lady saw a young woman stealing money from her purse in the shopping cart. She had just come from the bank next door and had $300 in a bank envelope. She yelled, and the thief ran away with it. By the time the manager got there, the robber was gone. He called it in, and the uniforms got here first. Based on the description, they thought it might be Haley and called me. This lady positively identified her."

"Stealing?" Trey said, lifting an eyebrow. "Are you sure it was Haley?"

Jon put his hand on Trey's shoulder as Beth held up Haley's picture that Trey had left at the police station.

"The lady swears it was her. One of the employees working that aisle also identified her. I've got another patrol car driving around the area, but no sign of her so far. We'll check with the bank, but have no reason to doubt this lady's story. She's a regular customer and one with means."

Trey's head dropped.

"You need us for anything?" Jon asked her.

"No. If I do, I know where to find you."

Jon tugged on Trey's arm. "Come on. Let's go."

As they got into Jon's car, Trey said, "I don't understand. Why would she steal? Why wouldn't she call us? Or answer her phone?"

Jon shook his head. Trey was in denial and needed to face the facts, regardless of how unpleasant. "My guess is Haley's probably using again and needed money. She's probably too embarrassed to reach out to you and Reece."

"My God," Trey said, shaking his head.

"But she's in the area," Jon said. "And she's alive."

Slowly, they drove around the vicinity, looking for Haley or clues as to where she might have gone. Jon wasn't optimistic but did it more for Trey's benefit. He was pretty sure that Haley had gone back underground.

When they passed a large municipal park, he pulled over and stopped. As they got out, he scanned the area. It was midday, and dozens of people were taking advantage of the nice weather. People with small kids, an older couple walking their little dog, and a group of teenagers loitering under the shade of a large tree. Why weren't the teens in school?

There were also a few homeless people. The closest one shuffled away as they approached. Thirty yards away, Jon spotted a disheveled man sitting on a bench next to a bulging black plastic garbage bag.

The man wore a dirty ball cap and sported an unkempt beard long overdue for a trim. He wore a tattered T-shirt and clutched the garbage bag as Jon and Trey approached.

"Just keep quiet and don't get too close," Jon told Trey. "Let me do the talking."

The man spotted them coming toward him and pulled the garbage bag closer. His eyes darted around the park, and he appeared ready to bolt.

Jon stopped when they were ten or twelve feet away, holding his hands up to indicate they meant no harm. "Excuse me. We're not here to hassle you. I just want to ask you a few questions."

He noticed the man had bruises and cuts on his face. Jon flashed a twenty-dollar bill he had palmed. "I'd be happy to pay you for your time."

The man cocked his head, eyes focused on the twenty.

"Stay put," Jon whispered to Trey. Jon took a few steps toward the man and held out the money. When the man nodded almost imperceptibly, Jon inched closer.

Still clutching his bag, the bearded man reached out and took the money. He stuffed the bill in the pocket of his tattered shorts, his gaze never leaving the two men.

Careful to keep his movements slow and non-threatening, Jon pointed to Trey. "We're trying to find his daughter and heard she might be around here. Would it be okay if he showed you her picture?"

The man looked at Trey, then back at Jon. Again, a slight nod.

Trey removed a picture from his pocket, slowly took a few steps until he was next to Jon, and gently handed the man Haley's picture.

With one hand on his bag, the homeless man took the photo with the other. Squinting, he brought it up close to his face and studied it. He looked at Trey and nodded. With his bony, outstretched arm, he looked like Moses, pointing to the promised land as he indicated the bench a few feet away. "Hers," he said. Then he pointed to the bench where he sat. "Mine."

Trey looked around, excited. "Where is she?"

Jon cut him off with a shake of his head. "Was she here earlier?" he asked.

Moses nodded and then pointed over to the edge of the park toward the Publix shopping center.

"Was anyone with her?" Jon asked.

The man shook his head excitedly. He reached up with both hands as if grasping something, then threw his hands out toward Jon as if discarding the object. He repeated the gesture, then pointed to the bruises on his face.

Jon felt his face flush as he interpreted what the man was saying. "I'm sorry," he said. "Can we get you anything?"

The man shrugged, then shook his head.

Jon reached into his pocket, pulled out another twenty, and handed it to him. This time, he took it without hesitation.

Jon took out one of his old business cards on which he had written his cell phone number. "Give me one of your cards," he told Trey. Jon gave them both to Moses. "Thank you. If you see her again, would you give these to her?"

Moses looked at the cards, stuffed them into his pocket, and nodded.

Jon turned and walked back toward the car, Trey beside him. "A lot of the homeless have severe mental issues."

"That was sad. What was he trying to tell you?" Trey asked.

"Somebody beat him up. Some punks get their kicks beating up homeless people. My guess is that's what happened to him."

"Oh my God. You don't think they hurt Haley, do you?"

"Don't know. Since the lady at Publix didn't mention anything about any cuts or bruises, I'm guessing she's probably fine."

No obvious signs of physical abuse didn't guarantee that, but he wanted to be upbeat for Trey. He didn't add that she felt well enough to take money from a stranger's purse and run. He guessed that the druggies who beat up Moses probably were in a car waiting for her outside the front door.

"He recognized her photo and called the other bench hers, indicating she slept there. I didn't see any signs of that, but it's not unusual for the homeless to carry everything with them."

Trey cringed when Jon referred to Haley as homeless. "So, she'll be back, right? I mean, if she was sleeping here."

"Maybe, but she's on the run. Remember, they saw her steal the money in the supermarket. We'll come back after dark and check."

12

It was mid-morning the next day as Jon pulled up to the front door of the Marriott Courtyard. Trey was standing outside, smoking. When he saw Jon, he finished his cigarette and stuffed the butt into the receptacle by the entrance.

"Morning," Jon said as Trey opened the car door. "Get any sleep?"

"Not much. You?"

"Couple of hours after I made my rounds at the marina."

Trey buckled in as Jon pulled out into the street, the exhaust rumbling from the big V-8 as they gathered speed. They were headed to Delray-By-The-Sea to pick up Haley's medical records.

Last night, they had gone back to the park to look for Haley. The park bordered a housing project, and Jon didn't want his friend there alone after dark. They saw Moses— as Jon called him—but no sign of Haley. Finally, well after midnight, they concluded that she was a no-show.

"Reece sends her love," Trey said. "I talked to her earlier this morning."

"She doing okay?"

"Yeah, just worried about Haley."

There was a lag in the conversation, then Trey continued. "She got a call from a collection agency this morning representing Delray-By-The-Sea." The embarrassment in his voice was palpable.

"Yeah?" A collection agency? As far as he knew, Trey and Reece were in good shape financially. Trey had done well working at the bank, and Reece had worked in real estate for years. He couldn't remember them ever having financial problems.

Another pause, then Trey continued. "Our insurance had run out while she was there, so we had to pay for Haley's care out-of-pocket. We took a second mortgage and kept up for a while but fell behind. Those places aren't cheap. They badgered us before Haley disappeared, then threatened to turn us over to collections. Apparently, they did."

Now, Jon understood all too well. Health care debt was the leading cause of personal bankruptcy in the United States. Even a well-to-do couple like Trey and Reece were susceptible.

As he turned in to Delray-By-The-Sea, Jon thought the place looked like a swank resort, with its clay-tiled roof and immaculately manicured landscaping. Palm trees swayed in the slight breeze. Hibiscus was blooming around a discreet sign that listed only the facility's name and address. It was the South Florida version of a treatment center he remembered in Atlanta. As Trey had said, not cheap. Treating addicts was a profitable business.

The curved, paved drive led to a building not visible from the street. They parked in the VISITOR area and walked up to the main entrance. Jon noticed the video cameras on the corners of the building. Inside, an attractive young blonde, smartly dressed, sat at a desk, looking like a concierge at a luxury hotel. Her name tag read TIFFANY.

"Good afternoon. May I help you?" she asked, displaying perfectly white teeth.

"I'm Trey Stevens. I'd like to speak with Kip Foster, please."

"Did you have an appointment, Mr. Stevens?"

Trey shook his head. "Not exactly. My daughter was a patient here. I met with Mr. Foster yesterday, and he told me I could pick up a copy of her medical record this morning. I had a few more questions I'd like to ask him."

She looked over at Jon, but Trey didn't introduce him. Jon met her stare with no comment. Flustered, she managed a thin smile, struggling to maintain her composure.

"If you'd like to have a seat, I'll call Mr. Foster's office and see if he's available," she said as she picked up the handset.

Trey looked around the empty lobby. Jon nodded toward the leather couch, and they walked over and sat.

Jon picked up a brochure on the table and watched as the receptionist spoke to someone on the phone, first nodding and then shaking her head as she talked. She hung up, staring at the phone as though willing a quick callback.

He turned his attention to the lavish, full-size color brochure in his hand. The cover featured a picture of Delray-By-The-Sea, replete with palm trees and a setting sun visible beyond.

He thumbed through it as he waited, skimming the slickly produced marketing piece. There were pictures of young people who looked like models in various settings. Multiple references to various accreditation agencies and organizations implied an official air of endorsement.

Out of the corner of his eye, Jon noticed that the receptionist was back on the phone. Jon looked at Trey and nodded toward her. As soon as she hung up, they headed over to her desk.

Appearing relieved she'd resolved the issue, Tiffany smiled and said, "Mr. Foster will be with you in a few minutes."

Ten minutes later, the double doors opened, and a young man with shoulder-length blond hair emerged, wearing jeans and a T-shirt bearing the word BELIEVE. Carrying a manila folder, he walked over and extended his hand to Trey.

"Hi, Mr. Stevens. Unfortunately, I only have a few minutes," he said. He shook Trey's hand, then offered his hand to Jon. "I'm Kip Foster. And you are?"

"Jon Cruz. A friend of the family." Jon ignored Kip's proffered gesture.

Kip withdrew his hand and turned back to Trey. "Uh, please, if you'll follow me. Let's go where we can talk privately."

Jon glanced around the empty reception area. What was wrong with out here? He bit his tongue as Kip led them through the double doors to a small conference room on the right. Trey sat, with Jon taking the chair next to him.

Kip sat on the opposite side of the table, placing a hand on the folder. He looked at Trey.

"As you requested, I've got a copy of her records covered by Haley's release. Tiffany said you had a few additional questions?"

"Yes. Yesterday, you said that Haley had discharged herself. AMA, I think you called it. Can you elaborate?"

Kip opened the folder and pulled out a sheet of paper. He slid it toward Trey. "I believe I showed you this yesterday," he said in a somewhat condescending tone. "Included in your copy of the records is the discharge form here. As you can see, Haley signed it, as well as her physician and me. It clearly documents that we advised her against leaving. Unfortunately, in Florida, we cannot legally prevent an adult from leaving unless we have a court order indicating otherwise. Since your daughter is over 18 and we have no such order, we had no choice but to let her go."

Jon looked at the form in front of Trey. As Kip indicated, it represented legal documentation that Haley was discharging herself against medical advice.

"Any idea as to where she went?" Jon asked.

Kip hesitated before answering, looking to Trey for permission.

"Well?" Trey asked.

Kip shook his head. "No, I'm afraid not. We returned her belongings, and she walked out the door you entered. I encouraged her to call you."

"She did have her phone, then?" Trey asked.

With a sigh, Kip pulled another sheet from the folder and slid it across the table to Trey. "According to this, also signed by her, yes." He pointed to the iPhone listed on the patient inventory sheet.

Trey looked at Jon.

Jon glanced at it, not surprised that the paperwork was in order. Delray-By-The-Sea had covered their bases. "She was here for what, six weeks? I'm assuming she got to know some of the other residents. Who did she hang out with here?"

Kip cleared his throat and turned his attention back to Trey. "Due to patient confidentiality, we're not allowed to discuss protected patient information."

Jon was in no mood for bureaucratic babble. "I understand that, Mr. Foster. But Haley's missing, and we're trying to find her. According to you, she just walked out the door. Where did she go? What was her state of mind? What else can you tell us to help us find her?"

Jon tapped his finger on the folder in front of Kip. "You have a release authorizing Haley's medical information to her father. Why don't you hand it over so he can review the contents, preferably while we're here?"

Foster blushed at being called out and narrowed his eyes. "That release only covers her information, not the names of other residents." He turned to Trey. "I'll need some photo ID, please."

Trey produced his driver's license and handed it to him.

"Excuse me while I make a copy. I'll be right back."

As soon as Kip closed the door, Jon took the folder and thumbed through it.

Trey was aghast. "What are you doing?"

"You have the authority. I doubt there's anything useful here, but I thought I'd check while we're here and have Mr. Foster's attention."

In addition to Patient Inventory, Discharge Form, and Medical Record Information Release forms, there was a copy of Haley's bill, dated last week, for an overdue balance of over fifty-five thousand dollars. He didn't see any patient notes.

Jon heard the doorknob, put the papers back in the folder, and slid it to its original place at Kip's seat. He purposefully left it upside down.

When Kip walked in, he noticed the upside-down folder. He looked at Jon, who returned the stare and dared him to comment. After a brief standoff, Kip seemingly decided to let it go.

Foster sat, putting his hand atop the folder. He slid Trey's license across the table. "We'll have your copy of the records ready for you tomorrow."

Wearing a thin smile, he turned to Jon. "You made me realize we have to make sure any information identifying other residents is redacted before releasing the records. They'll be ready tomorrow. Now, where were we?"

Trey repeated Jon's question as to Haley's state of mind.

"I can tell you that Haley was doing well. As you know, she was on track to finish her extension in another week. We were as surprised as you that she wanted to leave early.

I tried talking her out of it Monday after breakfast, but she was adamant about leaving. She didn't give any reason."

They spent another ten minutes talking with Kip, but he was not able to provide much more in the way of information. He did mention several places in Delray Beach that Trey might check, places that Detective Keller had already suggested.

"Anything else?" Trey asked Jon.

Jon nodded and locked his eyes on Kip. "You might want to reconsider turning this account over to collections."

"What are you talking about?" Kip said.

Trey said, "Somebody from a collection agency representing your facility called my wife this morning and threatened us."

Kip stumbled to respond. "Uh, I don't know anything about that. I'll have to check with our billing department."

"Why don't you do that," Jon said as he rose to leave. "It might save you some bad publicity and legal fees."

Back in Jon's car, Trey said, "Well, what did you think?"

"A waste of time. Not surprisingly, their documentation seems to be in order. When you get the rest of the records, give me a copy. I'll get a nurse friend to look through them."

"Now what?" Trey asked.

13

Valerie was meeting with Stuart in his office when Kip Foster barged in without knocking. He slammed the door behind him.

Stuart scowled. "We're in the middle of a meeting. I don't think I heard you knock."

"I need to see you. Both of you, actually," Kip said. "We've got a situation. Remember me telling you about Haley Stevens? The resident whose dad wanted to meet with me? Well, yesterday, he showed up—by himself. Real pleasant. We reviewed everything, and he asked for a copy of her medical records."

"Your point?" Stuart asked.

"Today, he shows up to pick up his copy. This time, he brings some asshole along. They just got through badgering me about her discharging herself, where she went, blah, blah, blah."

Kip glared at Valerie. "Then, the asshole threatened me, suggesting we reconsider turning the account over to collections. Seemed our collection agency called Mr. Steven's wife this morning."

Valerie squinted. "We talked about that, remember? Fifty-five thousand dollars, and it was already past due. I was just—"

Stuart shook his head and waved his hand. "It doesn't matter. We're simply following our policy. Did the asshole have a name?"

"Jon Cruz," Kip said.

Stuart cocked his head. "Jon Cruz? Are you sure? Describe him."

"Six feet and change. Short brown hair, kinda tan. Late forties, I'm guessing. Hard looking with an edge to him, maybe an ex-cop or ex-military. Someone you don't want to cross."

Stuart sat back in his chair. It had to be him. And the name was unusual enough. But what in the hell was he doing in Delray Beach?

"We're done here," he announced. "I need to make a few phone calls. If this is who I think it is, Mr. Cruz is going to be in for a rude surprise."

After they left, Stuart picked up his phone and called the Delray Beach police chief.

14

It was dinnertime, and Jon was in his usual spot at Hank's. Trey had gone back to the park to see if he could spot Haley.

Technically, Jon was off today. Although he only worked part-time, he took his security guard duties seriously and made rounds after dinner. He told Trey he'd be over to relieve him after he'd done so while it was still daylight.

He'd just finished eating when he felt someone's presence behind him. He turned to see a not-happy Detective Beth Keller. Although there was an empty stool next to him, she stood with her arms crossed.

"Can we talk?" It sounded more like an order than a request.

He looked around. It wasn't that crowded, but before he could comment, she barked. "Not here."

He looked to Addie for help, but she raised her eyebrows and turned to go down to the other end of the bar. Jon was on his own.

He stuffed the last French fry in his mouth, wiped his lips, and rose. Beth was already halfway out of the bar.

As soon as he crossed the threshold and the door slammed shut behind him, she turned and pounced.

"What the hell are you doing?" she said, spitting the words out.

He raised his hands in supplication, clueless. "I don't know what—"

"What were you thinking? Going into Delray-By-The-Sea and threatening them?"

He opened his mouth to speak but thought better of it. It was best to hear what she had to say and let her vent.

"My lieutenant just chewed my ass out. Know why?"

He shook his head. But he had a feeling she was about to tell him.

"Because ten minutes earlier, the chief had just chewed his ass out." She paused to catch her breath. "I know you think you're helping your friend, but that's our job. We're the police, remember? Not you, not anymore. All you're doing is sticking your nose where it doesn't belong, and you don't understand the consequences."

He could tell she was beginning to spool down, thank God, but it was still too early for him to speak.

"Delray Beach is a small town," she said. "Everybody knows everybody, especially when they're somebody."

He had to stifle a chuckle, wanting to ask her to dissect that sentence, but he didn't dare.

"Do not, I repeat, do not go back to Delray-By-The-Sea. With or without Trey Stevens. Do I make myself clear?"

He nodded. As Beth continued mumbling and cursing under her breath, he wondered who called the police chief. He doubted it was Foster, but who knew? He had clearly pissed someone off at Delray-By-The-Sea.

He replayed the conversation with Kip Foster. All Jon had done was suggest that they reconsider turning the account over to collections. He might have mentioned something about bad publicity and legal fees, but that wasn't really a threat. He'd done much worse in other situations.

He looked at Beth and decided it was safe to speak—maybe. But she wasn't in the mood to hear his definition of threat or his side of the story. "I'm sorry," he said. "I obviously didn't know what I walked into."

"Do. Not. Go. Back. There," she said as she wheeled around and walked away.

He walked back into Hank's. Addie walked over, but he shook his head and said, "Not now." He finished his beer and left without saying goodbye.

Daylight was fading when he got to the dock. Felix the cat was waiting on him.

"At least you're still associating with me," he said as he went on board to get Felix's dinner. Back at the bowl, Jon put the food in.

"Okay, buddy. Dinnertime." As usual, Felix waited before eating until he went back on the boat.

Maybe Beth was right, Jon thought, as he strapped his pistol on to make a quick circuit of the marina. They were no closer to finding Haley than when Trey rolled into town. In fact, it had been Beth that reported Haley's sighting at Publix.

He hadn't accomplished anything. He no longer had the power of a badge and access to the resources available to Beth. While he would do anything to find Haley, it might be better to step aside and leave that to the detective.

He made a fast loop around the property. Nothing was amiss, and few people were stirring. Only a handful of cars were parked in front of Hank's Galley. It was a quiet Wednesday evening.

Felix was gone when he returned to the boat, but the food bowl was empty. Jon shook his head, wondering where Felix slept and why he never saw the ginger cat anywhere else in the marina.

On board, he grabbed the bottle of tequila and two shot glasses to take to the park.

When he got there, he spotted Trey's rental car and parked behind it. Before he could get out, Trey walked back and got in.

"How was dinner?" Trey asked.

"Good. I told you I'd bring you something."

Trey picked up the bottle of tequila and smiled. "You did. Good thing I got a bite on the way over."

"Any action?" Jon asked as Trey poured each of them a shot.

Trey shook his head. "Moses is here. I think he lives here. No sign of Haley."

They each took a healthy sip. Jon scanned the park and saw Moses sitting on his bench, rocking. "Detective Keller came by the bar."

Trey perked up. "Any news?"

"Sorry, no." Trey seemed to deflate in front of him. "You know, maybe you should call her tomorrow. Stop by to see her."

Trey nodded. "When do you want to go?"

Jon gritted his teeth. "I'm kinda busy tomorrow. Besides, it might be better if you went alone."

Trey cocked his head, his face wearing a question. "Are you ditching me?"

"No, no. I just don't think I'm helping. Beth's your best bet. You need to stay close to her."

"I know you, brother. Something happened. Out with it."

"Look. I'll do anything to help find Haley. You know that. But I think your best shot is Beth, not me. I'll continue to work behind the scenes. All I'm saying is you might do better to leave me out of the point position. I'm not making any friends in town."

Trey finished his shot. "So, who did you piss off?"

Jon shook his head. "Not sure exactly. Somebody at Delray-By-The-Sea. They called the police chief, and I'm persona non grata there. All I'm saying is maybe I'm doing more harm than good."

Movement caught Jon's eye. He held up an index finger. "Moses's six. Check it out."

Two people were shuffling toward Moses from behind him. One was wearing shorts and a hoodie, the other shorts and a baseball cap pulled down low over his face. They kept scanning the area as they approached Moses, apparently looking for anyone watching.

Jon fingered his pistol. "Let's go see Moses. Easy on the doors."

They carefully opened the car doors and eased them shut. Jon pointed right, and they strolled on a path well to the right of Moses. They talked loudly, appearing to pay no attention to what was unfolding to their left.

The two thugs spotted them and stopped. After a few minutes, they seem to conclude the two older men posed no threat. They resumed closing in on Moses, who seemed oblivious to their presence.

They were within twenty yards of Moses when the hoodie guy pulled a baseball bat out from under his sweatshirt.

"Now," Jon said to Trey as he turned left and started running toward Moses.

"Hey," Jon yelled. The punks stopped when they saw Jon and Trey running toward them. When Baseball Cap reached into his pocket, Jon stopped, pulled out his gun, and pointed it at the two. "Take your hand out of your pocket. Now."

The two punks looked at each other, then turned and ran.

"Fuck," Jon said. Younger, and with a fifteen-yard head start, he knew he and Trey couldn't catch them. He put his pistol back into its holster as they turned and walked back toward the car.

"They were going to beat him up for the hell of it, weren't they?" Trey said.

Jon called Beth and reported what happened. A few minutes later, a patrol car pulled up behind them, followed by Beth in her unmarked.

A still-pissed Beth, followed by two uniforms, walked over.

"I thought I just told you less than an hour ago to butt out," she said.

Jon held his hand up. "Hear me out. That day we met you at Publix, we came over here and talked to that homeless guy." He pointed to Moses. "He recognized Haley's picture and told us she'd been sleeping here. So, we've been coming over at night to see if she returned. That's it."

"And you neglected to tell me that?" she asked Jon. She turned her attention to Trey. "After Mr. Stevens filed a missing person report?"

Jon realized he'd stepped into it again with Beth. He needed to dig himself out and cover Trey. "That was my fault. I came over here to tell Trey he needed to work with you. That's when we saw two punks—one with a baseball bat—approaching Moses. They saw us and ran, then I called you."

Trey corroborated the story. They described the two would-be attackers and pointed the direction they ran. Beth told the patrol officers to see what they could find.

"We've got it, Jon," she said.

"Thank you." Then, before returning to his car, he gave Trey a slight, almost imperceptible nod.

Picking up on the cue, Trey said to Beth, "Can we talk for a few minutes, Detective?"

At his car, Jon leaned up against it with his arms folded, waiting for Trey. He watched as Trey and Beth talked briefly, then shook hands. She went over to speak to Moses, and Trey returned to Jon's car.

"Shit flows downhill," Trey said. "Her lieutenant dumped on her, and you were next in line, huh?"

Jon shrugged.

"Hey, if you need to lay low in certain quarters, I understand. But I need you, Jon. Tonight proved that. I'll keep her in the loop, but I'm just one non-resident constituent. I know you'll do what's best for Haley. That's what counts."

15

The smell of fresh donuts filled the car as Jon pulled away from the curb on Atlantic Avenue. Knowing D'Lo was expecting food, he'd stopped at HoleyDonuts to pick up coffee and a bag of their classic donuts.

After his conversation with Trey last night, Jon continued focusing on finding Haley. When D'Lo called asking for a meeting, Jon didn't hesitate. He knew D'Lo would only call if he had new information. So, he'd told D'Lo he'd meet him this morning at Atlantic Dunes Park.

When working as a special agent, Jon always preferred meeting informants in busy places. Hiding in plain sight, he called it. It was usually safer and less noticeable. Old habits were hard to break.

Jon parked in the city lot across Highway A1A when he got to the busy oceanside municipal park. Holding two coffees and the donuts, Jon crossed the busy street to meet D'Lo.

He spied his former informant sitting in a beach chair in the shade of the lifeguard stand, an empty chair beside him. Jon noticed he was still wearing his DELRAY MEDICAL CENTER badge as he handed D'Lo a coffee and the bag.

D'Lo opened the donuts, closed his eyes, and inhaled. "Ummm. My favorite." Then, he took one out and offered the bag to Jon.

Jon shook his head and held up his coffee. "Coffee first."

They chatted for a while as Jon relaxed and enjoyed his coffee. Finally, D'Lo wiped his mouth and took a swallow of coffee to wash down another donut before speaking.

"Word is, your girl's working for Ramon."

"Working? What kind of work?"

"Don't know exactly. He's into lots of stuff. None of it good."

"Where would I find him?"

D'Lo studied his friend. "I'm not sure that's a good idea."

"I told you her father and I were in the Marines together."

D'Lo nodded.

"What I didn't tell you is that we were in RECON. We were on a classified mission in South America and got ambushed. I was wounded—badly—and Trey literally carried me to safety. He saved my life."

Jon paused to let everything sink in, then said, "I need to find her, D'Lo. I don't care what it takes."

D'Lo told him Ramon drove a blacked-out Escalade on twenty-six-inch rims, usually around Mayfield Homes.

Jon's ears perked up at that. Mayfield Homes was a seedy public housing project near the municipal park where Moses stayed. A blacked-out Escalade on twenty-sixes shouldn't be hard to find.

He told D'Lo about Haley being spotted at Publix and that she'd slept at the park nearby. He also told D'Lo about the run-in last night.

"That's what I mean," D'Lo said. "Be careful. Ramon don't screw around."

"Is Carlos part of his crew?"

D'Lo shrugged. "Not that I know, not anymore. Carlos knows his place, and he's careful not to cross Ramon.

Apparently, as long as he stays in his lane, Ramon doesn't bother him."

Jon nodded. Carlos may be easier to get to. And he knew how to find Carlos. "Anything else?"

D'Lo stuffed another donut into his mouth. "Word is Ramon tied in with a treatment center."

Jon wrinkled his brow. "What do you mean, *tied in with a treatment center?* Which one? How?"

D'Lo shook his head. "I don't know. All I heard was that he was connected to one. Not sure what that means. If I hear anything else, I'll let you know."

16

It was one-thirty in the morning when his phone buzzed. Jon was back at his boat and had just finished his late-night rounds at the marina. Earlier that evening, he'd already made a quick loop, but every so often, he liked to make rounds twice in one night. This was one of those nights.

Who the hell was calling at this hour? He looked at the Caller ID. Nora Jenkins, his nurse manager friend from the hospital.

"I didn't wake you, did I?" she said when he answered.

He heard voices in the background. "You working?"

"Yeah, I stepped outside to call you." Her voice sounded off.

"Everything okay?" When she didn't answer immediately, he thought maybe the call had dropped.

"You didn't hear this from me," she said. Her tone was serious.

The hair stood up on the back of his neck. His gut churned, like when a pair of uniforms appeared on your doorstep. "What is it, Nora?"

"EMS just brought in an overdose." She hesitated as if trying to find the words. "We tried, Jon, but couldn't revive her."

Her? Jon's heart stopped. He was afraid to ask. "Was it . . ." He couldn't say her name, but Nora knew. Why else would she have called?

"I'm sorry, Jon. No ID, but it was the girl in the photo you gave me."

Maybe Nora was mistaken. It could've been another girl who looked like Haley. "Are you sure?"

There was a long pause. Dead silence on the line, then Nora spoke, clearly and slowly, so there was no confusion.

"She had a butterfly tattoo on her left shoulder."

* * *

Daylight was creeping in from the east as Jon sat on *Trouble No More's* flybridge, drinking coffee. He hadn't slept. Couldn't. Haley was dead because he didn't get to her in time.

He heard car wheels on gravel as someone pulled into the parking lot behind him. Turning, he saw it was a black, unmarked, 4-door sedan. Beth stepped out and headed toward him. When she got to the boat, she stopped and saw him on the flybridge.

"Grab a cup," he said. "I've got a fresh pot of coffee up here."

He felt a slight movement as Beth stepped aboard, then heard her open the cabin door below. Minutes later, she joined him. She sat, poured a cup, and refilled his.

"You look like shit," she said, studying his unshaven face and bloodshot eyes. "You know, don't you."

He nodded once. "What happened?"

She told him that EMS got a call just after midnight. Someone dumped an overdose in Bird City. Bird City was a blue-collar residential neighborhood where the streets were named after birds.

A resident coming home late from work saw a big black SUV pull up and push her out. There was no license plate or other description. The neighbor called 911 to report it.

"They Narcaned her—twice," she said. "She crashed in the ER. They couldn't revive her."

She looked at Jon. "I won't ask how you knew. You probably wouldn't tell me anyway. Have you talked to her father yet?"

Jon's eyes watered, and he shook his head. He couldn't bring himself to deliver the news, even though he knew he had to.

"Why don't you shower and get dressed?" she said. "I'll drive you to his hotel, and then we'll take him to the station. He can ID her there."

Jon knew his friend wouldn't be satisfied looking at a digital image of the body on a screen, the way it was mostly done these days. He wouldn't be. "He'll want to see her."

"It's not necessary."

"I know, but I know Trey. He'll want to see her. I would."

"I'm sorry, Jon."

All he managed was a nod. "Give me ten minutes," he said, rising.

On the way to the Courtyard in Beth's car, Jon didn't trust himself to speak. He texted Trey.

On my way over. B there in 10.

Almost immediately, Trey texted back.

What is it?

Jon ignored it and set the phone down on the console, wondering how he would tell Trey.

When Beth pulled into the Courtyard, Trey stood out front, smoking a cigarette, looking for Jon's car. When he saw Jon riding in the unmarked and Beth driving, he started shaking his head. Jon was out the door before she put it in Park.

"No," Trey said. "Please, God, no." Tears were rolling down his face.

Jon walked over and put his arms around Trey. "I'm so sorry."

Looking over Jon's shoulder, Beth stood. "911 got a call around one this morning. EMS picked her up and took her to the hospital. They did everything they could, but they couldn't save her."

"Drugs?" Trey asked in a whisper.

Beth nodded. "I'm so sorry for your loss, Mr. Stevens. I know this is difficult, but I need you to identify her. We can do that at the station."

"No," Trey said. "I want to see her."

They were quiet on the short ride over to the hospital. At the Emergency Department desk, Beth flashed her badge, and the clerk waved them through. They went straight through the double doors down the hallway to the morgue, Beth leading the way.

Although Jon hadn't been to this morgue before, it wouldn't be his first trip to identify a body. His last trip was the hardest, but none of them were ever easy.

The attendant escorted them to a small, private room with a computer screen on a small table. Trey stopped at the door, shaking his head. "I want. To see. Her."

The attendant started to speak, then hesitated when he saw Beth nod.

"If you wish," he said to Trey in a calm voice.

They followed him into another room with stainless steel cabinets against the wall. Jon steeled himself as the attendant paused and looked at Trey to make sure he was ready.

Trey took a deep breath and nodded. The attendant opened a door and gently rolled a tray out. Carefully, he pulled back the sheet exposing only the face.

Trey gasped, his breath caught in his throat. He reached out and touched her, tears streaming down his face. "Dear, sweet Haley. My baby."

Jon stood there, uncomfortable, not knowing what to say or do. He looked at the attendant and Beth, who respectfully gave the grieving father a few minutes to say goodbye.

At last, Trey turned to the attendant and nodded. "Thank you," he whispered.

By the time Beth dropped them off back at the Courtyard, Trey had shifted into taking care of business mode, trying to dull the reality with something he could control.

"I need to get a flight out. I've got to call Reece first. I hate to tell her over the phone, but I don't see any other way."

Jon nodded. "I'll take you to the airport. Anybody who can be with her until you get home?"

Trey thought a minute, then said, "Her sister. I'll give her a call. What about my rental car?"

"Don't worry about it. Give me the keys. I'll take care of it."

Trey handed him the keys.

"Call Reece, then call the airline. I'll take your car to the marina and get mine, and then I'll come back over to take you to the airport."

When Jon came back to the Courtyard, Trey was pacing out front with his bag. He'd booked a Delta flight from Fort Lauderdale to Cincinnati that left in two hours. Fort

Lauderdale-Hollywood International Airport was only thirty minutes away, but they had to hustle to make it.

At the curb outside the departure entrance, Jon left his car running and got out to bid Trey goodbye. "Take care of Reece," Jon said as they embraced. "She needs you. Let me know if there's anything I can do."

"Just find out what happened," Trey said. His eyes were bloodshot from crying. He turned and ran toward the terminal with his bag.

"Don't worry," Jon said as he watched Trey leave. Finding who was responsible and seeing them punished was his only goal now that Haley was gone. That was the least he could do for Trey and Reece.

17

It was midday Sunday, and Stuart Westbrook was driving to Boca Raton to meet Cal Norman on his boat for lunch. The last thing he wanted to do on the weekend was have lunch with Cal. But when the boss called, you went, especially if the boss was Cal.

Cal was the CEO of Moren Health, the company that owned Delray-By-The-Sea. He'd called an hour ago and invited Stuart to lunch aboard his boat, docked behind his waterfront home in Boca.

Stuart had the top down on his 8 Series BMW convertible, one of the many perks of his position. The least he could do was enjoy the sunshine and fresh air on his way to what promised to be a corporate reaming.

He stopped at the gatehouse of the exclusive community and gave his name to the guard along with his driver's license. The woman checked it against the visitor's list, nodded, and handed the license back to him.

"Have a nice day, Dr. Westbrook."

He nodded. Drumming his fingers on the steering wheel, he waited for the gate to open. As soon as the opening was wide enough, he gunned the car and drove through.

At Cal's house, he parked on the circular drive in front. Rosaline, the housekeeper, opened the door. "Mr. Norman's out on the boat. I'll walk you out."

It wasn't necessary. He knew the way, and he'd been there enough that she knew he didn't need an escort. But he let her do her job and followed as she led the way.

WesTex, Cal's Horizon V72, was docked next to the seawall. She was a stunning boat. Admittedly, it was not particularly large by South Florida standards at seventy-two feet long. But still, Stuart knew it was over five million dollars' worth of boat.

Cal was sitting outside at the table on the main deck, talking on his phone. When he saw the pair approaching, he waved them aboard.

They made their way aft and waited as Cal wrapped up his conversation. Lunch was on the table.

"Could I get you anything else, Mr. Norman?" Rosaline asked when Cal set his phone down.

"No, thank you, Rosaline. How's your daughter?"

Her face lit up. "She's doing much better, thank you. She loved the balloons you sent."

Cal waved his hand, dismissing the compliment as if it happened all the time. "If you need anything or need to take some time off, just let me know."

"Yes, thank you." She turned and walked away.

"Her daughter just had her tonsils removed," Cal said. His phone rang, and he looked to see who was calling. He held up a finger. "I need to get this. It'll only be a minute. Sit. Eat."

Stuart sat opposite his boss and reached for a sandwich. The fattening of the lamb before slaughter. He took a bite.

"Did you get my message?" Cal said into the phone. He shook his head. Then, in a louder voice, "No, that's not acceptable." His face got redder. He was shaking his head and gesticulating wildly.

Stuart shook his head. Great. As if it wasn't going to be bad enough anyway. Now, someone and something was getting Cal primed to pounce. He wolfed his sandwich down before it happened.

"Goddammit, I don't care. Just do it." Cal slammed the phone down on the table in front of him. "What a bunch of morons."

He adjusted his expression and pasted a smile on. "Sorry about that. Thanks for coming out, Stu."

Stuart bristled. He'd always hated the shortening of his name. Hearing it irritated him, like running fingernails across a chalkboard. Cal was one of those who abbreviated everything.

Like I had a choice, he wanted to say, but kept his mouth shut. Cal wasn't interested in what anyone had to say unless it was what he wanted to hear.

Cal picked up the report in front of him and shook it at Stuart. "Your preliminary financials. Unless I'm missing something, you're not going to make your numbers this month. Again." He waited for a beat, inviting Stuart to speak.

Stuart cleared his throat. "We had to write off several unusually large accounts this month. It was an aberration, but we should be back on track next month."

Cal pounced. "Back on track for next month is too little too late. You'll still be behind year-to-date."

"We're pushing as hard—"

"Stu. The IPO is next month." The initial public offering stood to make Cal an even richer man. As one of Moren's original employees and CEO of their largest treatment center, Stuart also stood to reap a sizeable payday.

Again, Cal's face reddened. Stuart found himself hoping that the man would have a heart attack. If only.

"We have to finish *this* month strong to keep the offering price where it is," Cal said condescendingly. "We can't do it without Delray-By-The-Sea leading the way. What part of that don't you get?"

Stuart knew it was a rhetorical question. "I'll get with Valerie. We'll make it happen." He didn't know how, but that was the answer Cal wanted.

"Good. I'm counting on you. Don't let me down." Cal looked at the Rolex on his wrist. "I'm expecting a call in ten minutes. Anything else?"

Stuart had to stifle a chuckle. Cal made it sound like Stuart had requested the meeting. On his way to Boca, he'd planned on telling Cal about Jon Cruz, enlisting his assistance in shutting down the Stevens incident. But, after the way this meeting turned out, he didn't dare bring it up. Instead, he'd figure out how to handle it.

Stuart shook his head and rose. "I need to run by the office on my way home." He had no plans to do that but thought that'd be a good excuse to leave. "Thanks for lunch."

18

Jon decided to drive over to Fish Tale Marina to see Ricky.

When he got there, Ricky was standing outside next to a Mako center console on a trailer, talking to a man in deck shoes wearing shorts and a Huk T-shirt. His face was well-weathered, and Jon guessed he was the boat owner.

When Ricky saw Jon, a look of panic crossed his face. Jon hung back, waiting for Ricky to finish his business. As soon as they were done, the man climbed into a pickup and left. Only then did Jon walk over.

As soon as he approached, Ricky said, "I went to see the lady you told me to. Dr. Williams. I've got another appointment tomorrow." He seemed nervous about Jon dropping by unannounced in the middle of the day.

Jon nodded, pleased that Ricky had gone to see the psychologist Nora had suggested. Jon had made the appointment for him and told Williams that he'd be taking care of Ricky's bill.

"Good. But that's not why I'm here. I need to talk to Carlos."

"I . . . don't understand."

"I need you to call Carlos and set up a meeting. Today."

"I thought you didn't want me—"

"You're not. I'm going in your place."

Before Ricky could ask, Jon said, "Yesterday, I put my best friend on a plane back home to Cincinnati. His daughter overdosed, and some scumbag dumped her on the street in Bird City. She died in the ER, and I intend to find out who's responsible."

Ricky's head drooped. "I . . . I'm sorry."

Jon fixed him with a stern look. "That's what I don't want to happen to you. Call him and leave a message requesting a meet."

He stood there while Ricky called Carlos's number and did as instructed.

When Ricky hung up, Jon asked, "How soon does he call you back?"

Ricky shrugged. "Usually within an hour."

"Good. Soon as you get the details, call me."

Jon left and drove to Publix, where Haley had stolen the money. When he got there, he parked and looked at the map he'd brought. Mentally, he plotted a course around the area in an ever-widening circle. Before, he'd been looking for Haley. This time, he was looking for something else.

Three blocks away, he found it. St. Peter's Episcopal Church. A place where a runaway could've hidden in plain sight. He kicked himself for not thinking of it before.

It was early afternoon, so the parking lot was empty except for a few cars. He parked and followed the signs for the church office, listing the rector as Reverend Phillip Bryce.

Inside, a young woman sat at a desk. He noticed the office door behind her was cracked open. RECTOR'S OFFICE was on the nameplate.

She looked up and greeted him with a smile. "Could I help you?"

"Yes, I hope so. I'm Jon Cruz. Is Father Bryce in?"

"Did you have an appointment?"

"No, I'm sorry, I don't." He glanced at the rector's office, then said, "I was hoping he might have a few minutes. I'm trying to find out what happened to a friend's daughter."

He thought he saw a flicker of acknowledgment before she caught herself. She hesitated, then said, "Excuse me. I'll check."

She rose and entered the office, tapping on the door first. Jon heard a murmur inside. Then she walked out, followed by a man wearing a clerical collar. Trim, with sandy hair, he was younger than Jon expected and bore the unmistakable aura of a priest. He extended his hand. "Phillip Bryce."

"Jon Cruz."

Bryce motioned toward his office. "Please, come in and have a seat." The priest closed the door behind him and sat behind his desk.

"Thank you for seeing me, Father," Jon said. "I'll make it brief."

"Please, call me Phil."

Jon shifted in his chair. "Uh, that's not easy for me."

Phil cocked his head. "You must be Catholic."

"I went to Catholic school. My father was Hispanic and a devout Catholic. My mother, not so much."

Phil didn't comment. He appeared to be studying Jon's blue eyes and fair skin.

Jon chuckled. "I get that a lot. My mother was Scandinavian, and I got her looks. But I got my father's temper along with his name."

"What did you call your priest?"

"Padre. Anything else, and my father would have belted me."

Bryce smiled and shrugged. "Then call me Padre. I have quite a few Hispanic parishioners here at St. Peter's, and

I'm used to it. So, Melanie tells me you're trying to find your friend's daughter?"

Jon pulled out Haley's picture and handed it to the rector. Padre was better than most people at concealing his expressions, but it was evident he recognized Haley.

"Haley Stevens, my best friend's daughter. She was in a drug treatment program here in Delray Beach. A week ago, she checked herself out and never contacted her parents. She was spotted yesterday in the area."

"Hmm," he said, then handed the photo back to Jon. "How can I help?"

Jon stared at him for a moment as he weighed how to proceed. "Have you seen her?"

Padre folded his hands on his desk and adopted a poker face. "I would like to help, but I'm sure you know that clergy-penitent conversations are privileged."

Jon smiled. Padre had just unwittingly confirmed he'd talked to Haley. Nice was getting nowhere. He leaned across the desk.

"Haley's dead. Early yesterday morning, I took her father to the morgue to identify her body. Then, I put him on a plane home to Cincinnati, where he had to tell his wife they have to plan the funeral for their only child."

He sat back to let the words sink in. The expression of remorse crept over Padre's face like the sea fog stealing in over the Golden Gate.

"I . . . she . . . how?" He stumbled, searching for the right words.

"She overdosed. Some scumbag dumped her on the street in Bird City, three blocks from here. She died in the ER."

Padre put his face in his hands, emitting a primal cry. Jon felt a tinge of guilt about his blunt delivery, but he didn't have time to play games.

Finally, Padre looked up at him with bloodshot eyes. "We occasionally take in runaways. Feed them, give them a safe place to sleep—no questions asked. We offer emotional and spiritual support and encourage them to get help."

He looked down at his desk and shook his head. "She showed up two nights ago and left the following morning after breakfast. She didn't say much about her situation. We've learned not to press. I didn't know . . ." His words trailed off.

"Helping these kids is admirable, Padre, and I respect your efforts. You're providing a much-needed service in our community. But I want to find out who did this and make sure they don't do it again. Haley wasn't the first and won't be the last. Talking to others who knew her or were in rehab with her would greatly help."

Jon rose to leave and put his card on the rector's desk. "If you know of anybody, give me a call."

19

B ack in his car, Jon's phone buzzed. It was Ricky.
"When and where?" Jon asked.

"I'm supposed to meet Carlos at Peg Legs. Five o'clock."

Peg Legs was a local dive bar only a few miles from Hank's. Jon had never been in but had driven by it. From the outside, it made Hank's look downright respectable.

"Got it. If he calls with a change of plans, let me know. And Ricky? After five, don't answer any further calls from him. Understand?"

"Yessir."

"I'll talk to you tomorrow after your appointment with Dr. Williams."

Jon disconnected. He had just enough time to go back to the boat and get his pistol.

On *Trouble No More,* he changed clothes, putting on a ratty T-shirt and tattered shorts. He traded his good deck shoes for an old pair long since relegated to work duty.

Satisfied that he would fit in, he left and drove the short distance to Peg Legs. It was a dumpy, landlocked old-Florida bar, concrete block construction with fading paint and an asphalt shingle roof way past its prime. It wasn't particularly remarkable in a neighborhood of mostly older mobile homes in similar shape.

He was early and hoped Carlos wouldn't be looking for Ricky's car. He decided his vehicle would look out of place parked out front and might scare the dealer away.

He remembered passing a convenience store a block away, so he turned around and drove back. He pulled in and parked at the end of the building.

Inside, he offered the clerk, a middle eastern looking young man, two twenty-dollar bills to let him park there for an hour. Jon explained that he was going to Peg Legs but didn't want to park his new car there and risk getting it scratched.

The clerk looked at the money and Jon figured he was quickly doing the math. It represented four-hours' worth of pay for doing nothing—an easy call. The young man nodded, then pocketed the money.

Jon walked the short distance to Peg Legs and entered. The dark interior did nothing to dissuade him from his original assessment. A handful of people were seated at tables and another half dozen at the bar, none who paid him the slightest attention other than a cursory glance.

He went to the bar and ordered a Bud in the bottle. Not his first choice, but it wouldn't attract attention here. He gave the bartender a five and two ones, then walked over to an empty booth on the same wall as the front door. He took a seat where he had a good view of the entrance. More importantly, once someone came in, he could quickly position himself between them and the exit.

Jon knew he'd recognize Carlos, and he assumed Carlos would recognize him. He planned to approach Carlos and ask him to step outside to talk.

Five minutes before five, the door opened, and a pony-tailed, wiry Latino walked in. Carlos. He stopped inside the door for a moment, scanning the bar, obviously looking for Ricky. When he didn't see his customer, he walked over to a pair of empty stools, sat, and ordered a beer. He didn't notice Jon walking up behind him.

"Hey, Carlos."

Not recognizing the voice, Carlos turned, and his eyes widened when he saw not Ricky but the man who'd disarmed him and tied him up at Hank's.

"Easy. I just want to—"

Carlos bolted toward the door.

"Goddammit," Jon said. So much for his original plan. He turned and gave chase. He was halfway across the bar when Carlos went out the front door. By the time Jon got there, the door was almost closed.

He hit the door precisely as two burly guys opened it to enter the bar. Bodies went sprawling. Lying on the ground, Jon saw Carlos get into an old red Toyota Camry and race away before he could get to his feet.

"Hey, buddy. You need to watch where you're going," the taller one said, already standing and looking down at Jon. He extended his hand to his shorter but heavier friend and pulled him to his feet. They both stood, but neither offered to help Jon up.

"Sorry," Jon said as he got to his feet. He knew he could easily dispatch the two out-of-shape rednecks, but the last thing he wanted was to get in a row with locals. "I was trying to catch that guy who just drove off. He owes me money. Do you know him?"

They glanced in Carlos's direction, then turned their attention back to Jon. Their anger was now redirected to a new target.

"That little Mexican fucker? Nah, never seen him here before," the taller one said.

"Again, sorry I ran into you," Jon said. "I gotta go, or I'd buy you a round. Maybe next time?"

"No problem, man. We'll keep an eye out for him, though." Jon's new best friends turned and went inside.

Jon cursed his luck all the way back to his car. At least now, he knew what Carlos drove. He couldn't get the tag number, but it wasn't a black Escalade.

20

The next morning, Jon decided to go look for Ramon, the apparent drug kingpin in Delray Beach. As he walked through the marina parking lot to the bar for breakfast, he stopped to look at Lucille. The rear end was higher than the front, as if the front wheels were in a depression. He stepped closer and the reason was apparent. Her front tires were flat, the rims on the gravel.

What the hell? He looked at the left one but couldn't find any explanation. When he looked at the right tire, he found an inch-long cut, about the size of a knife blade. He returned to the other side and found the same on that tire.

What the fuck? Both cuts were in the sidewall, which meant no repair was possible. He'd have to buy two new tires at four hundred dollars apiece.

Someone had to have done it last night after he made his rounds. Carlos came to mind as the prime suspect. It was too much of a coincidence that Jon surprised him yesterday afternoon at Peg Legs, but how would Carlos have known where he lived and what kind of car he drove?

Of course, it wouldn't have been too hard to figure out that Jon worked at Hank's after the encounter with Ricky. From there to determine where Jon lived and what he drove wouldn't have been much of a stretch. Regardless, Jon was skeptical of coincidences.

He called Ricky and asked him to send someone to get Lucille. After the tow truck came and left with his vehicle, he went back into Hank's.

"You must've overslept," Addie said as she poured him coffee.

"No. Two flat tires."

"Two?"

"Don't ask. The usual, please." His typical breakfast was two eggs up with hash browns and bacon.

When Addie brought the food and a warm-up for coffee, she stopped to chat. "Sounds like your day is starting like mine ended yesterday."

"What happened?"

"City hall. The bastards."

He was surprised. Hank's had been in business for decades at the same location. Most of the city commissioners were regulars. The city of Delray Beach didn't usually bother Hank's.

Addie continued. "Sent me a notice that I need a structural and electrical evaluation before I can renew my business license."

"What? Where'd that come from?"

She shrugged. "They're blaming it on the Surfside thing." The twelve-story condo collapse in the Miami area had Florida rushing to enact more stringent standards for coastal buildings. All of the municipalities on the coasts were running scared.

"That's bullshit. That was a high-rise. You're one story."

"With a marina, which they claim is part of the issue."

"You call R.D.?"

R. David Stone had been Hank's attorney. When Hank passed, he'd left everything to Addie, who'd worked fifteen years for him. She'd been more family to him than his three kids, who'd little to do with him over the years.

They learned this at the reading of the will, where they had gathered at R.D.'s office like vultures finding fresh roadkill. With fake tears, they had huffed and puffed and threatened to sue Addie till the day she died.

What they didn't count on was that the old man was shrewder than they'd realized. R.D., who kept his boat docked at Hank's marina, also happened to be one of the top estate attorneys in South Florida.

Hank's will was heir-proof. Hank had left R.D a generous retainer, sufficient to defend Addie's claim for eternity. He had also left the painting that now hung in the bar, as a reminder to the ungrateful kids should they ever set foot inside again.

After spending prodigious amounts on frivolous lawsuits producing little progress, the heirs decided to cut their losses. Empty-handed, they quietly crawled back under the rocks from which they'd emerged.

Addie nodded. "He's looking into it."

"Don't worry. If anybody can fix it, R.D. can," Jon said.

At lunch, Ricky came to *Trouble No More,* driving Lucille.

"You didn't have to bring it to me," Jon said. "I could've got an Uber."

Ricky grinned. "And pass up a chance to drive this bad girl? Hope you don't mind. I took it to my appointment with Dr. Williams."

He smiled. Knowing Ricky, he took the long way, too. But he didn't mind. Ricky was one of the few people he trusted to drive Lucille.

"Thanks," Jon said. "Let's go to the bar, and I'll buy you lunch. Then you can drive me back to the boatyard to drop you off."

As they sat in Hank's, Ricky asked, "What happened? Joey at the garage said both tires had been cut."

Jon nodded. "Don't know. Whoever did it after I made rounds last night. At least they didn't key it or break a window." He didn't share his thoughts on who. He didn't want Ricky to think that he was somehow responsible.

After he took Ricky back to work, Jon moved a wireless camera on the boat and set it up so it would have a good view of his car. It was motion-sensitive and would text him if it detected movement.

He wasn't worried about anyone getting on the boat. It had an alarm, and besides, the gate was locked in the evening. He was a light sleeper, and the SIG was always beside him. Anyone breaking into his boat better be fast.

Satisfied the camera was working correctly, he shifted his attention back to finding Ramon. He remembered that D'Lo had told him Ramon drove an Escalade on twenty-six inch rims and hung out in the housing project known as Mayfield Homes, so he headed that direction.

The project consisted of a couple of non-descript four-story apartment buildings surrounded by a series of identical duplexes. A playground rounded out the complex. When he arrived, he circled the block, sizing up the area, and parked next to the playground. He sat there for a few minutes, observing.

A few people milled about in the park. Several families with small kids, a few pairs of young people, and a couple of singles, but no one appeared threatening. He checked the pistol in his waistband, ensuring his shirt covered it, and exited his car.

He walked over to a young man wearing a hoodie, who eyed him suspiciously. His hands were visible, and Jon spotted no sign of a concealed weapon.

"I'm looking for someone," Jon said. The man didn't reply, so he continued. "Ramon." He added, "I just want to talk to him."

The man shrugged. "Don't know him," he said, then turned to leave.

Jon watched as the man shuffled away. He didn't seem to be in a particular hurry, but Jon kept an eye on him until he was a safe distance.

Satisfied, Jon looked around the playground for someone else to question. As he looked, he felt something poking him in his right kidney.

"Don't move. You must be lost. Or crazy." The voice was that of a young male.

Shit. He couldn't believe he didn't see that coming. He was slipping. First, Carlos got away, and now this punk ambushed him. He'd let the man wearing the hoodie distract him so the gunman could get the drop on him.

"I told you, I'm just trying to find Ramon."

"You doan find Ramon, he find you."

Jon knew the man was right-handed since he was poking his gun on his right side. He calculated his next move.

"Nice ride you got parked over there," the man said.

Jon turned his head to the right toward his car and smiled. "The keys are in it."

The man chuckled. "You *are* crazy." He poked Jon and said, "Let's walk over there and see."

Jon feigned a step toward his right, then spun left, pushing the man's right hand to the side. Bringing his knee up, he grabbed the man's right wrist and slammed his arm down underneath the elbow. He heard the unmistakable crack of bone.

The man dropped the gun and screamed. "You broke my fucking arm. Police brutality."

Now behind him, Jon pulled out his gun and jammed it into the man's neck. "I'm not a cop, and you pulled a gun on me, asshole." He looked around and saw several sets of eyes on them, all at a safe distance.

He zip-tied the man's good arm to the playground fence. Keeping his eyes on the thug, he stepped over, picked up the man's gun, and cleared it. He stuck the magazine and the pistol in his pocket.

The man was whimpering in pain. "You fucked up my arm, man."

"You'll live. Send Ramon over to talk to me. I'll be over at the Waffle Hut."

At the Waffle Hut, Jon backed his car in to have a clear view of anyone entering the parking lot. Forty-five minutes later, he saw a black Escalade sporting twenty-six-inch rims turn in. The vehicle slowed as it passed in front of him, then stopped. Jon made a mental note to ask Beth if she had any further description of the black SUV that dumped Haley in Bird City.

The heavily tinted SUV windows prevented Jon from seeing the occupants, so he started the car. While he didn't think Ramon would be foolish enough to try anything in broad daylight, he remembered D'Lo's words. Be careful. Ramon don't screw around. He reached out and grasped the pistol he'd laid in the seat.

The Escalade backed up and then turned and pulled in nose first, the driver's side next to Jon. Jon held the pistol in his lap and pointed toward the SUV. He was poised to raise it at the first sign of trouble. The window lowered, and a tall young Hispanic guy with a ball cap on backward stared at him.

"You Ramon?" Jon asked.

"Maybe. You messed up my boy's arm."

"He pulled a gun on me. He's lucky that's all I did."

Ramon's eyes narrowed. "What do you want?"

"I'm trying to find out what happened to someone. A girl. White, mid-twenties, blonde hair. Her name is Haley. Witnesses say a vehicle like yours dumped her out in Bird City Friday night."

"Don't know what you talking about. Lotsa black Escalades in town."

"Carlos still working for you?"

Ramon shook his head, eyes narrowing. "He doan work for me."

"Who's he work for?"

"I don't know, don't care. I ain't seen him in months."

Jon tightened his grip on the pistol. "Somebody's lying to me. The girl I asked you about? Haley? She overdosed and was dumped in Bird City. She died on the way to the hospital. I want to know who's responsible."

Ramon's eyes widened, but he kept his cool. "I tole you. I don't know who you talking about."

"Tell me somebody who does."

"There a reward?"

Jon smiled. "The reward is you don't see me again."

Ramon glared at him. "You wastin my time."

Jon raised his window, put the car in gear, and drove away.

21

Back at the marina, Jon had just enough time to shower and change before Nora Jenkins arrived for dinner.

Convinced that Carlos or Ramon had information about Haley, he was frustrated with his lack of progress. He wished he hadn't invited Nora over since he wanted to talk about it with Beth. But that would have to wait. He'd promised to cook for his nurse friend, and it was too late to back out. Maybe a quiet evening with the vivacious redhead would do him good.

After getting dressed, he checked the spaghetti sauce simmering on the stove. He tasted it. Not bad. He added some salt, re-covered it, then called Beth. He got her voicemail and didn't bother to leave a message.

On his way up to the flybridge, he stopped to put on some music—Eva Cassidy, one of his favorites. Topside, he'd just gotten settled when he spotted the redheaded nurse walking out the dock toward him.

"Thanks for coming," he said after hustling downstairs to greet her as she walked up. She looked the part for dinner on his boat, wearing white shorts, a blue and white striped top, and boat shoes. It was the first time he'd seen her wearing something besides hospital scrubs, and he couldn't help but notice how attractive she was.

"Thanks for the invitation," she said as she stepped on board and looked around. "Nice. Do I get a tour?"

"Sure. You know anything about boats?"

She narrowed her eyes with a slight shake of the head. "I grew up in Michigan. On the lake by the same name. I sailed the Mac three times. You know what that is?"

He shook his head. Her well-worn boat shoes should've been a clue. But he liked the fact that she could give it right back to him.

The Mac, for short, was the annual Chicago Yacht Club Race from Chicago to Mackinac Island in July. It was one of the premier sailboat races in the world, and with the fickle weather on Lake Michigan, not for novices. In 2011, two experienced sailors died during the race when a sudden storm flipped their boat.

"Okay," he said. "Let me take my size ten out of my mouth and start over. How about I open some wine, give you a brief tour, and try to redeem myself?"

She laughed. "Nice recovery. That's a much better start."

They entered the main salon, where she sniffed the air and turned toward the galley. "Something smells good," she said.

"Nothing fancy. I hope you like spaghetti. Chianti okay?"

"I do, and Chianti is fine."

He stepped over to the galley to open the wine while she checked out the area. He noticed her gaze settle on the lone picture of Megan. She looked up at him, questioning, but said nothing.

He handed her a glass of wine. "Salud," he said, holding his glass up. He extended his free arm toward the steps leading down to the master cabin aft.

"My quarters," he said, leading her closer for a better view. He pointed out the head, the separate shower, and a small desk. A slight breeze flowed from the open rear companionway hatch.

"A lot roomier than my monohull sailboat," she said.

Back up on the main deck, they passed through the main salon back to the galley. He pointed down to the forward berth.

"V-berth up front with its own toilet/shower combo."

He paused at the steering station as they crossed to the wheelhouse door. "All the electronics have been updated, as well as the two Caterpillar engines at 435 horsepower each."

"Nice. What's your cruising speed?"

He laughed. "Maybe a little better than your sailboat. Around twelve knots. The six hundred gallons of diesel it holds gives you a six-hundred-mile range. Easy to get to the Bahamas and back, and comfortable."

"Who is that?" she asked, cocking her head to hear the music playing softly in the background.

"Eva Cassidy."

"Beautiful. I don't believe I know her."

"A lot of people don't, unfortunately. A voice like an angel. Sadly, she died at thirty-three."

He paused, collecting his thoughts. He'd stumbled on to Eva Cassidy after Megan died. And now, Haley. All died way too young.

"What happened?"

It took him a few seconds to realize Nora was asking about Cassidy. "Melanoma," he said.

"Wow. How sad."

The salon started to feel claustrophobic. He stepped through the wheelhouse door, anxious to get some fresh air, leading Nora outside. "Let's go up to the flybridge."

"This is my favorite perch," he said as they sat at the table there. He sipped his wine, then said, "Thank you for recommending Dr. Williams. My friend likes her, and I can already see where she's helping."

"That's good to hear. She's excellent. I never hesitate to recommend her."

When she realized he had caught her staring at the tattoo on his forearm, she said, "Interesting tattoo."

He didn't have to look. It was his only one—a compass rose with a watchful eye above the North arrow. Trey had one just like it, along with many others who'd served in Force RECON. "My souvenir from the Marines."

Changing the subject, he said, "So, you're a Great Lakes' girl. I must confess. The only part of Lake Michigan I've ever seen is what I could see from the Chicago lakefront."

She chuckled. "You and a lot of other people. It's a beautiful lake but can be very unforgiving. Just like any other large body of water. Don't turn your back on it and don't take it for granted."

She told him about sailing the Mac, then directed the conversation back to him. "So how did you end up living on a stinkpot in Delray Beach?" she asked with a mischievous grin, using the derogatory term sailors use for powerboats.

He wasn't going to let that pass. "I like to get from point A to point B in a reasonable amount of time and not be dependent on which way the wind is blowing, unlike you snailboats."

She grinned at the derisive term powerboaters used for sailboats.

"When I retired, I wanted a change," he said. "I found this boat in Jacksonville. It needed updating, but I could afford to upgrade everything at the price I paid and still come out ahead. I changed the name to *Trouble No More* and headed south for the Keys. Had to lay up here while a storm passed and decided to stay."

"Changing the name of a boat is bad luck, you know."

He shrugged. "I've heard that. But the name was *Sundance*—too hokey for me."

"Maybe sometime you could take me out," she said.

He nodded. "I'd actually thought about that this evening. I nixed that idea since I didn't know how much of a boat person you were." He held up his hands. "No assumptions—I just wanted you to be comfortable, so don't slug me. Now that I know better, we'll have to do that next time."

Back down in the galley, she offered to prepare a salad and set the table while he started the pasta and got the bread ready for the oven.

When everything was ready, they sat. She took a mouthful of spaghetti. "Delicious," she said. "An old family recipe?"

"Right off the internet. I thought it would be easy and safe. Better than crow, right?" He grinned.

"I'm surprised. I figured you for seafood."

He shook his head. "Seafood is my favorite, but I wasn't sure where you stood on that either. Damn—I'm getting off to a rocky start."

She laughed. "I love seafood—if it's fresh."

"The only kind I serve. Maybe we can go out and catch dinner?"

"That'd put you in the plus column."

"Glad I asked instead of sticking my foot in my mouth again."

After eating, they returned to the flybridge for an after-dinner glass of wine.

"I was surprised when you invited me over," she said. "I didn't think you were serious that day at the hospital."

"The least I could do. I appreciate your help. It's been a rough few days."

"How's your friend Trey doing?" she asked, genuine concern in her voice.

He shrugged. "As well as can be expected. I wish I had some answers for him." He told her he thought Trey's daughter fell off the wagon and got in with the wrong crowd after she left Delray-By-The-Sea.

"Pretty common, unfortunately," Nora said.

He glanced at Megan's picture, a gesture she caught but didn't pursue. "Trey doesn't believe it," he said.

"Denial?"

Jon shook his head. "I'm not sure. He'd been down this road more than a few times before with Haley. He believed this time was different."

"What do you think?"

"I don't know. You know how high the recidivism rates are for drug rehab. But why else would she drop out so close to the end, especially if she was doing well?"

"Have you looked at her medical record?"

He wrinkled his brow. "Not really. I told Trey to get a copy from Delray-By-The-Sea, but then everything happened, and I forgot about it. I'm not sure I'd be able to decipher it anyway."

"I'd be happy to take a look at it if you want."

He nodded. "Thanks. I'd appreciate that. I'll get him to send me a copy."

She finished her wine and looked at the clock. "It's been a wonderful evening, but I probably need to go. I've got a staff meeting at six in the morning."

He eyed her with a mischievous grin. "If you promise to give me a second chance. I do learn from my mistakes."

"Ball's in your court, sailor," she said with a grin.

"Good. I'll walk you out."

22

It was a slow night at Hank's as Jon sat at the bar, waiting for Addie to bring him a beer. When she walked over and set his beer down, he could tell that something was bothering her.

"You look like someone stole your dog," he said.

"I don't have a dog."

She didn't walk away, a sign that meant she wanted to chat. He took a drink from his beer and waited. With Addie, you had to be prepared to listen patiently and not interrupt.

"Delray's finest came by earlier," she said. "To let me know they're going to be increasing patrols here."

Sounded like a good thing to him, but obviously, Addie didn't see it that way. He nodded but didn't speak, awaiting her assessment.

"'Due to the increased drug activity,' they said. That's going to be great for business, with a patrol car sitting out front."

Before he could comment, motion distracted him. Ricky walked up beside him and stood at the bar.

"What's the po-po doing out front?" Ricky asked.

Addie snorted and stormed off.

"Did I say something wrong?" Ricky asked.

Jon shook his head. "Bad timing."

Addie brought a soda over, sat it in front of Ricky, then walked away without speaking.

Jon looked at Ricky with a critical eye. The mechanic's eyes were clear, and his speech normal—good signs. "You clean?" he asked, wanting Ricky to look him in the eye and answer.

He met his gaze without wavering. "I've been going to Dr. Williams. Doing what you told me. I swear."

"Good. You don't want to give the cops an excuse to stop you."

Ricky took his soda and walked down to the other end of the bar to sit next to a friend.

Jon was almost finished with his beer and about to leave when Beth walked in and sat next to him. "I called you earlier."

She nodded. "But that's not why I'm here."

Addie walked over, but before she could say anything, Beth waved her hand across the bar and said, "Nothing for me. I'm on the clock."

Beth's tone prompted Addie to nod, then make her way back down to the other end of the bar. Jon sensed that she wanted to get as far away as possible.

"Consider this an official visit," Beth said.

Jon raised his eyebrows, wondering what this was about. "Okay?"

"You been over to Mayfield Homes lately?"

"Maybe. Why?" He didn't like where this conversation was headed.

"It's a yes or no question. Your evasive answer indicates you have."

Beth was in full detective mode, raising alarms. "And?" he said.

"Some punk came down to the station. Said you broke his arm, and he wants to file charges. I'm here to get your explanation."

Jon held his hand up. "You're kidding?"

"Do I look like it?"

"I was just asking a few questions, and he pulled a gun on me. I bet he failed to mention that part. He wants to file charges? Bring it on."

She stared at him. "What questions were you asking?"

"Jesus, Beth. I asked his buddy how to get in touch with Ramon. Next thing I know, some dickhead sticks a gun in my back."

"Any witnesses?"

"Yes, but good luck in getting them to testify. Tell you what. Let's go down to my boat and I'll give you his gun. Run the prints. You'll find mine and his. I'm betting you'll find a match for his. He probably has a felony conviction and doesn't have a permit. Last time I checked, pointing a firearm at someone is a felony in Florida. You should be arresting him, not harassing me."

She shook her head. "What do you want with Ramon?"

Jon was pissed, now. "I'm just trying to find out what happened to Haley Stevens since obviously it's not a priority with your department. Why aren't you talking to Ramon? Or his ex-sidekick, Carlos? Did you get a description of the black Escalade that dumped Haley Stevens out on the street in Bird City?"

"Who said it was an Escalade?"

He gave a nonchalant shrug. "I just assumed it was. You told me it was a big black SUV."

He avoided her stare, chiding himself for the slip. He finished his beer, then rose. "Let's go. I want to give you the gun before anymore bullshit happens."

Without speaking, they walked down to *Trouble No More*. Beth followed him on board. He went to his safe, removed the gun and magazine, and handed them to her. "Anything else?"

"I'm just doing my job, Jon. Let me do it. Quit poking around where you have no business." She crossed her arms. "What did you want to talk to me about?"

He shook his head, no longer in the mood to chat. "Not important."

She stood for a minute, then said, "Okay." She turned and left.

He poured himself a tequila and went up to the flybridge to calm down. What the hell was happening? Addie gets harassed. Then Ramon's punk wants to file charges against him?

He looked at his phone and saw that Trey had called. He punched Trey's number.

"Hey." Trey's voice was still a flat monotone.

"Sorry, I was in Hank's without my phone. I just saw the missed call." Jon started to ask Trey how he was doing, then realized how stupid that sounded.

Trey's voice took on a hard edge. "We got another call today from the collection agency on Haley's bill."

Jon squeezed the phone so hard he thought he'd crush it. He couldn't believe Delray-By-The-Sea was still harassing them. Obviously, they didn't take his warning seriously.

"I'm sorry, buddy. I'll go over there in the morning and take care of it. I promise."

"Thanks."

"Anything else I can do?"

"No. We haven't finalized plans for her service yet. I'll let you know."

Jon hesitated, then continued. "I know you've got a lot on your plate right now, but could you email me a copy of her medical record? I want to take another look at it." He still couldn't bring himself to say Haley's name out loud.

"I'll try to get it to you this evening."

"Thanks. Give Reece a hug for me. And let me know if I can do anything else."

Those assholes from Delray-By-The-Sea. First thing in the morning, he was going over there to put a stop to this crap.

23

The following day, Jon drove over to Delray-By-The-Sea. Tiffany, the same perky blonde, was sitting at the desk. Her eyes widened when he walked up, sensing trouble. Before she could speak, Jon said, "I need to see Kip Foster. I'm Jon Cruz."

"Uh, did you have an appointment with Mr. Foster?"

Jon folded his arms across his chest, hardening his stance and his voice. "I don't. I need a minute of his time regarding Haley Stevens. As you probably recall, her father and I met with him Thursday."

She nodded while reaching for her phone. "Let me call his office."

He didn't move, listening to her side of the conversation.

"Jon Cruz is here at my desk and wants to speak with you about Haley Stevens. He and Mr. Stevens were here Thursday, remember?"

She looked up at Jon and shook her head as she spoke into the phone. "He's standing right here in front of me. I don't think that's going to work, Kip."

Although he couldn't hear what Kip said, Jon guessed that Foster had told her to say he was busy and to ask him to call for an appointment. Jon smiled to let Tiffany know she made the right call.

"I'll tell him," she said into the phone, then hung up.

Looking at Jon, she said, "He'll be right out. If you want to have a—" He shook his head and stared before she could finish, indicating he wasn't moving until Kip Foster showed.

In a few minutes, the bearded man crashed through the double doors and strode over to Jon. His T-shirt of the day read BELIEVE.

Not bothering with formalities, he said, "I am in the middle of a meeting, Mr. Cruz. If you'd like to set up an appointment, Tiffany here will be happy to assist you."

Jon stepped forward and pointed his finger inches away from Foster's chest, careful not to touch him.

"Not necessary. Your collection agency called the Stevens yesterday evening. If they call again, I won't bother coming back to see you. I'm going straight to the *Miami Herald* and every television station in South Florida. I don't think you want to make those headlines. Your choice."

He spun and walked out.

When he returned to his boat, he went up to the flybridge and sat, still fuming about the treatment center's handling of Stevens's account. He knew Delray-By-The-Sea was a business, but turning a collection agency loose on grieving parents was the height of insensitive.

Turning his thoughts to his conversation with Addie last night, he called R.D. Stone, the attorney.

"Hi, Jon. What's up?"

"I'm assuming Addie has called you about the city harassing her. What the hell is that about?"

R.D. told him he'd talked to several people at city hall. Everyone was dodging the issue and not forthcoming about the source of the complaint regarding a code infraction.

"I think I know the source," Jon said. He told about his visit to Delray-By-The-Sea with Trey Stevens.

"Jon?" He recognized Beth's voice coming from the dock. He shook his head and looked down. She was standing there with a uniformed officer next to her.

"Let me call you back, R.D. I've got a visitor," Jon said.

He went down to the main deck and stepped off the boat onto the deck. The officer wore a Palm Beach County uniform and held an envelope.

"Jon Cruz?" the uniform asked.

"Yes." He looked at Beth. "What—"

The deputy stepped forward, handing him the envelope. "This is an official criminal trespass warning. Under penalty of law, you are hereby prohibited from appearing on the premises of Delray-By-The-Sea. If you do so, a warrant will be issued for your arrest."

Jon shook his head, took the envelope, and looked to Beth for an explanation.

"Thanks, Karl," she said to the uniform. As soon as Karl got into his vehicle, Beth lit into Jon. He let her get it out of her system before trying to speak.

"Impressive," he said. "I left there less than an hour ago. I guess the wheels turn fast when you piss off the wrong person."

She exhaled and looked away. She turned back to face him and said, "I asked you not to go back there. And you promised you wouldn't."

"Trey called. Delray-By-The-Sea turned his account over to a frigging collection agency. They called again yesterday. Jesus, Beth, they haven't even buried her yet."

Her expression softened as she shook her head.

He continued with his side of the story. "All I did was tell the bearded freak Foster that if the Stevens got another call, I was going to the *Miami Herald* and every television station in the area. That was it. Then I left."

"They told the chief you threatened him. Did you touch him?"

"I'm not stupid, Beth. I pointed my finger at him but did *not* lay a hand on him."

"Do you know who the CEO of Delray-By-The-Sea is?"

"No, and I don't give a shit."

"Maybe you should. It's Stuart Westbrook, M.D., who also happens to be close friends with the police chief and everybody else who's somebody in Delray Beach."

"Dr. Stuart Westbrook?" Jon repeated. "He's at Delray-By-The-Sea?" Couldn't be. The last time he'd heard that name was in Atlanta. Two years ago.

"The one and only. And that explains how you ended up with that." She nodded toward the envelope in Jon's hand. "And why my tit's in a wringer with the Chief."

Damn, he thought. The shit was flowing downhill at Delray Beach PD and burying Beth. He felt guilty about giving her a hard time earlier. That also explained why the city was suddenly after Addie. All because of him.

"I'm sorry, Beth. I'm just trying to find out what happened to Haley Stevens and protect her parents. I didn't mean to start a shitstorm for you."

"Well, drop your cowboy act. Quit poking the fucking bear and let me do my job—while I still have one. And Jon? Do not violate that criminal trespass warning in your hand. If you do, I promise I'll arrest you myself."

She turned to leave, then stopped and spun around. "I like my job, and I'd like to make it to retirement."

"I understand."

As soon as she left, Jon called R.D. "I know who it is."

24

After Jon finished explaining everything, R.D. said, laughing, "I'll say this for you, you go big. It all makes sense now."

R.D. told him not to worry about Addie, that he'd take care of that. "Nobody at city hall, including the mayor, will mess with her. She's got more friends in high places than he does. That was just for the mayor to appease the police chief. I told Addie the patrol car wouldn't be there after a few nights. The police chief is just sending a message for his poker buddy. He doesn't have the resources to keep that up."

"What about the collection agency harassing the Stevens?"

"If the debt's legit, which you seem to think it is, they have the right to call within the limits of the law. But I know the CFO. I'll call her and appeal to her sense of fair play."

Jon waved the piece of paper the deputy had delivered. "What about the criminal trespass warning? Does that mean I'm not allowed to have contact with them?"

"No. All it means is that if you step foot on their property, they can have you arrested for trespassing. A TRO or a temporary restraining order is a more serious step. That means you can't have contact with a person or persons. But, for that, they have to convince a judge. Just do yourself a favor and don't go over there."

After hanging up with R.D., he went to his desk. Digging through the stack of papers on the corner, he looked for the Delray-By-The-Sea brochure he'd picked up the other day with Trey.

He found it and stared at the lavish, full-size color booklet in his hand, this time paying more attention.

The cover featured a glamour shot of the facility, complete with palm trees and a setting sun visible beyond. He opened it and slowly thumbed through the pages of the expensively produced marketing piece.

Almost every page contained pictures of primarily young people in various settings. On the tennis court, out by the pool, gathered around a bonfire on the beach. Along the way, references to multiple accreditation agencies and organizations implied an official air of endorsement.

The theme also focused on the key to their success, the Treatment Plan. An entire two-page spread was devoted to this revolutionary tool, tailored to meet their residents' individual needs.

There he found a picture of a distinguished-looking gentleman touting the merits of their approach. It was Stuart Westbrook, M.D., Ph.D., the CEO and Medical Director who held degrees from three different Ivy League schools. According to Dr. Westbrook, the copyrighted Delray Treatment Plan was responsible for the numerous success stories depicted in the brochure.

"Bullshit," Jon said out loud. Westbrooks' highly touted treatment plan didn't save Megan.

Westbrook had been her physician at Atlanta Recovery Haven, the addiction treatment center in Atlanta. After her tragic demise, he confronted Westbrook at his office. In a rage, he threw a chair through the good doctor's window. That was the early end of Jon's otherwise stellar career as a special agent with HHS-OIG. And another step down into the abyss that began with Megan's death. So much for Westbrook's celebrated treatment plan.

As he flipped to the back cover, he noticed that Delray-By-The-Sea was the flagship of Moren Health, a for-profit chain of treatment centers headquartered in Boca Raton, Florida. He tossed the brochure down and spent the next hour browsing the internet for information about Moren Health.

Cal Norman, a wealthy oilman from West Texas, founded the privately-owned health care company. Delray-By-The-Sea had been one of Moren's first acquisitions and was the flagship of the nationwide chain of addiction treatment centers. Cal was taking the company public, and an IPO was in process.

Moren Health was a Wall Street darling, with numerous flattering articles in the financial news, poised to dominate the burgeoning treatment space. Westbrook was riding the wave.

He was puzzled. Westbrook had prospered. On the other hand, Jon had lost everything. Yet, Westbrook was acting irrationally with Jon, going after him and anyone associated with him. Why? How could he possibly be a threat to Stuart Westbrook? It appeared to be excessive for a personal vendetta.

His inbox chimed, and he saw that Trey had emailed him. It was Haley's medical record. He checked to make sure it was there, then called Nora. It was too voluminous to print, and he wanted to forward it to her to check for any anomalies. He didn't expect to find anything but wanted to cover the bases.

His call went to voice mail, so he left a message saying he was sending Haley's medical record over and to call him once she'd seen it.

Then he called D'Lo. Again, voice mail. Hell, does anyone talk on the phone anymore? He sent D'Lo a text and asked him to call.

He also thought about how to get Westbrook to lay off Addie and Beth. He'd considered appealing to him directly, but now that he couldn't go to Delray-By-The-Sea, he had to find another way. If Westbrook wanted to go after him, fine, but leave them out.

Still convinced that the drug dealers had information about Haley, he was determined to talk to Ramon and Carlos. He didn't think Carlos knew anything about Haley. His gut told him Ramon was the key, but he wanted to bounce everything off Beth first.

He also owed her an apology. She had the misfortune of befriending him, and he'd taken out his frustrations on her. When he called, he was surprised she answered. "Would you like to go for a boat ride?"

There was a pause, then Beth said, "Not dinner at Mediterraneo?"

Jon chuckled, remembering the last time he'd tried to apologize with dinner at her favorite restaurant. "If you'd rather. But I was hoping for something a little more private, so we could talk."

This time Beth laughed. "You're not worried about me tossing you overboard?"

"I like living dangerously."

"How about tomorrow? You can make it a sunset cruise. And, I expect a bottle of Cakebread."

He sighed. Cakebread chardonnay was her favorite. It was a big butterball, not cheap, and getting harder to find. "Deal. See you here at four?"

"I'll be there. Make sure it's properly chilled."

25

That evening at Hank's, things were slow enough that Addie came out from behind the bar with a glass of water and sat next to Jon as he ate dinner.

"Ricky doing okay?" she asked.

He looked at her, wondering how much she knew. Probably more than he realized. The standing joke at the marina was that nothing went on around here without Addie knowing.

"Far as I know," he said before stuffing the last onion ring in his mouth.

"Thanks for helping him," she said. "He's had a rough ride."

Jon nodded. He knew the boy was an only child and had lost both parents in a boating accident when he was younger. As far as he understood, Ricky didn't have any relatives left. He wiped his mouth, then stood. "Time to go to work."

Addie laughed. "You don't like it when somebody calls you out for being nice, do you? Don't worry, I won't tell."

When he returned to the boat, Felix wasn't on the dock waiting for him. He looked around, but the cat was nowhere to be seen.

Not the first time. "Must have a hot date," he said out loud as he stepped onboard. Inside, he picked up his phone and saw that he had a message from Nora and a missed call from D'Lo. He went to voicemail and played her message.

"I skimmed through Haley's medical record. First pass, I didn't see anything unusual, but I'll go through it again when I have more time. It looked like she was doing well up until the day she discharged herself. I'm working tonight. Give me a call tomorrow."

Her assessment squared with what Trey had told him about Haley. So, why would she discharge herself? He made a mental note to call Trey and ask him again about that. Something about that didn't fit. He pressed D'Lo's number.

"J.C. What's up?" D'Lo said when he answered.

"I need to talk with Carlos. I tried to talk with him, but he slipped me." He told D'Lo about the aborted meeting at Peg Legs.

D'Lo chuckled. "Don't worry. He's a regular there. You might try again but without warning."

Jon thought about the rednecks he ran into at the door. They said they'd never seen Carlos there before, but probably different times. He trusted D'Lo's information.

"I don't think he's who I want, but I want to make sure. Ramon is the one I want. I talked to him but didn't get anywhere."

D'Lo let out a hoarse, throaty laugh. "I heard you didn't make a friend. He's gonna be a hard one to get to. I can't help you there, but be careful."

"Thanks for the tip on Carlos. Later."

He texted Trey and asked him to call when he felt like talking. He still hadn't figured out what to do about Westbrook. Maybe Beth would have some ideas when he saw her tomorrow. He looked at his watch and decided he had time to change and take a quick ride by Peg Legs to see if he could catch Carlos.

By the time he got there, the daylight was fading as he slowly drove past. Carlos's battered red Toyota was parked out front. He pulled into the parking lot, careful to park as far away from anyone else as he could.

Made sense. Bars were like churches. The early service attendees were a different group from the mid-day crowd. He pegged the rednecks as the afternoon shift at Peg Legs. A few beers after work, then home to mama before dark. Carlos was probably more often there nights.

Inside, Jon saw his quarry sitting at the bar. He walked over and stood behind him, blocking his escape.

Carlos seemed to sense a presence, turned, and was face-to-face with Jon. His eyes widened as he appeared to consider bolting.

Jon leaned in, intentionally invading his personal space to let him know he wouldn't get away so easily this time. "No need to run," Jon said quietly. "All I want to do is talk. I'll even buy your beer." He gave him a quick minute to consider his options.

Cornered, Carlos nodded. Jon eased onto the empty stool next to him, staying on guard until he was sure the dealer wasn't playing him.

"Two more," Jon said to the bartender, pointing to Carlos's beer.

After the bartender set the beers in front of them, Jon pulled out Haley's picture and put it on the bar in front of Carlos. "La has visto?" You ever seen her? He watched his expression and saw no sign of recognition as Carlos shook his head.

"She's dead," Jon said. "She got drugs from somebody. I want to know who."

"Yo no," Carlos said, shaking his head and reverting to Spanish. "Lo juro," he said, crossing himself. Not me. I swear.

Jon took Haley's picture and placed it in his pocket. He pulled out a scrap of paper on which he'd written his cell phone number and handed it to Carlos.

"You call me if you hear anything. I'll pay. Entiendes?" You understand?

Carlos nodded with enthusiasm.

Jon pulled out a twenty and laid it on the bar. He rose to leave and added, "And stay the hell away from Ricky."

26

The next morning, before breakfast, Jon's phone buzzed.

"Cruz," he said when he answered.

"This is Phillip Bryce. At St. Peter's."

"Morning, Padre. You're up early."

"After your visit, I instructed our staff to inquire about Haley. Every morning, I always stop by to check on the new arrivals. This morning, they told me that a new girl mentioned she knew Haley at Delray-By-The-Sea. I—"

"I'm on my way."

"Don't bother. She's gone."

"Gone? Do you know—"

"Please. Let me finish. I talked with her briefly. I told her a friend of Haley's family would like to talk with her. She knew Haley was dead and was adamant that she wouldn't talk to anyone. She was anxious, so I decided to continue my rounds and then come back to her. When I got to the other side of the room, I turned around, and she was gone. The only information she gave was her first name—Lexi. That's all I have. Sorry."

Jon shook his head. "Any idea where she might have gone?"

"No, we never really know where they come from or where they go. We've learned not to ask too many questions. But I've asked the staff to notify me immediately if she returns."

"You think she'll be back?"

"Hard to say. We've established St. Peter's as a safe refuge for people like Lexi and Haley, and a high percentage come back."

"If she returns, would you please call me ASAP?"

"Yes, but I'll not allow you to talk to her unless she gives permission. We've worked hard to earn their trust, and I won't jeopardize that."

Jon was tempted to ask if he wanted her to end up like Haley but thought better of it. Padre was a good person at heart, trying to do the right thing, so he let it slide.

"I understand. And I appreciate your calling. Let's hope she returns."

* * *

At four o'clock, Jon had *Trouble No More* ready to go out. He'd gone to three wine stores to find Beth's chardonnay, which was in the fridge. On the way home, he'd stopped by 3G's deli on Atlantic to pick up a platter. Now, all that was missing was the detective.

Ten minutes later, he heard footsteps on the dock and went out to greet her. He was surprised to see her dressed casually in white cropped pants, a red-striped V-neck top, and boat shoes. She was carrying a bottle of red wine.

"Nice to see you out of uniform," he said. He opened the boarding door for her as she stepped on the boat. Looking down at her feet, he added, "I didn't know you owned boat shoes."

"How would you? You've never invited me out boating."

This was not her first time on his boat, but she was right. This was the first time he'd taken her out.

She handed him the wine. "This doesn't get you off the hook for the Cakebread."

He turned it around to see the label. A Paso Robles Cabernet. "Nice. Thank you. Your Cakebread should be chilled by now. Let's get a couple of glasses, and then we'll shove off."

She followed him inside, where he opened the chardonnay and poured. She nodded her approval as he held up his glass.

"To friends," he said. He walked over to the controls and started the engines to let them warm up.

"What can I do?" she asked.

He wasn't sure about Beth's nautical bona fides, but after his boating faux pas with Nora, he wasn't about to ask. Fortunately, the tidal current was minimal at present and there was only a faint breeze, so he didn't need much help.

Trouble No More was parked in her slip bow-first with the dock on the port side. They went out on deck, where he led her around, pointing out the various lines as he removed the spring lines and draped them over the hooks on the pilings. She nodded, indicating her understanding.

Satisfied that she knew the basics, he asked her to keep the last line taut until he got up to the helm on the flybridge. Comfortable they were ready to leave, he told her to step on board with the line as he backed out of the slip. She soon joined him topside with the wine.

As they cruised past the homes and businesses, she said, "This is nice. It seems like another world on the water. And thanks for the Cakebread. It's delicious."

He toasted her. "Thanks for coming." He was silent for a minute, then continued. "How's Owen?"

Owen was a criminal defense attorney she'd been dating. She hadn't mentioned him lately, and Jon was curious.

She sipped her wine before answering. "We decided it wasn't a good match. I arrest them, and he gets them off. Opposite sides of the fence. But it was a mutual and civil parting."

He nodded. "I can see that would be a problem. Sorry it didn't work out."

She shrugged. "Probably best. My line of work isn't conducive to a healthy relationship anyway. How about you and the nurse?"

He wondered how much she knew. "We enjoy each other's company. It helps that we're both about helping people."

Beth sat up straight and her eyes narrowed.

Before she could speak, Jon held his hand up. "Sorry, that didn't come out right. You, I believe, help. Owen, let's just say he helps people, too—just the wrong ones."

She cracked a smile at that.

"Look, losing Haley was personal," he said. "I want to find out who and why. I'm convinced there's more to it."

"I'm sorry about Haley. But you can't go around threatening people. We have procedures."

"No one's above the law. Even Dr. Stuart Westbrook."

"I agree. And the process is the same for everyone. But when dealing with well-connected people, we have to be careful not to skip any steps. I do what I can. I'm just asking you to let me do my job and not interfere."

"Being a security guard is a lot easier."

Now it was Beth's turn to laugh. "Something to be said for that line of work, I suppose."

Lights were starting to come on along the Intracoastal as dusk settled. Jon turned the boat around and headed back to the marina.

"Trey's also convinced that there's more to the story. For example, why would Haley check herself out so close to finishing the program? And why wouldn't she contact them?"

"Addicts relapse all the time. Nothing unusual about that. She was probably embarrassed to call them. Sometimes those closest are the last to see it."

He tensed at Beth's words as he thought about Megan but didn't want to go there. "I know. But Haley had been in multiple programs, so this wasn't Trey's first rodeo. He's not naïve about the process."

"What do you think?"

Jon shook his head. "I honestly don't know. I'm trying to learn more about why she left, where she went, etc. My gut tells me Ramon is somehow involved, which is why I wanted to talk to him." He decided not to mention anything about D'Lo or Lexi.

"That wouldn't be surprising. But, as much as I'd like to nail the bastard, I can't roust him for no reason."

"Did you get any more information about the vehicle that dumped her in Bird City?"

"Not a lot. A large black SUV—an Escalade, as you guessed." She paused, observing him.

He remembered his previous blunder and, this time, said nothing, maintaining a neutral expression.

Beth relented and continued. "No plates, no description, no driver, or other occupants. Know how many black SUVs there are in South Florida?"

Remembering Ramon's similar comment, he said, "I'm guessing more than a few. But Haley was dumped on the street like garbage. How many others like Haley?"

She looked at him and shook her head. "Too many. It's out of control. We're overwhelmed. First responders get calls daily. Palm Beach County alone averages more than one overdose death a day."

"Jesus. Any pattern?" He wondered how many had been at Delray-By-The-Sea.

"I wouldn't call it a pattern. More like a profile. Usually under thirty, previous addicts, runaways, slightly more males than females, in and out of treatment programs, most from out-of-state. Unfortunately, that's a sizeable population in this area. As far as addicts being dumped, yes, many of those are also. But different places, vehicles, etc."

"Do you track which treatment programs?"

She snorted, shaking her head. "Impossible. This county has over 200 treatment centers, with an equal number of recovery homes—which, by the way, are unregulated."

"Unregulated?"

"Yep. If you want to open a recovery home, all you need is a business license. No licensure, no monitoring, no anything."

They soon arrived back at the marina. After they'd got the boat docked and secured, they took the deli platter and wine up to the flybridge.

"Thanks for the ride," Beth said as they got comfortable.

"Next time, maybe we can get an earlier start and go out on the ocean."

"I'd like that. Besides, you still owe me a sunset." She refilled their glasses. "Now, tell me. What's between you and Westbrook? Your going to Delray-By-The-Sea obviously hit a nerve. Why?"

He took a swallow of wine, weighing how much to tell her. "My daughter was in rehab at the treatment center in Atlanta where he was the medical director. He was her doctor. We had a disagreement, and apparently, he carries a grudge. But I didn't even know he was at Delray-By-The-Sea when I went there."

She nodded, waiting for him to continue.

"If Westbrook wants to come after me for whatever reason, bring it on. But leave the Stevens out of this. Harassing them for paying Haley's bill? That's just cruel."

"I agree that was uncalled for. And I relayed that to the chief. But to be fair, it's a business. They have a right to get paid."

"That's the problem. It is a business, and that's all. Now, Westbrook's after Addie, too. Trying to get to me by bullying her."

Beth's surprised expression told him that she wasn't aware of that. "What do you mean?"

He told her about the city harassing Addie on inspections. And increasing the police presence out front of the bar.

"I wasn't aware of that."

"Ask her. You know as well as I that Delray Beach has never screwed with Hank's. Now, this bullshit? Again, if Westbrook wants to go after me, fine. But how do I get him to leave Hank's out of this?"

She digested this latest information, then cocked her head. "You said you and Westbrook had a disagreement in Atlanta. About what?"

He hesitated and stared off into the distance. His voice got quiet. "Right after Megan finished the program there, she committed suicide. Him and his damn treatment plan."

"I'm sorry. I didn't realize . . ." She hugged herself, sensing there was more.

His throat clenched and he forced himself to continue. "Next thing I know, I received a bill from his treatment center. I went to his office and told him he was more interested in profit than fixing my daughter. And . . . I threw a chair through his office window."

She put her hand to her mouth, staring at him, her eyes reflecting a multitude of emotions: shock, pity, and a touch of worry.

"I wanted to throw him through it as well."

She moved over next to him and put her arm around him, pulling him beside her. His tears fell onto her arm.

"I'm so sorry, Jon. I didn't know. No wonder you reacted the way you did to Trey getting a call."

They sat that way for a few minutes, with her comforting him while he tried to regain his composure.

Finally, he pulled away and said, "I'm sorry I got you in trouble with your lieutenant."

She shrugged and shook her head. "No worries. He's a dickhead, climbing the ladder. His biggest concern is how it affects his chances for a promotion."

He allowed a thin smile at her sloughing it off. "There's more to this than my history with Westbrook," he said. "I didn't know he was here until you told me, and I'm willing to bet he didn't know I was in town until I showed up at his place with Trey. Do you think it's a coincidence that when the money ran out, Haley Stevens checked herself out and disappeared? I'm betting she's not the only one."

He thought about D'Lo's comment that Ramon was working with a treatment center. Lexi said that she and Haley went to a recovery home. Something was going on here, and he hadn't yet put all the pieces together.

He shook his head. "I get that you have to go after the street dealers and be careful about harassing the big shots. But I want the people pulling the strings. The real criminals are working at that resort called Delray-By-The-Sea or in their corporate office in Boca."

"You may be right. But I can't go after Delray-By-The-Sea just because you have a hunch. I need proof."

"Who's fighting for these kids?" he asked.

"Good question."

27

At a quarter of seven, Dr. Stuart Westbrook and Rachel, his wife, pulled up to Dial's entrance. The waterfront restaurant on the Atlantic was the trendiest and most expensive in the area. Two valets swarmed over the Jaguar before Stuart had come to a complete stop, one on each side.

Cal had invited them to dinner. He told Stuart to make reservations at the restaurant on the beach that Rachel liked. Dial was a popular place, and as a regular, Stuart had connections and could get a table with little notice.

Stuart looked over as the valet opened Rachel's door. He grinned as she swung her legs out to exit the vehicle. Rachel, eleven years younger and in excellent shape, was wearing a short black dress, and he knew the young man was getting an eyeful.

Inside the restaurant, the stuffy, older maître d' was scowling as he looked down at his list. As he looked up to see who had interrupted him, he smiled as he recognized the handsome couple.

"Good evening, Dr. and Mrs. Westbrook. Good to see you. The other member of your party hasn't arrived yet, but I'll be happy to go ahead and seat you."

The man took three menus and asked them to follow. He wound his way through the crowded dining room, then stopped at a four-seat table set for three in a private nook facing the water.

Perfect, Stuart thought as the man pulled a chair out for Rachel. Stuart sat next to her as she stared out at the waves rolling in just beyond the restaurant. Although twilight was fast approaching, many beachgoers were still out walking.

A young waiter appeared at their table, asking if they'd like something to drink while they waited for the other party.

Rachel turned and said, "Gin and tonic. Bombay Sapphire, please." The waiter nodded and looked at Stuart as she turned her gaze back to the ocean.

"Macallan. Neat."

"Is the eighteen satisfactory? We also have a twenty-five."

Stuart nodded, then the waiter stepped away.

"Nice view," Rachel said, turning to look at her husband.

"Obviously. By the way, you look stunning tonight. I'm sure the valet enjoyed watching you get out of the car."

She beamed, and he saw a bit of a blush in the dim light. She knew that the little black dress was one of his favorites. "Thank you, Dr. Westbrook."

It was a term of endearment that she'd used with him since he graduated from medical school. She flashed him a sly grin and raised her eyebrows. "You must be fishing for dessert later?"

He forced a grin and raised his eyebrows to match. Although sex was usually top of his list when it came to his young wife, it wasn't first tonight.

When the waiter brought their drinks, Stuart looked at his watch, a Patek-Phillipe that Rachel had given him when he opened Delray-By-The-Sea. It was thirty minutes after seven, not unusual for Cal. He was annoyed by Cal's chronic tardiness but resolved to accept what he considered a character flaw. They enjoyed their drinks, and he tried to relax, aided by the whisky.

"Sorry I'm late, you two." The big, Texas voice boomed as Cal walked up. He leaned over to kiss Rachel, then stepped back, his eyes taking her in. "You get more beautiful every time I see you."

Still holding her hands, he glanced over at Stuart. "Stu, I hope you realize how lucky you are."

Stuart cringed. Cal was relentless in using that nickname. "I am fortunate, indeed," he said with a forced smile. Cal released her hands and shook his before sitting.

The waiter appeared, and before he could speak, Cal said, "Bring them another round. You still have any of that Pappy 15?" When the waiter nodded, he added, "Good. Make that neat, with a glass of water on the side."

Stuart shook his head. Dinner would be charged back to Delray-By-The-Sea, and a shot of the Buffalo Trace bourbon would cost more than the meal. He realized that was the real reason Cal wanted to come here. He didn't patronize any place more than once if they didn't carry his drink of choice.

"Well, I sure appreciate y'all coming out to see me on such short notice," Cal said. "I've got to go to Texas tomorrow evening and wanted to have dinner with y'all before I left."

They made small talk while Cal drained his first drink. After everyone had ordered dinner, he asked the waiter to bring another round. Stuart declined. Since he and Rachel both ordered seafood, he ordered a nice bottle of Sancerre for them, knowing that Cal would continue to drink the super-premium bourbon with his steak.

Halfway through dinner, Stuart was surprised to look up and see a familiar face approaching, one he hadn't seen in a while. It was Jon Cruz.

He looked the same, Stuart thought. A few more gray hairs, maybe a few more pounds. But he was still in good shape. He hadn't let himself go.

"Hello, Stuart," Jon said, his voice even. "Sorry to interrupt, but I was having dinner and thought I'm come over and say, 'hello.'"

Stuart looked around, hoping to attract the attention of their server or the maître d'. In a slightly louder voice, he said, "I'm sorry, Mr. Cruz, but we're having a private dinner here if you don't mind."

Raising his voice to match Stuart's volume, Jon said, "Since I got your little message, I couldn't come by your office and talk to you civilly. So, I'll say it here. I'm politely asking you to lay off. If you've got a problem with me, deal with me directly. But leave my friends out of it. Don't have your buddies do your dirty work for you."

"Is there a problem here, Dr. Westbrook?" the maître d' asked, appearing out of nowhere.

Before he could answer, Jon said, "I was just leaving." He turned and walked away.

Shamefaced, the maître d' said, "I apologize, Dr. Westbrook. I can assure you that person will not be allowed in here again."

"Thank you, Javier."

"What the hell was that about?" Cal asked as the maître d' walked away.

Stuart flicked his hand as if warding off an insect. "Sorry. Just a disgruntled acquaintance with a vendetta. Not important."

"Who is he?"

"Jon Cruz. We had a disagreement when I was in Atlanta, and now he's trying to cause trouble for me here."

"What's he doing here?"

Stuart shook his head. "Apparently, he lives in Delray Beach now. I didn't realize he did until a few days ago."

Cal's eyes narrowed. He looked over at Rachel and smiled. "I'm sorry. I don't want to ruin a wonderful dinner talking shop. Let's retire to the bar for a nightcap."

On the way, Rachel excused herself to freshen up. When she was out of earshot, Cal leaned over to him. "Come over to the house for breakfast in the morning. We need to talk."

28

Stuart sat across from Cal on board *WesTex*, watching him eat breakfast. Another fucking weekend meeting. Sipping his coffee, he wasn't hungry. His stomach was churning as he anticipated Cal's grilling him about Jon Cruz.

"Tell me about the guy at the restaurant last night," Cal said.

Stuart carefully explained that Cruz's daughter was his patient in rehab at Atlanta Recovery Haven, where he was the medical director at the time. She had completed her treatment plan, and he had discharged her. A week later, she committed suicide.

"Sad, but not unheard of in our business," Cal said.

"I know, but that wasn't the end of it. He hired an attorney and sued. Our insurance company offered him a settlement, but he wanted retribution, not money. He showed up, angry and blaming me. Then, he threw a chair through my office window."

"Jesus."

"I declined to press charges in return for him dropping his lawsuit. Apparently, he also lost his job as a result, which is why I say he has a vendetta against me."

"What sort of work did he do?"

He hesitated. "He was a Special Agent with HHS-OIG."

Cal raised an eyebrow. "A federal agent? With Health and Human Services OIG?"

"Ex-federal agent. I checked. Shortly after the incident in Atlanta, he was forced to take an early retirement."

Cal cocked his head. "So, what's that got to do with Delray-By-The-Sea?"

Stuart shifted in his seat. This is the area where he had to tread lightly.

"We had a resident—Haley Stevens—who relapsed after leaving our program. Sadly, she overdosed and died. Turns out, she was the daughter of Jon Cruz's best friend. Cruz showed up with the father, threatened my resident counselor, and caused a scene. Given his violent history, I called the Delray police chief and asked him to do something, so he issued a criminal trespass warning to Cruz. If he sets foot on our property, we can have him arrested."

Cal narrowed his eyes. "I'm not liking this. Should we be worried?"

Stuart cleared his throat. "I don't think so."

Cal studied him. "You don't think so? Why the hesitation?"

Stuart chose his words carefully. "As you know, we have strict guidelines for payment. Stevens was behind. So . . . we 'encouraged' her to leave the program. She discharged herself AMA." He added, "But, our documentation is completely in order. We have a signed, witnessed release."

"What's the problem, then?"

"We, uh, referred her to the local recovery home that we use for such situations."

"Delray Serenity House?"

Stuart almost said, *where else?* Delray Serenity House was Cal's idea, a recovery home owned by Ramon and financed by Cal. It was a below-the-radar revolving door for Delray-

By-The-Sea, serving as both a receptor and a source for patients. Instead, he nodded.

Cal slammed his hand on the table, rattling the silverware. "Goddammit, Stu. You've got a former federal agent—OIG of all things—in your backyard, and he's on the warpath? You've got to get a handle on this."

"Maybe we should lay low for a while until the dust settles. Cool things with Delray Serenity House. If we need to refer a patient out, send them elsewhere."

Cal shook his head. "Unacceptable. We can't afford the hit on the bottom line. Plus, if this gets out, we can kiss the IPO goodbye. God knows what other repercussions." He pointed his finger at Stuart. "*You* have to contain this. Now. Understand?"

"I'll handle it."

"You better." Cal wiped his mouth and threw the napkin down on the table. "Anything else you need to tell me before you leave?"

Stuart stood. "I'll take care of it," he said as he turned and left.

All the way home, he fumed. What Delray-By-The-Sea did was common practice throughout Moren. Cal had set up a network of recovery homes to service all of Moren's treatment centers.

But the message was clear. Cal was not going to take the fall. He'd throw Stuart and every other CEO under the bus first. Somehow, Stuart had to force Jon Cruz to back down. And soon.

Far from acceding to Cruz's clumsy request at Dial, Stuart intended to step the pressure up another notch.

29

Saturday afternoon, Jon was cleaning the deck on *Trouble No More,* when his phone buzzed. His first reaction was to ignore it, then thought it might be Addie. But when he looked at the caller ID, he was surprised to see it was Ricky.

He picked it up and answered. "Cruz."

"I've been arrested."

What now? He'd believed that Ricky was doing well.

"It's not what you think. They stopped me for rolling through a stop sign. They tossed the car, but there was nothing in it. I was so nervous, I flunked the sobriety test, so they hauled me in for suspicion. I'm clean, Jon. And the tests will prove it."

"You at the County Detention Center in West Palm?"

"Yes."

"Do not say anything to anybody. Not a word. I'll call Stone. Sit tight." He disconnected and called R.D. Stone's cell phone.

"Stone Law."

"R.D. Jon Cruz."

"Hi Jon, what's up?"

He explained what'd happened to Ricky.

"That's bullshit. Is he at County?"

"Yes, he just called."

"Don't worry. I'll take care of it."

He walked over to Hank's to tell Addie. Beth pulled up in her unmarked as he got to the front door. As soon as she got out, he pounced, hands out and palms up. "Me. Addie. Now Ricky? Really?" he said in an accusatory tone.

"What are you talking about?"

"Your people picked up Ricky. Claimed he failed a sobriety test. Now they're holding him at County waiting on blood tests. But don't worry, R.D.'s taking care of it. I guess Stuart Westbrook's running the department these days." In the dim light outside the bar, he saw Beth's face flush with anger.

"Speaking of the devil," she said.

"Oh, so R.D.'s a devil, now?"

"I wasn't speaking about R.D., although you might need him, too. I was referring to Dr. Westbrook. That's why I came by."

He cocked his head. "Why would I need R.D.?"

"Dr. Westbrook is threatening to file for a TRO."

Jon's nostrils flared, and he felt his cheeks flush. A temporary restraining order. "For what?"

"He's claiming that you violated the spirit of the criminal trespass warning by publicly threatening him at Dial yesterday evening."

He spat and shook his head. "The criminal trespass warning specifically stated that I was not to set foot on Delray-By-The-Sea property. I didn't. Plus, I was respectful, and I did not threaten him."

"He claims he has witnesses. His wife and his boss."

"That was his boss?" He thought back to the other two people at the table. One, obviously Ms. Westbrook, was an attractive woman in a black dress. The other was an older, big man who looked like he just got off a horse. Neither of them said a word.

Beth nodded. "Cal Norman. CEO of Moren Health, Delray-By-The-Sea's parent company. And one of the richest people in this zip code, which, as you know is not all a poor area."

"This is crazy. Why has Westbrook got such a hard-on for me? I'm no threat to him."

"Maybe you are?"

"How?"

"I don't know, but he's going after you with both barrels. Anyway, I just wanted to give you a heads-up. I've got to get back to work."

He stood there, digesting the heated conversation as Beth drove away. When he told her he was no threat, she had said that maybe he was. But why?

30

Inside Hank's, Jon went to his usual spot. Addie met him with a beer and dinner.

"What was that about? Beth not coming in?"

He looked at her and sighed. As usual, Addie didn't miss anything. "We had a little disagreement. And, no, she's working."

She lifted a single eyebrow but didn't pursue it.

"I was coming over to tell you Ricky's been arrested." Watching her connect the dots, he added, "She didn't know anything about it. But I've already called R.D., and he's handling it."

Addie's phone rang. "Hank's. Addie speaking." She nodded, then offered Jon the phone.

Puzzled, he looked at her for an explanation.

"Phillip Bryce. Says he knows you."

He took the phone. "Padre?"

"Can you come to my office? Now?"

"I'm in the middle of dinner. Why?"

"She's back. And she's agreed to talk to you. Only you, and only in my presence."

"I'll be there in ten minutes." He hung up and wolfed down another couple of bites. When Addie came over, he pushed his plate across the bar. "I've gotta run. Later."

Fifteen minutes later, he pulled into St. Peter's and parked next to what he assumed was the rector's car, the only vehicle there.

He tried the door to the church office, but it was locked. When he knocked, Padre opened the door and motioned Jon inside. He stuck his head out and looked around outside, then closed it..

Jon followed the priest to his office. Inside, a young girl sat, hands together. Thin, to the point of unhealthy, with stringy brown hair, she wore tattered shorts and a faded T-shirt. Her eyes darted around the room, then locked on Jon. It was the same look that Carlos wore in Peg Legs, and he thought for a second she was going to bolt.

"Jon, this is Lexi. Lexi, this is Jon Cruz, the man I told you about." Padre's voice was calm and soothing.

"Hi, Lexi. Pleased to meet you," Jon said. When he stuck his hand out, she reluctantly took it. Her hand was cool and lifeless. She released his hand almost as soon as he touched her as if it were toxic. She looked at Padre, and he nodded slightly.

Jon tried to mimic Padre's demeanor to put her at ease. "I'm sorry about Haley. I used to live next door to them. Her father and I were in the Marines together. Her mom and dad want to know what happened, so anything you can tell me would be appreciated."

When she glanced at Padre again, he said, "It's okay. He's a good person. You can trust him."

Lexi told how she met Haley at Delray-By-The-Sea, where they were both in rehab. Both were from the Midwest and had been in various other programs before landing there.

"The morning Haley left, she came to my room," Lexi said. "She was upset and told me she was leaving. Her parents were behind on payment, they told her. If she signed a release saying she was discharging herself, they would arrange for her to go to a local recovery home, which would be much cheaper."

"Who told her that?" Jon asked.

She shook her head. "I can't. They killed her, and they'll kill me."

Padre frowned, then gently asked, "Can you tell him what you told me? About you?"

Jon guessed that she had a similar experience. "Did the same thing happen to you, Lexi?"

She teared up and nodded. "The next week. There're others, too." She was wringing her hands.

Nodding, Jon leaned forward, anxious for her to continue.

"They picked me up and took me to a house somewhere. One of the other girls there told me Haley had been there, too, but she'd escaped."

Questions flooded his brain, but he knew he had to proceed carefully. He didn't want to rush her and overwhelm her. *Easy,* he told himself as he took a deep breath. "How many people like you were there at the house?"

She shrugged. "Five or six."

"The others at the house. Had they been at Delray-By-The-Sea, too?"

Lexi nodded. "I think so. The one who knew Haley, she'd been there three times."

"Do you know her name?"

There was so much he wanted to ask. Knowing he had a limited window to ask questions, he carefully considered what to ask next.

"What did you do at the house?"

She shook her head and started wringing her hands. She glanced at Padre and shook her head twice. Jon didn't know if it was withdrawal or the questions or both. He could feel the anger welling up inside but knew he had to appear calm and in control.

"You said they picked you up at Delray-By-The-Sea. Do you know who?"

Jon sensed she knew but wasn't saying, so he tried another angle. "What were they driving when they picked you up?"

She considered the question for a few seconds, then seemed to decide she could safely volunteer that much. "A black Escalade." She folded her arms and started tapping her foot. Lexi was getting anxious.

Padre shot Jon a glance, then said to her, "I think that's enough for tonight. Maybe we can talk again later?"

Jon still had unanswered questions, but he didn't want to frighten her away. Taking the cue, he stood to leave. "Thank you, Lexi. You've been very helpful and very brave to talk to me. If that's okay with you, I'd like to pass this information along to her parents. Nobody else, I promise. And I won't tell them where I got this."

Her eyes widened, and she shook her head vehemently. "No. Please don't. They'll find me."

Jon was pretty sure she meant the bad guys, not the Stevens. Whichever, she was terrified. "All right, I won't. But maybe we can meet again?"

Still tense, she shrugged. Not a no or a yes.

He hoped Padre could convince her to come back. "Thank you again, Lexi. Padre," he said as he walked out.

31

When he returned to Hank's, Jon was relieved to see R.D. Stone sitting at the bar. Ricky was beside him. They were laughing and chatting with Addie.

"Glad to see you," Jon said to Ricky. "And you, R.D. Thanks."

"All the tests were clean," Ricky said. "I told you."

"Once I mentioned unlawful arrest, false imprisonment, and compensation for my client here," R.D. said, putting his hand on Ricky's shoulder, "they couldn't get us out quick enough."

"Good," Jon said, sitting on the empty stool beside R.D.

"Everything okay?" Addie asked Jon as she brought him a beer.

"Better. Beers on me," he said, gesturing toward R.D. He stared at Ricky's empty glass, then looked up at his young friend.

Ricky held up his glass. "Soda. All I've had tonight and all I'm going to have. We're on the same track."

He didn't feel good about Ricky in a bar even though Dr. Williams had given him the okay. He'd mentioned it to Addie and knew she'd keep a close eye on him when he wasn't around.

He pulled out his phone and looked at the screen. No calls. He'd called Beth on the way back to Hanks and left a message asking her to call him ASAP. Maybe sending a text would be better.

At Hanks. Need to talk

Addie jerked her head back. "He has his phone, and he texts. What have you done with Jon?" Her comment prompted laughter from Ricky and R.D.

He looked at her and shook his head. When he didn't take the bait, she walked back down to the other end of the bar.

"I gotta go," R.D. said, finishing his beer. "I need to prepare for an early Monday morning court date."

"I need to talk with you about a personal matter—if you've got a couple of minutes?" Jon said.

Ricky stood with his soda and nodded toward the end of the bar. "Thanks, R.D. and Jon. I'm going over to talk to my buddy."

"What's up?" R.D. asked after Ricky walked away.

"Apparently, Dr. Westbrook is threatening to file for a temporary restraining order." Jon told him about the confrontation at Dial and his subsequent visit from Beth.

R.D. chuckled. "You really pissed him off, didn't you? Don't worry about it. If he files for a TRO, it'll require a hearing before a judge, and I doubt he wants that. In the meantime, don't go to Delray-By-The-Sea, and try to avoid him."

"Thanks, R.D. Send me a bill."

R.D. shook his head and stood to leave. "Pro bono. I'm not going to let them get away with this."

Jon's phone buzzed. He grabbed it and answered without looking, thinking it was Beth. "Are you on your way over?"

A male voice said, "Obviously, you were expecting a call from someone else. I'm in Cincinnati."

Jon stumbled, confused for a moment, then realized it was Trey. "Sorry. I had just texted Beth and thought it was her. You okay?"

"Is that music I hear in the background?"

"Yeah, I'm at Hank's."

"I don't want to interrupt anything. It can wait. Give me a call later."

Trey's voice was off, which piqued Jon's curiosity.

"Everything okay?"

"Just wanted to chat. Later."

Before Jon could answer, Trey hung up. He stared at the phone in his hand, then set it on the bar.

It buzzed again. This time he looked. Beth. "Hey. You coming by?" he asked when he answered.

"An hour or so. What do you need?"

"I'd rather not say on the phone. By then, I'll be on the boat. Why don't you meet me there." He disconnected and put the phone on the bar.

Addie brought his dinner over. "Somebody steal your dog?" she asked.

"What?" he said, then realized she was parroting his line from the other night. "Too many loose connections rattling around." He pointed to his head.

She didn't pry. She nodded, then turned and walked away.

As he ate, Jon tried to process what he'd learned that evening from Lexi. Something sketchy was going on at Delray-By-The-Sea. It sounded like they were linked with a recovery home that was recycling patients. The whole thing smelled like a rehab mill.

That fit with what Beth had told him on the boat. Recovery homes were designed to facilitate an addict's reentry into drug-free living. Since they weren't regulated, anyone could open and operate one—even a drug dealer.

Using it as a dumping ground to recycle patients in and out of more expensive and highly regulated treatment facilities was illegal. A financial connection between the two was a clear conflict of interest, especially if it was used to recruit patients. But—and this was a big but—it would be totally under the radar.

Thinking the worst, he shuddered to think what else could be going on at such a place. He remembered Lexi's reaction when he asked what they did there. Remembering D'Lo's words about Ramon when he said he'd heard Haley was "working" for Ramon. *He's into lots of stuff. None of it good.*

He finished his dinner and told Addie good night.

At the dock, he went through the gate and looked around for the ginger cat. "Felix, where are you?"

He stood there for a few minutes, calling him again. He hoped if Felix could see or hear him, he'd show. But as he looked around, there was no sign of the cat. Dejected, he went aboard and called Trey.

"What's going on?" he asked when Trey answered.

"Touching base. Any progress?"

He didn't want to get Trey's hopes up, but he wanted to share his conversation with Lexi without betraying her confidence.

"Actually, I did have a small breakthrough this evening. I can't say much about it just yet, but I've located someone who was in Delray-By-The-Sea with Haley. I'm hoping this person can provide me with more information."

"Great. I need some good news."

He didn't like Trey's tone. There was more to this call than Trey was letting on. "What are you not telling me?"

Trey hesitated. "I've been having some health issues and my doctor's run a bunch of tests. I met with him this afternoon to go over everything." Another pause. "Not good. It's pancreatic cancer. Stage IV."

"Fuck." That was all Jon could say at the moment. He knew enough to know that pancreatic cancer was a death sentence. Stage IV meant it had metastasized, making the prognosis even bleaker. That explained why Trey looked so emaciated when he was down.

"How long?" Jon asked.

"Months if I'm lucky. Weeks if I'm not."

"How are you feeling?"

"Not too bad, physically. Just a lot to handle emotionally. Trying to get things in order."

"Are you getting another opinion?"

"No. My guy's thorough. He spent a couple of hours with Reece and me going through it all. He offered, but I'm done."

"Anything I can do?"

"Not really. I know you're doing all you can to find out what happened. We've set a date for Haley's service." He gave Jon the date. "Hope you and the detective can make it."

"You know I'll be there. And I'm sure Beth will, too. Soon as we make our arrangements, I'll let you know. If I can do anything . . ."

"I appreciate it. Talk to you soon." The call disconnected.

Jon slumped in his seat and shook his head as he stared at the phone, wishing the news away. Why? Hadn't Trey and Reece suffered enough? He set the phone down. It's a discussion he intended to have with Padre over a beer sometime.

He heard the crunch of gravel as a car pulled into the parking lot. He looked down to see Beth's unmarked. When she got out, she automatically looked up to the flybridge and spotted him. With a limp hand, he waved her onboard, then went down to greet her.

"Are you done for the night?" he asked.

"No, but I could use a drink," she said as she followed him into the main cabin.

"You're reading my mind," he said as he poured two stiff shots of tequila. "Salud," he said. He led her topside, where they sat at the small table on the flybridge.

Neither said anything for the first few minutes as they sipped and let the liquor course through their veins, diluting the stress.

"You look distracted," she said.

"Sorry. I just got off the phone with Trey."

"How are they doing?"

He gritted his teeth and shook his head. He shared Trey's news with her.

"Oh my God, I'm so sorry. And on top of everything else."

He gave her the dates for Haley's service. "They want you to come, too."

"Of course. I'll have to get approval, but that shouldn't be a problem. So that's why you called."

"No. Actually, I do have some good news." He told her about meeting someone who'd been at Delray-By-The-Sea with Haley. The person had also been taken to a recovery home where there were others, including Haley, who'd also been there. He withheld any identifying details other than the fact that the person was picked up by a black Escalade.

"Delray-By-The-Sea is a rehab mill," he said. "They are a predatory criminal enterprise working with a known drug dealer who I'm betting is Ramon. God knows what else is happening to these victims. These people need to be stopped."

She took another drink and looked at him. "Where is the home? And why do you think that Ramon is working with them?"

He started to say that Ramon drives a black Escalade but realized how vague that would sound. Plus, she would want to know how he knew that. He wanted to say that the word on the street is that Ramon is working with a treatment center, but then Beth would want to know where he heard that. He wasn't going to give D'Lo up.

"I don't know where it is. And it makes sense that maybe Ramon is working with them."

She nodded. "Interesting. Certainly possible, but I need to talk to your source."

Jon shook his head. He knew this would be Beth's response.

"This person is frightened for their life. They would barely speak to me. I'm working on getting them to talk to you, but it's going to take time. In the meantime, something needs to be done. Jesus, Beth, did you hear what I said? There are at least another five or six victims at this recovery home. For all we know, there's more. Delray-By-The-Sea has cameras outside their front door. What about getting the video?"

"Where is this place? According to your source, other people were there, but no names. Who picked your source up? No ID, just that they drove a black Escalade, which proves nothing. I could ask for the video, but they won't give it to me, claiming it would violate patient confidentiality. Without something concrete, no judge is going to force them to do so."

"Why can't you pay them a visit? Rattle their cage?"

"You haven't given me anything, just rumors and speculation. You haven't even told me where you found this person. You already know how wired Westbrook is with my chief. What do you think will happen if I go there with nothing but baseless speculation?"

He took a deep breath. Beth was right, and he knew it.

"I know you're frustrated," she said. "But you know how this works. I need details. If you think this person is credible, I need to talk to them. I need something solid to proceed." Cocking her head, she added, "Just don't do anything else stupid."

He nodded, resigned to admit she was right. Beth's phone chimed. She looked at it, then stood. "Sorry, I've got to go. Maybe next week when I'm off we can get together and do some serious drinking. In the meantime, get me something concrete."

He stood and watched her leave. He looked at his empty glass, tempted to have another. Probably should do rounds first.

32

Halfway around the marina, Jon's phone vibrated. Nora.

"Cruz."

"Did I catch you at a bad time?"

"Working. Doing my rounds."

"I'm just leaving the hospital. Thought you might want to have a nightcap."

He wasn't really in the mood for company. On second thought, he hoped it might help his spirits.

"Sure. I should be done in half an hour. If I'm not back when you get here, just make yourself at home."

"See you shortly."

When he got to the boat, Nora sat on the aft deck, still wearing her scrubs. The bottle of tequila and two glasses were sitting on the table.

"I waited for you," she said. She poured a shot into each glass. "Salud. Based on your tone, I wasn't sure you wanted company."

"Sorry. Not you. It's just been a shitty day." He told her about Trey. When he finished, she shook her head.

"That's not good. I'm sorry. Wish I could be more encouraging."

"Nothing you can say. I know the score. Pancreatic cancer killed a coworker of mine a few years ago. Three weeks after he was diagnosed, he was gone."

He took another sip and said, "I just wish I could find out what happened to Haley before . . . Trey's gone."

"How's that going?"

He shared a little about his conversation with Lexi, leaving out the details. He also told her about his discussion with Beth. "But my source refuses to talk to anyone. Unless I can get her cooperation, Beth won't touch it."

"So, what do you think is going on?"

He shook his head. "Not sure. That's why I want you to look over Haley's records. There's more to the story than a relapse. Delray-By-The-Sea is crooked. I'm convinced now that I've talked to someone else who was there with Haley."

A cool breeze stirred, indicating rain was coming. Nora wrapped her arms around herself.

"Let's take this inside," he said. "If it's not too late. It's getting cooler out here."

She nodded and rose. "I don't go in until three tomorrow afternoon."

They went into the main salon, where only a single light was on. He saw her glance at Megan's picture, but she didn't comment. "I can turn on some more lights," he said.

"No, this is fine."

They sat at the corner of the small dining table, one on each side.

"Enough about my day," he said. "Tell me more about Nora."

She chuckled. "You already know I grew up on Lake Michigan. And I'm a boat rat. Not sure there's anything more to tell."

"Everybody has a story. Try me."

She told him about growing up in a small Michigan town, wanting to get as far away as she could as soon as she could. She went into nursing, figuring that would be a ticket to go anywhere she wanted. After spending a couple of years at a Chicago hospital, she was tired of the Midwest winters and wanted to move elsewhere. She went to work as a travel nurse, taking assignments all over the country. Her last gig as a traveler was at Delray Medical. At the end of that assignment, they offered her a full-time position.

"How about you?" she asked. "You keep steering the conversation to me, but you've told me very little about you."

"Not tonight," Jon said, yawning.

"I better go," she said, standing. "I'm keeping you up." She held her arms out for a hug. Next thing he knew, his arms were around her waist, and her arms were around his neck. It felt good, and neither seemed in a hurry to turn loose.

Still holding him, she leaned her head back so she could look him in the eyes. He looked down at her green eyes and was lost. Their lips touched, gingerly at first, then with increasing urgency.

* * *

The next morning, the smell of fresh coffee woke Jon. Groggy and confused, he turned to see the bed covers in complete disarray. Blue scrubs and a bra were thrown over the chair by his desk. Interesting. He didn't own either.

The brain fog started to clear. He smiled as he remembered last night, realizing it wasn't a dream. It had been a long time since he'd been with someone. He hoped she enjoyed it as much as he did.

He slipped on a pair of shorts and a T-shirt. After stopping at the head for his morning pee, he padded into the galley. There stood the attractive redhead pouring coffee. She was wearing one of his shirts and nothing else.

"Good morning," Nora said, turning to face him. Her shirt—his shirt—was completely unbuttoned. All he could see was bare skin. "How do you take your coffee?" she asked.

"Uh, black, please."

"Me, too," she said, handing him a steaming cup. "You okay?"

He nodded and sat in the same place he did last night. She joined him at her spot.

"That was an . . . interesting evening," he said. "You okay?"

She put her hand on his arm. "I hope you thought it was more than interesting. I thought it was wonderful. And, yes, I'm fine. Don't worry. I'm not going to ask you to marry me."

That started him laughing. Then, they were both giggling like teenagers on a first date.

Once they stopped, he said, "For the record, it was off-the-chart wonderful."

He got up to get the coffee pot. When he returned to the table, he filled her cup first. As he did, his eyes drifted to her chest, and he almost overflowed her mug. His open shirt draped over her naked body left little to the imagination. His pulse quickened, and he felt a stirring below his waist.

"My shirt looks so much better on you," he said, licking his lips.

She grinned. "I'm glad you think so, but I don't think it's the shirt you're staring at. Not fair. You have on more clothes than I do."

With an unsteady hand, he poured himself another cup of coffee and sat on the same side of the table as her. When their bare legs touched, he felt a spark and was convinced she felt it too. She leaned over and kissed him, her hand snaking underneath his T-shirt, stroking his bare chest, then sliding down to his shorts. His breath quickened as he stood, took her hand, and led her back to bed.

Afterward, as they lay there, she ran her finger over the scar on his chest. "What happened?"

"Another souvenir from the Marines. A long story for another time." Changing the subject, he said, "To be clear, I thought that was also off-the-chart wonderful. But I'm famished. As soon as I can stand, how about I cook breakfast?"

"Yes, to both," she said, grinning as she leaned over and kissed him.

Later, as they ate, she nodded toward the lone picture. "Your daughter?" she asked.

His eyes narrowed, and he nodded. "Megan."

"She's beautiful."

He looked at Megan's picture wistfully. "She was."

An awkward silence crept into the salon.

"I'm sorry," she said. "I didn't mean to pry."

He shook his head and stared at the picture. "It's okay. Happier times." He exhaled, then looked at her. "Her mom and I drove up to Atlanta for her graduation. We had admitted her to a treatment program there, supposedly one of the best in the country."

That was Megan's third program. He remembered that it had been a hard ninety days—on everyone. But they were convinced that the third one was the charm. All of them were hopeful and full of optimism.

"She looked so good, sober and drug-free. On the way home, we stopped and spent the night in St. Simons Island, at the same mom-and-pop motel on the beach we visited every year. Erika—her mother—took that picture there."

Nora put her hand on his arm but didn't speak.

He placed his hand on top of hers. "That's the last I want to remember."

"What happened?" she asked in a soft voice.

"The worst that can happen to a parent," he said, shaking his head and staring off into the distance. "That's the part I wish I could forget."

They sat there for a few minutes, not saying anything. At last, he looked at her. He'd never voiced this before and wasn't sure he could now. His voice breaking and tears sliding down his cheeks, he continued.

"Two days after we got back to Jacksonville, I had to go to Dallas. While I was gone, Megan killed herself at home. Erika found her." He started sobbing and couldn't stop.

Nora slid over and wrapped her arms around him. "It wasn't your fault," she said, stroking his head.

"I . . . should've . . . known," he said between heart-wrenching sobs.

"You couldn't have. Nobody—not even you—could have known."

Nora took him to bed, only to lie down to hold and comfort him. Much later, propped up on her elbow, she studied him. "I need to get dressed and go to work. Are you going to be okay?"

He nodded. "Thank you." He exhaled. "For listening. That's the most I've talked about it. To anyone."

She put her arms around him, holding him close. "I'm glad you felt comfortable sharing with me. Anytime. But you've got to quit blaming yourself."

He nodded, then got out of bed to start cleaning the kitchen. By the time he'd finished, she had emerged wearing scrubs and holding his shirt over her arm.

"Thanks for the shirt," she said, offering it to him.

He walked over and stood in front of her. "Keep it—if you want. It looks good on you." He shifted his weight from one foot to the other before continuing.

"This is new territory for me. Forgive me for bumbling around, but I'm not exactly sure what the proper protocol is. I wouldn't blame you for running."

She reached out and took his hand. "There is no protocol, Jon. And I'm not running anywhere. We are two consenting adults who enjoyed each other's company. But there's no obligation on either side. I want to see you again, and I hope you want to see me. Let's leave it at that for now."

He nodded toward the shirt. "I'd like to see you wearing that again. You're easy to be with. Thank you."

He leaned down and kissed her like he meant it.

33

After Nora left, Jon poured himself a fresh cup of coffee. On his way out, he noticed the Delray-By-The-Sea brochure on his desk. He grabbed it and went up to his usual spot on the bridge.

Sipping his coffee, he pondered the fascinating turn of events with Nora. It was indeed an interesting evening—and morning. Scary, as well. Certainly not what he expected at the beginning of dinner. He was drained emotionally but also felt better, like a weight had been lifted off his shoulders.

Why Nora? He had told her things he'd never shared with anyone. Odd, since he hadn't known her that long. There was clearly a mutual, physical attraction, but it was more than that. Recalling her words before she left, he decided that would have to do for now until he had more time to process his feelings.

He turned his attention to how best to utilize the information he'd learned from Lexi. As he flipped through the brochure, an idea struck him. Moren Health owned Delray-By-The-Sea. Maybe they were the key to stopping Westbrook?

He went online to refresh his memory on Moren Health. Based in Boca Raton, it was founded by Cal Norman, the oil man from west Texas. Delray-By-The-Sea was his first major acquisition. He had subsequently purchased forty other drug treatment centers across the country, building a national chain about to go public.

Jon wanted to go straight to the top—Cal Norman. He wasn't sure he could trust any of the minions between Cal and Stuart Westbrook. But Jon knew cold-calling someone like Cal would get nowhere. To get to someone like him, he needed an introduction. A connection like Warren Thompson.

Warren, a wealthy hedge fund manager in Ft. Myers, was a friend of Jon's. Somebody like Warren was more likely to be able to open a door for Jon to talk with Cal.

He called Warren's cell phone.

"Jon, how are you?" Warren said when he answered. "You in town?"

"I'm fine, thanks. Still over on the east coast. How are you?"

"No complaints. We need to get together. It's been too long."

"I agree. That's why I was calling. I want to run something by you. I was thinking I could drive over for the day when you've got a few hours."

"I'd love to. But I'm leaving in the morning and won't return for two weeks. How about then?"

He shook his head. He didn't want to wait two weeks. He looked at his watch. Ten o'clock.

"I'd really like to do it sooner if possible. What about today? I could meet you and Micah at the Veranda at one. Assuming they're still open for lunch on Sundays." Since Hurricane Ian, Jon knew things were still not back to normal in Southwest Florida.

"They are, and that works for me. Micah's working, but I could meet you there at one."

"Great. I'll see you then."

Jon disconnected. More than just an intro, which he could have suggested on the phone, he wanted to run his plan by Warren. Besides, he hadn't seen him since Ian devastated that area in late September. The two-and-a-half-hour drive each way would give him time to think.

He showered and left the marina thirty minutes later, heading south on I-95 to 10th Street, which turned into the Sawgrass Expressway. At I-75, he took the east ramp to the Everglades toll plaza. Once through there and on the arrow-straight stretch of I-75 known as Alligator Alley, he set the cruise control on eighty. It was a boringly straight shot, especially in Lucille, but heavily patrolled. He'd learned the hard way to set it and forget it.

At one o'clock, he pulled into the parking lot at the Veranda, an iconic downtown Ft. Myers restaurant for over forty years.

Warren was already seated at a table in the corner and stood when he spotted Jon. They clasped hands and exchanged a heartfelt man hug. "How was your drive?"

"Boring, as usual," Jon said. "You're looking good. How's Micah?" Micah was Warren's wife.

"Great. She sends her love and says you owe her. You look happy. What's going on with you?"

Jon blushed, thinking about Nora, surprised that it showed. He shrugged. "A lot. One of the reasons I wanted to talk to you." He told him about Trey and Haley, giving him a brief synopsis of how he'd gotten to the reason behind his visit.

"I'm convinced Delray-By-The-Sea and a local drug kingpin are in cahoots. I've got a good source, but she won't talk to the cops. So, they won't do anything. Since a larger company owns Delray-By-The-Sea, I thought about going to them and see if they can do anything."

Warren nodded. "Makes sense."

"Therein lies the problem. I want to go to the parent company CEO but don't have an in. I was hoping you could help."

"Sure. Who is it? I might know them."

"Moren Health, based in Boca Raton. Cal Norman is the CEO and founder."

"I've heard of them. Got an IPO coming up, I believe. I maybe met him somewhere along the line. Big guy, Texas drawl?"

Jon nodded. "That's him. I've never formally met him, but he was at dinner with someone I know the other night. Think you could get me an audience?"

"What's your pitch?"

"You know me, straight up. I have information about questionable activities involving Delray-By-The-Sea and wanted to give him a chance to deal with it internally. There's some indication that their management may be involved. That's why I wanted to avoid them and go to corporate."

Warren pursed his lips. "That may work, especially if they're close to going public. Nobody wants bad press at this juncture. I'll give him a call and let you know."

On the way back across the Alley, Jon thought about his pitch to Cal, framing it around possible unsavory press relating to Delray-By-The-Sea. Unsure of how much Cal may know, he wasn't sure how or if he should explain his experience with Stuart Westbrook. He had to be prepared and wanted to avoid the appearance of a vendetta.

Warren called as Jon was exiting I-95, almost home. "You wanted soon, and you're in luck. Cal just called me back and said he could meet with you tomorrow morning at nine."

"Thanks, that's awesome. I'll be there."

Warren gave him the number for Cal's assistant to call for directions and to confirm.

Jon immediately called the number. After explaining who he was and why he was calling, she told him she'd text directions to Mr. Norman's house in Boca Raton.

"They'll have your name at the gate. Oh, and Mr. Norman is very impatient with anyone who's late."

"Don't worry," Jon said. "I am, too."

* * *

At a quarter to nine, Jon turned into Coral Isle Cove and stopped at the gatehouse of the exclusive community. He'd never been here before, but it had the appearance of a typical high-end community in Boca Raton located on the Intracoastal waterway.

He gave his name to the guard along with his driver's license. She checked it against the visitor's list, nodded, and handed his license back, giving Lucille the once-over. He swore she turned up her nose at the unassuming sedan in a conclave of exotic cars.

"First left, then the second right. Mr. Norman's house is the third driveway on the left-Bahama Breeze. Have a nice day, Mr. Cruz."

The smell of money permeated the air in this well-manicured community. Many of the mansions weren't visible from the streets, hidden behind hedges and fences and trees, with only the roofs or top stories visible. Occasionally, he got a glimpse of large boats parked behind them. Here, the mansions had names, not numbers.

When he got to the driveway marked Bahama Breeze, he entered. As he rounded the curve, a blue Lamborghini was parked in front. He parked next to it and walked up to the front door. Before he could ring, the door opened, and a neatly dressed woman greeted him. He guessed that the front gate had warned her.

"Good morning, Mr. Cruz. Mr. Norman is expecting you. If you'll follow me, I'll take you to him."

Walking through the house, Jon felt like he was in a museum. Art of various forms—paintings, ceramics, fabric—lined the walls and filled the space. When they got to the rear of the house, he was greeted with the sight of a massive yacht docked there.

WesTex was the name on the transom. She led him on board and up to the rear deck, where the tall Texan he recognized from the restaurant was sitting in front of a stack of papers.

"Thank you, Rosaline," he said, dismissing her. He stood and extended his hand. "Cal Norman."

"Jon Cruz," he said, shaking Cal's hand. "Nice office."

"Thanks. I have a real office in town, but I try not to go there more than necessary. Too many meetings and interruptions. Have a seat. Coffee?"

"Thank you. Black's fine."

Cal filled a cup for Jon and then refilled his.

"I appreciate you taking the time to see me," Jon said.

"Warren tells me you want to talk about Delray-By-The-Sea."

Cal didn't waste time getting to the point. As he'd told Warren, he was going to play it straight up with Cal—no subterfuge. Now, he was even more convinced that was the way to go.

"I do. You should know that I lost my daughter to drugs. She'd been in and out of multiple treatment programs—none Moren."

"I'm aware of that. I'm sorry for your loss."

That disclosure took him by surprise. He wondered how much more the man knew about him.

Cal soon answered that. "I was at dinner the other night with Stu when you stopped by the table. When I asked him what that was about, he gave me his side of the story. I wanted to hear yours. That—and Warren's call—are why you're here."

He nodded. This was going to be delicate. He figured Westbrook had tried to pass it off as retaliation, so he chose his words carefully.

"My behavior in Dr. Westbrook's Atlanta office was regrettable. I'd just lost my daughter. I was distraught and lashing out at the world. That doesn't excuse my actions. I apologized and withdrew my lawsuit. As far as I'm concerned, the book is closed on that incident."

Cal nodded. "I appreciate your honesty. That night at Dial, you seemed to imply that Stu was causing trouble for your friends."

Jon paused to regroup. Cal kept steering the conversation in a different direction than he wanted. He had to wrestle it back and get to his reason for the visit.

"A close friend just lost his daughter, Haley Stevens, who had recently been a patient at Delray-By-The-Sea. Their daughter hasn't even been buried and they've turned the account over to collections. When I went with him to get a copy of her records, I recommended they reconsider doing that. As a result of my suggestion, Dr. Westbrook seems to believe I pose a threat."

"Why do you think that?"

"He got a criminal trespass warning prohibiting me from going there. And there's reason to think he may be using his influence to pressure my landlord, employer, and several friends in retaliation. That is what I was referring to at the restaurant."

Cal leaned forward. Jon held his hand up.

"My friend is not blaming your facility. His daughter discharged herself against medical advice, all properly documented. He's just a grieving father trying to comprehend what happened."

Cal nodded and seemed to relax. "Go on."

"While researching Haley's demise, I ran across another former patient who knew Haley. This person revealed some disturbing information that I thought you should know."

Cal listened as he finally got to his reason for being there.

"They stated that they were encouraged to discharge themselves to a recovery home associated with Delray-By-The-Sea," Jon said.

Cal shrugged. "As far as I know, that's not unusual. Most treatment centers work with such places as part of the broader treatment process."

He leaned forward. "That's where it gets interesting. Another half dozen patients at the home, including Haley, had similar stories. In fact, some had been in and out of Delray-By-The-Sea multiple times. The kicker is a known drug dealer runs this home."

Cal's eyes widened at this bit of information. He couldn't tell whether his reaction was recognition or surprise.

"How do you know this is true? You said this is one patient? No offense, but drug users are not always the most reliable sources. Have you gone to Stu with this?"

Jon nodded. "To address your first question, I found this person extremely credible. They have nothing to gain by fabricating this. As for your last question, I didn't go to Dr. Westbrook because I believe some of their staff may be involved. Those reasons have nothing to do with my history with Dr. Westbrook. That's why I wanted to talk to you directly. I think it's only fair you have a chance to investigate it discreetly and get out in front of any potential bad press."

Cal narrowed his eyes, clasped his hands, and rested his chin on them. "This is disturbing. May I ask why you think Delray-By-The-Sea management is involved?"

"I'm in the process of vetting what I've learned. I'd rather wait until I have more concrete information."

"Fair enough. I appreciate your bringing it to my attention, and I certainly intend to explore this further. Any chance I could speak with your source?"

Jon shook his head. "Unfortunately, no. They are frightened of retribution."

"Hmmm," Cal said, nodding. "Any other details you can give me?"

"No. As a private citizen, there's only so much I can do. For example, I have a description of the vehicle that picked my source up at Delray-By-The-Sea but no license plate. Those are things that law enforcement would have to get."

Cal shifted in his chair. "I hope you haven't involved them. This could be very damaging to our reputation. And, the evidence seems rather thin at this point."

"No, I haven't. Again, I wanted to speak with you first."

"I appreciate your consideration. Before you speak to anyone else, let me see what I can find out, confidentially, of course." Cal produced a card and handed it to him. "This is my cell. If you find anything further, please call me anytime. You've already talked to Becky, my assistant. She always knows how to find me."

Jon stood and gave Cal his old business card. He'd marked through the title and office information and written in his cell number. "My cell phone. Thanks again for your time."

Cal looked at the card, then up at him. "Special Agent. Health & Human Services. Office of Inspector General? Impressive."

"Retired."

"What do you do now?"

"Bought a boat and moved down here. Live on it up the waterway at Hank's. Glad to be out of the rat race."

"What kind of boat?"

"Nowhere near as nice as this," he said, chuckling. "An old Grand Banks. Comfortable, good enough to get me to the Bahamas and go fishing."

"Grand Banks makes fine boats. Years ago, I owned one. I have a house in the West End. The fishing is coming back. I just don't get enough time to enjoy it." Cal stood. "Thanks again for bringing this to my attention. We'll be in touch."

34

S tuart was in a foul mood, irritated at being summoned to the boss's boat once again. As usual for a Monday, he had a full calendar. He tried to beg off, but Cal was insistent.

At Cal's house, Rosaline escorted him to *WesTex,* where Cal held court as usual. After depositing him on board, he and Cal watched in silence as she made her way back to the house. As soon as she was out of earshot, Cal leaned over the table.

"I had a visitor this morning bearing troubling news. Remember Haley Stevens?" He sat back and waited for an answer.

What the hell? "Who came to see you? Her father?"

Cal folded his arms, still waiting for an answer to his question.

"She was a patient," Stuart said. "I told you about her the other day. Her family got behind on payment, so at our suggestion, she discharged herself, and we sent her to Delray Serenity House." He added, "Moren's policy."

Red-faced, Cal said, "There is no such 'policy.' Is it true she overdosed and died not long after she left?"

Suddenly, he realized who had met with Cal. "Jon Cruz. That son of a bitch. That's who came to see you. What did he say?"

Cal sneered. "He's got a source. Another former patient told him you're using a recovery home he claims is owned by a drug dealer. They also told him it's filled with former Delray-By-The-Sea patients."

Stuart narrowed his eyes. "Who told him that?"

"I don't know. He wouldn't say, but somebody is talking. And why are you provoking him by trying to pressure his friends?"

Stuart felt his face flush at being called out for his ploy to ratchet up the stakes by leaning on Cruz's friends.

Punctuating the air with his finger, Cal said, "You've got a real problem here, Stu. And you have to fix it. If this gets out, we can kiss the IPO goodbye."

He sat back. "He's bluffing. I told you he has a personal vendetta. He'd have gone to law enforcement if there was anything to it. But he hasn't. I'd know."

Cal shook his head, disgusted. "You think because you're pals with the local police chief, you'd know? Jon Cruz is a retired federal agent. The feds could already be involved."

He considered Cal's point but discarded it. "We would've gotten wind of it one way or the other."

"I'm not convinced. And if he's bluffing, where'd he get that information? Do not underestimate him. I'm betting he knows more than he said. And quit screwing around with his friends. Instead, focus on finding out who's talking. Tell them to put a sock in it or else."

On his way back to the office, he called Ramon. "We need to talk," he said when Ramon answered.

"Sure. Want me to come over to—"

"Hell no. Stay away from here. The usual place. One hour." He disconnected and banged his fist on the steering wheel. "Fucking Jon Cruz," he said out loud.

He thought about what Cal had said about the feds. Maybe his poker buddy, the police chief, didn't know everything. He looked up and checked his rearview mirror, wondering if someone was following him.

How did the hell did Cruz get in to see Cal? It didn't matter. The shit had hit the fan. And Cal would throw Stuart and everybody else under the bus before it was over. He had to figure something out. Soon.

Back at Delray-By-The-Sea, he had his assistant get Kip to his office stat.

"Just how many motivational T-shirts do you have?" he asked the resident counselor as soon as he walked into his office.

Kip closed the door behind him. "I've got one for each—"

"It's a rhetorical question. I need to know who Haley Stevens associated with while she was here. Someone else who went to Delray Serenity House."

Kip nodded. "How soon?"

"I've got a meeting in an hour."

Kip started to protest, but Stuart's hard look gave him pause. Instead, he rose. "I'm on it."

"Oh, and no more patients go there."

Kip scrunched his face up. "We always send everyone there. What's the problem?"

He shook his head. "A moratorium until I can figure out what's going on. Send them to Kettering House."

"Ramon's not going to be happy."

"I don't give a damn. I'll deal with him."

An hour later, Stuart drove to Delray Beach Memorial Gardens, the municipal cemetery formerly known as Pine Ridge Cemetery. It was a convenient spot, and easy to see if either of them was being followed.

He drove through the main gate on Southwest 8th Avenue, looking for Ramon's black Escalade. They met at different graves to avoid setting a pattern and to evade others.

He spotted the SUV parked alone on one of the side streets in the cemetery. He drove toward it and parked thirty yards past. When he got out, he spotted Ramon standing at a grave in the distance, looking down as though contemplating memories of the occupant.

Casually, glancing around to ensure they were alone, he made his way over to Ramon. He handed him a sheet of paper with the names that Kip had compiled. Ramon took it and stuck it in his pocket without even looking.

"Somebody's talking," Stuart said.

"Nobody here."

He shook his head at Ramon's feeble attempt at humor. "Somebody on that list is talking about our arrangement." He had gone over the list with Kip. Together they'd marked out names they thought couldn't be Cruz's source—timeframes didn't fit, people who'd left the area, etc.

"What am I supposed to do?" Ramon asked.

"Find out who and persuade them to keep quiet."

Ramon nodded and cocked his head. "Persuade?"

His expression sent a chill down his spine. "Nothing violent. Just a warning."

Ramon's expression changed from anticipation to disappointment. Stuart didn't doubt that the man was capable of violence, probably more so than he wanted to believe. What he now saw was a glimpse of Ramon's sadistic side.

He glanced over at the SUV. Though he couldn't see through the heavily tinted windows, he knew at least two well-armed thugs were inside watching their boss. At the slightest provocation, they would emerge and deal with any threat.

"We don't need to encourage any more attention to former patients," Stuart said.

Ramon chuckled. It was a hollow laugh. "We're in business, doc. They're customers—mine and yours.

They're the ones who buy and use, not me. If I don't sell them product, they'll buy it from someone else. On your side, you get a lot of repeat business. As soon as they can scrape up more money, they're back in for more rehab. It'd be bad business to hurt customers, wouldn't it?"

He thought about asking Ramon if he had anything to do with Haley's overdose, then decided against it. He didn't want to know. "Let me know when you find them."

As he turned and walked back to the car, his gut was churning. Things were spinning out of control, and he was being marginalized. To hell with Ramon and Cal. It was time he came up with a plan for Stuart.

He was reminded of the ancient proverb: The enemy of my enemy is my friend.

Maybe he needed to take a fresh look at the big picture and rethink who his enemies were.

35

Jon stopped by St. Peter's when he got back to Delray Beach from Boca Raton and talked briefly with Padre. No one there had seen Lexi again or knew anything about her whereabouts. After leaving, he called Nora.

"Hey, got time for a quick cup of coffee?" he asked when she answered. "I'm just leaving St. Peter's."

"Sure—unless we get slammed before you get here."

Ten minutes later, he was sitting with Nora at the Starbucks in Delray Medical.

"What were you doing at St. Peter's?" she asked.

"Just stopped by to chat with the rector."

She raised her eyebrows. "I didn't realize you were religious."

He chuckled. "I'm not. Have you had a chance to look at Haley's records?"

She nodded. "And I thought you just wanted to see me. I've looked through them. Nothing out of the ordinary that I could see. Any more from your source?"

He shook his head, disappointed that she didn't find anything. "No. I'm at a dead end, although I did meet with Westbrook's boss this morning. Maybe he can do something."

"His boss?"

"Cal Norman. CEO of Moren Health, who owns Delray-By-The-Sea."

She shifted in her seat. "How did you get in to see him?"

"A friend of mine made the introduction. Cal seemed interested in what I had to say, but who knows?"

She shrugged, looked at her watch, and stood. "Hope it helps. I need to get back to work. We're short-handed today. But I'm off tomorrow night. Maybe we can have dinner?"

"I'd love to, but I'm going to Cincinnati for Haley's service. Won't be back till late. How about the day after?"

When he returned to the marina, he was surprised to see Beth standing by her car. He parked beside her. Her expression was fixed and unreadable, and she didn't look at him when he walked over.

"What's going on?" he asked.

She showed him a photo on her phone. It was a picture of a dingy piece of cloth lying partially in the water. On it were the ragged letters J O, which trailed off into something indecipherable. A lifeless hand was nearby. "Is this your source?"

He studied the picture, trying to make sense of it. He looked up at her. "What is this? And what makes you think that?"

"Apparent overdose. Tox report's not back yet. A fisherman found the body washed up near the George Bush Boulevard bridge on the Intracoastal. The ME thinks the vic wrote this in blood on their shirt before they died. That's the first two letters of your name."

He cocked his head, his gut churning as he tried to keep his emotions in check. He hoped to God it wasn't Lexi. "So? Lots of Johns and Joes out there. Whose hand?"

"No ID yet. I was hoping you could help."

He stared at the picture. The hand didn't belong to someone still in this world. "Male or female?" he asked, holding his breath.

"Male."

He silently breathed a sigh of relief. "Not my source."

"Anything else can you tell me about *her?*"

He shook his head and stared at her. "How many more will it take?"

"I can assure you this is a priority."

He almost said, *some priority,* but he wanted her to go with him to Haley's service. "I hope so. Are you still going tomorrow?"

"Yes. I already cleared it with my lieutenant. And Jon?" She got in her car, but before she closed the door, she looked up at him.

"I know," he said. "Don't do anything stupid."

36

Haley's memorial service was at Masons Funeral Home in Kenwood, just northeast of Cincinnati. On the flight up, Beth had shared with Jon what little she'd learned about Haley's demise.

The cause of death was fentanyl overdose. Someone dumped her on a corner in Bird City. The only witness described a black SUV that stopped, shoved her out, then drove off. An Escalade, but no license plate, no identifying characteristics, and occupants unknown.

Jon was surprised that it was fentanyl, not oxycodone. Beth had told him that the latest craze was dealers selling fentanyl as OxyContin. M-30s, they called it. In addition to more kick, fentanyl was cheaper, easier to manufacture, and easier to move. But considerably more dangerous.

The thought enraged him that another human being could dump her like so much garbage on the street. They could have just as easily taken her to the hospital. Maybe they didn't want her to survive? Maybe they didn't care.

He was missing something but couldn't put his finger on it. Putting himself in the dealer's shoes, he could understand the why. Once the addicts no longer served their purpose, the dealer discarded them quickly and efficiently. Recycling and abusing addicts were their business, requiring a steady stream of victims. That was the key. Overwhelmed by his grief and anger at what had happened to Megan and Haley, he'd focused on the disposing of victims. What he needed to concentrate on was the supply side of the equation.

The graveside service immediately followed at the cemetery adjacent to the funeral home. At the conclusion, he and Beth waited near the end of a long line to offer their condolences to Reece and Trey.

Jon had thought Trey didn't look good inside the softly lit funeral home but realized he looked even worse in the daylight. He'd lost weight, his skin was sallow, and he seemed unsure of his balance when walking. The cancer was taking its toll.

He fidgeted, standing in line, shifting his weight from one foot to another. This was the first funeral he'd attended since Megan's. He'd never been a fan of funerals and swore after Megan's he'd never go to another. Never say never.

When it was their turn, Trey hugged him. His strength was a fraction of the old Trey and Jon's heart ached at the decline.

"Thank you for coming," Trey said.

"It was a nice service. I'm so sorry, Trey."

Trey nodded. "You're coming by the house, aren't you?"

"Of course. We'll see you there."

Trey released him and turned to Beth while he stepped over to Reece. Her eyes were wet and bloodshot, and she clutched a tissue.

She embraced him and said, "Good to see you. Thank you for coming."

"I'm so sorry, Reece. I wish the circumstances were different." Not knowing what else to say and anxious to keep moving, he added, "We'll stop by the house on our way to the airport."

He moved forward and outside the tent to wait for Beth. She soon joined him, grabbed his hand, and squeezed it. He held on to it like a drowning man.

"Thank you for coming," he said. "It meant a lot to them. And, to me."

"You'd do the same for me."

When they got to Trey and Reece's house, a large crowd had already gathered. In the living room, they had constructed a shrine of sorts. Pictures and artifacts from various stages and events in Haley's too-short life.

He picked up a picture of Haley and Megan, taken when they were about ten. Two loving, stable families, two beautiful innocent girls. What happened?

Trey walked up next to him, putting his arm around his friend to console him. "Sorry, Jon. We shouldn't have put that one out."

He shook his head, tears welling up. That was Trey—comforting his friend at his own daughter's funeral. Putting his arm around Trey, he said, "No. I'm glad you did. Happier times. That's what we need to remember."

They stood that way for several minutes, others respecting the moment and keeping their distance.

As the crowd started to thin, Beth cornered Jon. "We have to leave soon. I know the timing is not good, but I'd like to speak privately with Trey and Reece for a few minutes before we do."

He nodded. "Let me see what I can do."

He found Trey and expressed Beth's desire to chat with them before they had to leave. Trey told them to go down to the basement rec room. He'd get Reece and meet them there.

When Reece and Trey entered the room, Beth spoke. "Again, I'm sorry for your loss. I know the timing isn't good, but I need to ask you a few questions before we leave."

"Is this about Haley?" Trey asked, holding Reece's hand as they sat.

Beth nodded. "It is. Did your daughter ever mention any names of people she'd met in rehab?"

Reece said, "Occasionally. Usually, just first names. Why?"

"Any you recall?"

Reece thought about it, then nodded. "The last time we talked. She said she was going to miss her friend Lexi."

Shit, Jon thought. Why didn't he think of asking that? He could feel Beth's eyes boring into him.

"Did she say why she was going to miss her?" Beth asked.

Reece shook her head. "No. I just assumed that it was Lexi leaving the program."

"Any other names you remember?"

"No. I remember Lexi because she mentioned her the last time—" Reece started sniffling. Trey put his arm around her shoulder.

Beth stood. "I'm sorry. I know this isn't easy. Just one last question. Jon has told me that you both believed this time was different and that you didn't think she checked herself out. Why?"

"It was different," Trey said. "She'd been in several other programs, so we were especially skeptical this time— and wiser. Two things were unlike before. One, this was the first time she'd made it this far in rehab. Every other time, she'd bailed well before the end. Two, the last time we visited, she was doing so well. She was looking forward to us coming down for her 'graduation,' excited about a new beginning. The difference was obvious."

He looked over at Reece, who nodded, then back at Beth. "We'll never believe that Haley checked herself out and disappeared without getting in touch."

"Thank you so much for taking my questions. Again, I can't tell you how sorry I am for your loss." She turned to Jon. "We really need to go."

They said their goodbyes, went upstairs, and called an Uber to take them to the airport.

On the ride to Cincinnati/Northern Kentucky International Airport, Jon said, "That was sneaky."

"Just doing my job. That name sound familiar?"

"Maybe."

"That photo I showed you yesterday? It's a homicide. If you know anything that could be related, I'd appreciate your *voluntary* cooperation."

She emphasized the word voluntary. He recognized the implied threat. With an active homicide investigation, she could haul him in for questioning, forcing him to disclose anything he knew about Lexi now that she had a name.

"I'll give it some thought," he said.

"I'm cutting you some slack under the circumstances. But we're going to have a conversation soon. Since this is a homicide, I'm getting a lot of pressure."

They didn't talk much on the flight home. He was drained emotionally, and now he had to worry about giving up Lexi. His thoughts returned to his conversation with Beth on the flight up to Cincinnati.

He'd mentioned that he asked his nurse friend to look at Haley's medical record, and she'd not found anything unusual. Beth lapsed into detective mode, questioning Nora's qualifications and wanting to know how well he knew her. He had gotten defensive, so Beth had dropped it.

He looked over at her, staring out the window. "Maybe I should have someone else look at Haley's medical record."

She turned and stared at him. "Where'd that come from?"

"Just thinking about it. It wouldn't hurt to get a second opinion."

She had not asked to see the records as far as he knew. She still considered Haley's death due to a relapse. He had to agree that was the logical explanation.

But Trey's insistence that he didn't believe she checked herself out, along with Lexi's information, had changed his mind. Unable to interview his source, Beth had discounted Jon's theory. Now, with Lexi's name and the Stevens's disclosure, maybe she was coming around. Still, he wasn't counting on Delray PD.

He thought about asking Beth if she knew anyone who could review Haley's records, but then it hit him. Micah, Warren's wife. She was a nurse. He made a mental note to send them to her without any comment. A second, unbiased opinion should ease everyone's concerns.

He hadn't told Beth about his meeting with Cal, not wanting to provoke her wrath. Despite Cal's assurances, he wasn't convinced their meeting would amount to anything. If he heard from him, he'd have the conversation then.

He closed his eyes to take a little nap before they landed.

37

The next morning, Jon emailed Haley's medical record to Warren and Micah. He asked Micah if she'd please review it, looking for any irregularities.

While he was on the computer, he decided to search for recovery homes in the area. He remembered Beth saying there were over two hundred but hoped he could narrow the list.

Multiple cities were cheek to cheek in South Florida, packed in like sardines. North of Delray Beach was Lake Worth, West Palm Beach, and others. It was worse to the south. First was Boca Raton, then Pompano Beach, then Ft. Lauderdale. One couldn't tell where one town ended, and another started.

He didn't know for sure that the place Lexi mentioned was in Delray Beach but figured that would be a good starting point. He was surprised to see over almost fifty recovery homes listed in Delray Beach alone. And those were the ones listed. Who knew how many more there were since no regulations or reporting requirements existed?

Further confusing was that they went by a variety of names. Halfway houses, transitional homes, sober living houses, recovery homes, etc. The list went on forever. Somehow, he needed to narrow the possibilities, but the only one who could have done that was Lexi.

Although Padre had said he'd call if she showed, Jon thought it was worth checking with him. He also wanted to give him a heads-up about the Stevens disclosing Lexi's name to Beth.

"Morning, Padre," he said when the priest answered his cell phone. "Any news on Lexi?"

"I'm sorry, Jon, no. She hasn't been back since we talked to her. But that's not unusual."

"I'm still trying to figure out where that house is. She may have some clue."

"I wish I could help. I've notified everyone here to let me know if she returns. You'll be the next to know."

He told him about the latest overdose, and Beth asking the Stevens about Haley ever mentioning any names. "When she asked me, I didn't confirm or deny it, but I'm going to have to come clean with the detective. They're calling that latest overdose a homicide, and I can't withhold information related to a homicide."

He ended the call and tapped his pencil on the table, trying to figure out where to go next. He replayed his conversation with Lexi, looking for clues he'd missed. She implicated Delray-By-The-Sea but with few details. She'd mentioned what sounded like a recovery home with other victims. In fact, she used that term when describing her last encounter with Haley. But, there were just too many to check.

His gut told him Ramon was involved, but again, Jon had nothing concrete to go on besides a black Escalade. As Ramon and Beth had wryly pointed out, there were many of those in South Florida. Maybe D'Lo knew something that he didn't realize he knew. He called D'Lo and was surprised when he answered.

"J.C. What's up?" D'Lo said.

"Hey, how 'bout breakfast?"

Jon couldn't help but grin when he heard the hoarse laugh on the line.

"You know my weakness. I'll meet you in fifteen."

When he walked into the Waffle Hut, he saw D'Lo sitting in the back booth. After they had ordered and had a full cup of coffee, Jon explained his predicament. He told D'Lo about Lexi, sharing what she'd told him.

"I've hit a wall and am not sure where to go. I'm convinced Delray-By-The-Sea is the treatment center working with a dealer whom I believe to be Ramon. I'm guessing the house she mentioned was a halfway house or recovery home, but I don't know for sure."

Between bites, D'Lo nodded.

"Do you know how many of those places are in this area?" Jon asked.

D'Lo chuckled. "Not exactly, but I'm guessing too many to go knocking on doors."

"That's an understatement. Hundreds. I need to find someone I can talk to who's been in Delray-By-The-Sea and some type of recovery home. Someone who knows who Ramon is and might have known Haley."

D'Lo smirked. "Is that all?"

He shook his head, frustrated. He realized he was asking a lot.

"Haley and this other girl are two victims I know of. Lexi specifically said there were five or six more at this house. I've got to do something. And, to top it off, Haley's father is dying. I want to give him the peace he deserves, but right now, that's not looking likely."

D'Lo's set his jaw, but his big brown eyes softened. "I wish I had something. I'll keep poking, but Ramon runs a tight ship. It's not going to be easy to find someone willing to talk."

That evening, Jon sat at the bar, eating dinner but more like rearranging the food on the plate. His feeling of helplessness was dragging him down. Even Addie noticed something was bothering him, but she didn't press.

He was on his second beer when Beth sidled up next to him and sat. Addie brought her a beer, and he sensed an unspoken communication between the two before Addie walked away.

"You okay?" Beth asked.

"Yeah. Fine." After a few seconds, he shook his head. "No, not really."

"What's the matter?"

"I'm frustrated and angry and don't know what to do. For one of the few times in my life, I do not know what to do. There are innocent people like Haley in this town who are being abused and taken advantage of by a corporation and some sleazy drug lord named Ramon. And I can't do a damn thing to stop them. Nothing. So, here I sit, eating and drinking, doing nothing."

He took a long drink from his beer, then looked back at Beth. "Sorry you asked, huh?"

Gently, she shook her head. "I don't know what to tell you. Other than I know exactly how you feel. It's why so many cops eat their guns."

He snorted. "I feel like Sisyphus."

"Every so often, the boulder doesn't roll back down the hill," she said. "That's what keeps me going."

He nodded. "I guess that's as good as it gets in this life."

"We need to talk. About Lexi."

Beth's phone vibrated. She looked at it, then stuck it back in her pocket as she rose to leave.

"Saved by the bell. I've got to go. But, next time." She put her hand on his arm. "Go easy tonight. Please."

Still upset when he walked back to his boat, he went to punch in his gate code and noticed the gate wasn't locked. It was supposed to lock automatically when it closed.

He opened it, then slammed it shut. Nothing. The light on the keypad worked, so it had electricity. "Fuck," he said out loud. This thing was a pain in the ass. He'd just had someone service it a few weeks ago, and they'd replaced a circuit board. He'd recheck it in the morning in the light of day and place a service call if he couldn't get it working.

On the dock, he looked around for Felix. Still no sign of the cat. He hated to admit that he'd grown fond of the aloof feline. He tried to convince himself that Felix had found a home, but his gut told him otherwise. In some ways, not knowing was worse. But, nothing he could do about that, either.

As he stepped on board, he felt his phone buzz. It was a text from Warren asking him to call when he could. He poured a shot of tequila and went up to the bridge to call.

"Hey, I've got you on speaker with Micah," Warren said when he answered.

"Hey, Micah. How are you?"

"Good. Sorry I missed you when you were over the other day. I had a chance today to look through the medical record you sent me. A couple of things I thought you'd find interesting."

She told him that when a patient discharged themselves against medical advice, a physician had to document that they had counseled the patient and specifically advised them why, medically, they shouldn't leave. She was unable to find any such documentation. Furthermore, nursing notes had to agree with the physician's assessment. Again, no such documentation was in the record she'd received.

"Maybe those pages were missing?" he asked.

"Possible, but the page numbers were in order and didn't reflect any missing pages."

"Did the records mention referring her to a recovery home?"

"None. They end with her leaving AMA."

"If they referred her out, wouldn't that be in her records?"

"Should be. Any type of post-discharge referral should be documented."

Why was that not in the records? Lexi had explicitly said that another girl at the home recalled Haley being there and that she'd escaped.

"Anything else?" Jon asked.

"I'm not a doctor, but the general tone of the notes reflected that the patient was making significant progress and had a good attitude."

"Thanks, Micah. I appreciate you doing this and responding so quickly. Dinner is on me next trip."

He ended the call and sat, confused. Why had Delray-By-The-Sea not documented sending her to a recovery home when they were so meticulous about everything else? And how had Nora missed this? According to Micah, these were obvious omissions.

He thought back to his conversation with Lexi. Before Haley left Delray-By-The-Sea, she told Lexi that she was told to discharge herself, and then she'd be sent to a recovery home.

The following week, they told Lexi the same thing. She was then picked up by a black Escalade and taken to a home. When she got there, the other girls said that Haley had been there but escaped.

He had to find that home.

38

The next afternoon, Jon drove to Peg Legs to find Carlos. Sure enough, his beat-up red Toyota was parked outside.

Although there was no need to hide Lucille this time, Jon was still concerned about some drunk scratching his car or worse, trying to kidnap her. As he entered the parking lot, he saw someone leaving a nice roomy spot at the end of a row near the front door. He parked, got out, and locked the doors.

He stepped inside the dimly lit dive, allowing his eyes to adjust for a minute. Carlos was sitting at the bar, his back to Jon, the stools on either side of him occupied.

The guy on the left was huge and engaged in an animated, alcohol-fueled conversation with his buddy to his left. The man on Carlos's right was much smaller and apparently by himself.

Jon pulled out a twenty, then walked over between Carlos and the person on his right. He laid the twenty on the bar in front of the slight fellow, at the same time putting his left hand firmly on Carlos's left shoulder.

"Hey, buddy," Jon said to the stranger. "Let me buy you a couple of drinks so I can sit next to my friend here."

He felt Carlos stiffen as he looked up and saw him.

The little guy looked at the money and said, "Sure thing, man." He palmed the twenty, grabbed his beer, and went to an empty stool halfway down the bar.

"No need to rush off," Jon said, squeezing Carlos's shoulder hard enough to make him wince. He motioned to the bartender and held up two fingers as he sat beside Carlos.

He lowered his voice. "No te preocupes." Don't worry. "I just want to buy you a beer and have a little chat."

Carlos cast a furtive glance at the door.

"Ni lo pienses," Jon said. Don't even think about it.

Carlos glanced at the door again, then looked at him. He felt Carlos's shoulders relax slightly, so he removed his hand but remained ready to react quickly.

The bartender brought two Budweisers over. He gave him a twenty and told him to keep the change.

He turned to Carlos. "I know you used to work for Ramon, but I take it you two aren't pals anymore." He watched Carlos's expression closely for tells and saw his eyes narrow.

"I know Ramon has a deal with Delray-By-The-Sea. When they kick patients out, he gives them a place to stay."

Carlos's eyes widened, indicating he was on target. He gave him a few seconds to digest the news, then leaned a little closer. "I want to know where that place is."

Carlos's expression changed from surprise and acknowledgment to fear. Jon was convinced he knew where it was, and he also understood the risk of telling.

He pulled out one of his old business cards and put it on the bar in front of Carlos. He gave him a minute to read it and saw him swallow. "We're going to take Ramon down. If you help me, you will get a pass. If you don't, you're going down with him. What's it going to be?"

Carlos shook his head. "Ellos me matarán." They'll kill me.

Jon tapped his card with his finger and stood. "You've got twenty-four hours to think about it. If you don't call, I'll know you've made your choice." He turned and walked out.

39

Jon was making his rounds early that evening when his phone rang. He expected it to be Nora but was surprised to see it was Padre. He stopped to answer. "Is she back?"

"You better get over here. Now." Padre disconnected before he could say anything else.

He ran to the boat to get his car keys. In five minutes, he was heading to St. Peter's. Nearing the church, he passed a gathering of police vehicles at the park, blue lights flashing, along with an ambulance and a uniform directing traffic.

He turned the corner and parked beside an unmarked police car in front of the rector's office.

He walked in and was surprised to see Beth standing in the office. Padre, sitting at his desk, was visibly upset.

"What's going on?" Jon asked.

"Father Bryce found another apparent overdose victim and called 911. EMT got here first." Beth shook her head. "There was nothing they could do. She was dead when they got here."

Padre looked up at him, his expression confirming Jon's worst fears.

"Lexi?" Jon asked but knowing the answer.

"We don't have a confirmed ID yet, but Father Bryce recognized her as Lexi Martin, who'd been here Saturday."

He nodded. "How?" he asked, teeth clenched.

"Autopsy won't be complete for a few hours, but ME's initial call was an overdose."

"Fuck," Jon said, forgetting he was in the priest's office. "I apologize, Padre."

Bryce shook his head. "I'm sorry, Jon." Only Jon understood the priest's remorse was as much for Haley as it was for Lexi.

"We'll get out of your hair," Beth said to Bryce. "Thank you for your help. We may have more questions later."

She nodded toward the door, and Jon followed. By her car where they were alone, she stopped. "She was your source."

He nodded. "I talked with her briefly the one time she came here. The only thing I knew was her first name—Lexi." He looked at Beth. "If I'd given you her name earlier—"

"It wouldn't have made any difference. All any of you had was her first name, nothing else. And, who knew if that was really her name. Even the rector didn't know how to find her."

She looked around. "I didn't want to say anything in front of him, but there's more. This is between me and you—no one else. We're officially withholding this information until we have a suspect."

He knew that was often the case in a homicide. Law enforcement would withhold certain information that only the perpetrator would know. It served two purposes. One, it was a way to validate if a suspect was telling the truth, and two, eliminate potential copycats.

"You have my word," he said.

"I think it was a homicide. There are signs she'd been tortured."

His sadness morphed into anger. "Tortured?"

"I can't go into any detail, but it was obvious. We'll know more once the autopsy is complete."

"Are you going to do something now?" His anger boiled over. "I gave you the information I got from Lexi. I told you what was going on. And what did you do? Nothing."

She held up her hand. "Not fair, Jon. I know you're upset. But you, of all people, know that we just can't pick someone up based on unfounded rumors. We have procedures to follow."

"How many more is it going to take?"

She fired back. "Besides me, who else did you mention your 'unnamed' source to?" She put air quotes around *unnamed.*

"Oh, so now you're interrogating me?"

Her voice was stern and professional. "This is a criminal investigation. I'm doing my job and I'm asking the questions. I repeat, who else did you tell?"

He shook his head. "Only three people, and I didn't give her name or gender to anyone. Bryce, you, and Cal Norman. That's it."

He didn't mention D'Lo, but he knew D'Lo didn't say anything to anyone.

"You didn't tell me you talked to Cal Norman."

"I didn't think it was important." Cal had to be the source of the leak. But how did Cal know Lexi was Jon's source?

He stared at Beth, meeting her glare head-on, wanting her to feel the intensity of his emotions. "There are others, you know. Besides Haley and Lexi. Maybe they're alive— for now. These places are completely under the radar, here in your backyard. Do you think they're all just sitting around holding hands and singing 'Kumbaya?' God knows what they're being forced to do. Besides being recycled again and again through rehab as soon as the families can raise more money."

His nostrils flared as he took a breath, then continued. "Trey and Reece, who you met, just buried their daughter. The one thing he wants to know before he dies is what happened to her. I'm trying to get him an answer. Maybe you should ask Cal Norman who he talked to after I spoke with him."

40

That evening at home, Stuart sat at the bar with his martini as Rachel prepared dinner. Technically, it was just vodka with olives—no vermouth—but he always called it a martini. He thought that sounded better than saying vodka.

He took a swallow and shook his head. Valerie had given him Delray-By-The-Sea's latest financial statements before he left the office. Unfortunately, the bottom line still wasn't where it needed to be to satisfy Cal.

He knew she kept various cushions in reserve for emergencies. But when she handed the financials to him this afternoon, she made it clear she'd depleted everything she had squirreled away. Moreover, she warned that they were uncomfortably close to fraud, a line she was unwilling to cross.

The television on the corner wall was tuned to the local news, which Rachel watched every evening. He paid little attention to it unless it affected Delray-By-The-Sea. Everything else was noise.

"Did you hear that?" Rachel asked. She'd stopped what she was doing, still holding a cooking spoon, and riveted to the small screen.

"What?" he turned his head to see what had drawn her attention.

On screen was an attractive thirty-something blonde with a microphone. The chyron read ANOTHER SUSPECTED OVERDOSE DEATH IN DELRAY BEACH. There were flashing blue lights, ambulances, squad cars, and yellow Do-Not-Cross tapes in the background. The camera was positioned to maximize the drama.

He thought he recognized the church in the background. It looked like St. Peter's Episcopal, and he tried to remember exactly where it was.

"They found another young woman," Rachel said. "Unidentified. She was dead at the scene. That's so sad."

Hope to hell it wasn't another one of our former patients, he thought. That was the last thing he needed.

He watched as the reporter interviewed Rev. Phillip Bryce, the rector. The camera cut to a police department spokesman, who said the identity of the person was being withheld until the next of kin were notified.

Stuart shrugged and turned his attention back to the financial statements.

41

Early the following evening, back on *Trouble No More*, Jon prepared to make a quick loop around the marina. Last night had been tough. First, the news about Lexi, then the heated exchange with Beth.

He knew he'd been unreasonable. She couldn't just go out and pick someone up on speculation, which was all he had now that Lexi was dead.

Nora had called this afternoon and wanted to come over. He didn't want company, but by the time they hung up, he'd thought it might be a good diversion. Besides, he wanted to question her about Haley's medical records.

She was coming over as soon as she left the hospital, so he wanted to finish work before she arrived. He got his pistol and phone, then went out on the deck. He stopped, sniffing the salt air in the light breeze while he scanned the marina. Looking up into the clear night sky, he could see the blinking red and green lights of an aircraft heading south, probably on approach to Fort Lauderdale-Hollywood International Airport.

As he stepped off the boat and onto the dock, he couldn't help but look for Felix. It had been almost two weeks, and still no sign of the wary orange cat. Rationally, he had to accept that Felix was probably not returning. In his heart, he wanted to believe Felix had found a nice home. But, every day that passed, that became harder to accept.

As he walked around the property, he kept an eye out for the cat as he thought about how best to question Nora's review of Haley's medical records. He didn't want to get into another confrontation but did not want to admit he'd had someone else look at them. Yet, he was curious as to how she had missed what Micah had so easily found.

When he returned to his slip, Nora was sitting on the aft deck of his boat, wearing her scrubs. An unopened bottle of wine sat on the table. He apologized for being late. "Been waiting long?" he asked as he leaned down to kiss her.

"Just arrived." She nodded toward the wine. "I haven't even opened it yet."

"I can fix that," he said. Inside, he put his pistol away and put on Eva Cassidy, switching the outside speakers on low. He grabbed a corkscrew and two glasses on his way out.

"Good choice in music," she said when he returned. "You've got me hooked on her."

She spied the corkscrew in his hand and added, "It's a screw-top."

He looked at the wine and then at the corkscrew and shook his head. "Habit," he said, not used to the fact that more wineries were moving in that direction. He opened the bottle and poured them each a glass.

"What's your favorite song of hers?" she asked before taking a sip.

He didn't hesitate. "Nightbird."

She nodded. "I love that one, too. Who else do you like?"

"All of the blues greats. Albert King, Elmore James, Buddy Guy. Stevie Ray Vaughan wasn't too shabby, either.

Another one who died way too young. And, of course, Muddy Waters."

She laughed at the last name. "*Trouble No More*. You told me that's where you came up with the name."

"How's your week?"

She told him it was pretty quiet so far. The usual runny noses, sprains, and cuts. Nothing exciting. "And yours?"

"Okay." He wanted to tell her about Lexi but wasn't ready to go there. "Beth and I had words last night after she busted my chops for not telling her that I went to see the CEO of Moren Health."

She nodded. "You told me that when you stopped by the hospital for coffee. Then, I had to go back to work before you could tell me more. What happened?"

"I told him he should know what was going on at Delray-By-The-Sea. Give him a chance to fix it."

"What is going on there?"

He gave her a brief overview, saying he had reason to believe they were connected with a drug dealer to take advantage of their patients and families.

"That's pretty serious. What was his reaction?"

"He said he'd look into it. I'm not expecting much, but we'll see."

Since he hadn't told her about Carlos, he skipped over that. Instead, he wanted to steer the conversation toward Haley's medical records.

"I finally had a chance to look through Haley's medical records. You said you looked at them and didn't see anything exceptional, but I have a question. Probably because I don't know what I'm looking at. The only thing I saw related to her discharge was what looked like a standard form with signatures. That was it. No discharge instructions. No referrals. I know whenever I was in a hospital, they always did that sort of thing."

She shifted in her seat and took a sip of wine, appearing to recall her review. "I remember seeing the discharge form. I was reviewing it at work, so I didn't dig any deeper once I saw that." She shrugged. "I'll be happy to take another look if you want."

He shook his head. "No, I was just curious. So, should there have been more documentation?"

"Normally. Now, you've aroused my curiosity. I'll take another look. This time, at home. With no interruptions. Are you looking for anything specifically?"

He was surprised that she'd not been more thorough. He recalled his original request and decided that maybe it was his fault for not being specific enough.

"I don't know. I'm getting mixed signals on whether she'd quit the program so close to the end when she was doing so well. I'm just grasping for anything that might lead to answers. What do you know about recovery homes?"

"I know what they are. There are a ton of them in this area. Why?"

"Do the treatment centers have ones they usually work with? You know, like when I asked you for a referral for a drug abuse counselor, you immediately had someone in mind."

She shrugged. "I guess. You'd have to ask."

That gave him an idea. He'd promised Beth that he wouldn't defy the trespass warning prohibiting him from going to Delray-By-The-Sea. But the court order didn't say anything about phone calls, especially if they were from someone else.

He held up his glass. "Enough work for tonight." He moved closer, leaned over, and kissed her.

When they separated, she said, "I don't have to go in until tomorrow afternoon."

"Good. You can cook me breakfast this time."

42

After Nora left the next morning, Jon set his sights on how to approach Delray-By-The-Sea to find out which recovery home they may be aligned with.

Certain that his name had been blackballed by the entire staff, he knew he would get nowhere calling. He contemplated giving them an alias, but a stranger calling out of the blue with a query might spook them. Plus, with caller ID, they would know it was him.

He considered asking Nora to call, but that could backfire since the hospital employed her. That could cause unnecessary trouble for her.

Addie could pull it off, but they might need to call back. If it pointed to Hank's, that would be a red flag. It would be better if it were someone in the mental health field. Someone like Phillip Bryce.

He grabbed his phone and clicked on Padre's number.

"Morning, Padre. How are you?"

"Fine, Jon. And you?"

Jon explained that he was still trying to find out which recovery home Lexi had referred to when they talked. But, with hundreds in the area, he didn't know where to start. He wanted Padre to call Delray-By-The-Sea under the guise of finding out which recovery home they might use. Then Jon could pay them a visit, hoping to learn more.

"Why don't you just call them?" Padre asked.

Jon took a deep breath. He explained that since he'd been there with Haley's father, they would probably be reluctant to talk with him. Padre was hesitant, questioning that it seemed unethical for him to call under false pretenses.

"How much do you know about recovery homes?" Jon asked.

"I'm familiar with what they are and their purpose in treating addiction. As you point out, there are hundreds in our area alone."

"Don't you think it would be good for you—as a counselor to those suffering from addiction—to know which ones are legitimate?" Jon was setting a trap.

Seeming to sense that, Padre hesitated. Unable to argue with the logic, he said, "I suppose so."

Even though he was on the phone, Jon grinned. "Look at it this way. I'm just helping you do your homework."

Padre agreed to call Delray-By-The-Sea Monday and ask to speak to someone about recovery homes. Jon guessed that he would be directed to Kip Foster. Padre would then say he was vetting some of the more widely-used homes in the area for his counseling practice since they were largely unregulated. Jon would then visit the homes unannounced, saying he was researching such facilities for a friend in the Midwest.

* * *

Monday afternoon, Padre called. "I spoke with a Kip Foster at Delray-By-The-Sea. When I told him why I was calling, he seemed suspicious at first but then warmed up. He said they didn't utilize recovery homes often, but when they did, they used Kettering House."

"Where's that?"

"It's here in Delray Beach. He gave me the name of the Director there, Lewis Adams. I took the liberty of calling him."

Jon swore to himself. At first, he wished Padre hadn't called but then decided it might give him an opening to follow up on.

Padre continued. "Interesting conversation. He said that they don't normally get many referrals from Delray-By-The-Sea. He volunteered that the last one had been five or six months ago. Until Friday."

"This past Friday?"

"Yes. He said that was the first one they'd gotten in months. This would seem to rule out Kettering as the place Lexi mentioned."

Jon shook his head. He'd go by and check that one out, but there was no doubt that Kip had given Padre a red herring.

"I'm guessing Mr. Foster didn't give you any other names."

"No, he didn't. I also called one of my colleagues. She was familiar with Kettering and confirmed they have an excellent reputation."

Jon gritted his teeth. He knew that Padre was just trying to help, but he wished he'd stuck with the script and not tried to play amateur detective. Too many questions in too many places would attract attention and might tip off the people Jon was trying to find.

"Thanks. I agree that Kettering doesn't sound like the one I want. I'll let you know if I learn anything more."

"Damn," Jon said out loud after he disconnected. Back to square one. Which home was Delray-By-The-Sea using?

43

Kip Foster barged into Stuart's office without knocking, slamming the door behind him. "We've got a problem," he said, plunking down in a chair at Stuart's desk. PERSEVERE was splashed across today's T-shirt.

Stuart was tempted to reprimand the bastard for interrupting but decided to hear what he had to say first. He steepled his hands and stared at Kip, indicating for him to continue.

"I just got a call from the Rector at St. Peter's Episcopal," Kip said.

The church's name sounded familiar, but Stuart shrugged as if to say, *so what?* He glanced at the computer monitor on his desk, looking at the stock ticker.

"He wanted to know what recovery home we used."

That got Stuart's attention. He straightened, putting his hands flat on the desk, focusing now on Kip.

"I told him we didn't use them much, but I told him Kettering House. That's who we use for overflow when Delray Serenity House is full."

"Yes, yes. I know. Why was he asking?"

"He claimed he was just vetting homes for his counseling practice, but it sounded fishy. You know where

St. Peter's is?" Kip didn't wait for an answer. "That's where they found Lexi Martin's body."

Stuart tensed, trying to maintain his composure. Now he remembered why St. Peter's sounded familiar. It was on the news bulletin Rachel had caught at home last night. Where they'd found a body but no name.

"Lexi Martin? They didn't give a name last night on the news. How do you—"

"They just announced it. It was her."

Jesus. It was Lexi Martin. One of the names on the list of Haley's friends that Kip had compiled. The list that Stuart had given Ramon. Kip was in full panic mode.

"Keep your voice down," Stuart said in a measured tone. He was trying to calm his racing heart and be reassuring to Kip. "An unfortunate coincidence, nothing more." He didn't believe that for a second but had to project confidence.

"I don't like this," Kip said. "It's getting out of hand. And we're right in the middle of it."

He leaned forward, meeting Kip's eyes. "On the news, they said it was an overdose. Our patients are addicted to drugs, Kip. That's why they come to us. Relapses and overdoses are not uncommon. Every treatment facility has that happen occasionally. It's the nature of what we do. You know that."

Kip exhaled and leaned back in his chair. He stared at him, then nodded. "You're right. I guess I overreacted, what with Haley and all."

Stuart extended his hands, palms up. "Good. Thanks for the update. If you hear anything else, let me know." He folded his hands on the desk, signifying the meeting was over.

Kip stood to leave.

"Oh, close my door on your way out, please."

As soon as the door shut, Stuart pulled out his phone and called Ramon's number.

"Sup?" Ramon answered.

"We need to talk. This afternoon."

"It's after five o'clock. How 'bout tomorrow?"

He looked at his calendar. Tomorrow was already overbooked. He had to leave the day after for a conference in Orlando. Besides, what was so important that Ramon couldn't meet today?

"Tomorrow is out, and I have to drive to Orlando for a conference the next day. We need to talk before I leave, so it's got to be today. It won't take long. Pick a time, and I'll meet you at the usual spot."

Ramon grumbled, then said, "Four-thirty. Don't be late." He disconnected.

Arrogant prick. Stuart slammed his phone down on the desk. Ramon needed to understand who the boss was.

He shifted his attention to his computer and searched online for news about Lexi Martin's death. Everything he read said that it was considered an overdose. There was no indication of foul play and no other details.

For a brief moment, he thought about calling the police chief. But he nixed that idea, deciding it might attract unwanted attention.

When he got to the cemetery, he found Ramon's Escalade near the back and parked behind it. As he got out, he spotted him standing alone beside a grave. He walked over and followed Ramon's gaze to a simple grave marker.

CICELY WILLIAMS
FEBRUARY 8, 1924 – JULY 22, 2021

"Ninety-seven. Cicely lived a long life," Ramon said.

"Unlike Lexi Martin, who was on the list I gave you. Please tell me you didn't have anything to do with that."

"Only thing I heard is she overdosed. Guess we lost a customer, but that happens sometimes, right?" Ramon fixed his vacant stare on Stuart. "What's in Orlando?"

"I'm speaking at a conference. You didn't answer my question."

Ramon sighed and shook his head. "You asked me to find who was talking. I did. I told her to put a sock in it and that she needed to leave town. Took her to the bus station and gave her the cash for a one-way ticket to Atlanta. I hung around to make sure she boarded. End of story."

Stuart was stunned. That was the second time in a week that he'd heard the phrase *put a sock in it*. Cal had used the expression when he'd met with him. Before that, he couldn't remember the last time he'd heard anyone say that. And it certainly wasn't a gang-banger like Ramon.

He studied Ramon, looking for clues. Ramon met his stare evenly, seeming to dare Stuart to challenge him. It was not the look of someone intimidated.

Stuart felt increasingly uneasy with Ramon. He had intended to tell Ramon that Delray-By-The-Sea was no longer sending patients to his sober home. Now, he didn't feel comfortable sharing that. Besides, he had the eerie feeling that Ramon already knew.

"We got a question from a local counselor about the sober home we use," Stuart said. "We told them Kettering House. But the timing seems suspicious. Everything I've seen says the same about the Martin woman—overdose, but I thought I'd check."

Ramon seemed nonplussed about the mention of an inquiry. His face remained expressionless, and he said nothing.

"Thanks for the update," Stuart said. Nervous about turning his back on Ramon, he walked back to his car. He kept a wary eye on the Escalade, half expecting the goons inside to burst out firing at him.

44

Jon was sitting at the bar in Hank's, having dinner later than usual. He'd gone by Kettering House; as expected, it was a dead end. Totally legitimate. It was not Ramon's place.

The twenty-four hour deadline he'd given Carlos had expired without any contact from him, so there was no help there. D'Lo had called and left a message that he might have some information in a few days. Jon felt like he was back where he started.

Addie came over with a beer which surprised Jon. He looked again at his. It was almost full. She set the frosty mug down in front of the empty stool next to him. He turned in time to see the detective taking her seat.

"Anything to eat, Beth?" Addie asked.

"Thanks," Beth said, taking the beer. "A grouper plate, please. I'm hungry. No lunch today." She helped herself to one of Jon's onion rings. When she finished it, she held her beer up toward him. "Cheers."

Jon held his up. "Cheers."

They sat there in silence for a few minutes, drinking their beer, Beth pilfering several more of his onion rings before Addie brought her dinner.

Jon finished his food and slid the plate away. "I was out of line the other night," he said. "Sorry. Maybe we should set aside one day a week as apology day for me."

Beth smiled. "Apology accepted. And, yes, that might not be a bad idea."

"I was—am—frustrated. The Lexi thing hit me hard. I took it out on you."

"I understand. I'm used to it. Tell me about Lexi."

He told her about his one conversation with Lexi and what he'd learned. He didn't leave anything out.

"She didn't give you any names? Any other details?"

He shook his head. "I had the distinct feeling that she knew more than she was saying, but Haley's death scared her. Did you talk to Padre?"

"I did. He corroborates what you just told me."

He told her about the issues Micah found with Haley's medical records, issues that Nora had missed.

"Did you ask her about it?"

He nodded. "She acknowledged that she'd done a cursory review while she was at work. She offered to go back and take another look."

"Do you believe her?"

It was a question he had asked himself multiple times, not always sure of the answer. "Yes. I do. When I asked her about what was missing, she agreed and wasn't evasive. I admit I was pretty vague with my instructions when I gave them to her."

"Sounds like you two are spending a lot of time together."

He shrugged. "We enjoy each other's company." He got the impression Beth was skeptical and wanted to pursue it, but she let it drop.

It was getting noisy. He looked around and realized the place had filled up after Beth arrived. She almost finished eating.

"You off the clock?" he asked.

"Never off the clock, you know that. But, officially, yes."

"It's getting loud in here. Finish your dinner and let's go down to the boat where we can talk."

She ate the last few bites, then Addie came over to clear her spot.

"We're going to the boat," Jon said. "You're busy, so we'll free up a couple of spots for you."

Addie nodded once. "I'll put it on your tab."

Beth reached for her wallet to pay.

"Oh, no," Addie said, looking at him. "He's picking it up."

He nodded, not about to start an argument with these two.

On board *Trouble No More,* he and Beth stopped in the galley to get drinks before going up to the flybridge.

"Wine? Tequila?" Jon asked.

"Definitely a Tequila night."

Jon grabbed two glasses and the bottle of El Tesoro. Topside, he poured them each a healthy shot. "I'm still trying to find Ramon's recovery home."

He told her about getting Padre to call Delray-By-The-Sea. Seeing her bristle, he held up his hand. "Let me finish. I just wanted to find out if they would give up anything, which they didn't. He didn't mention my name, and I haven't gone near the place—or Dr. Westbrook."

He told her Delray-By-The-Sea had given Padre the Kettering House as their preferred recovery home. But the Director told Padre they got a referral two days ago, which was the first in five or six months. "I went by there to check, but that's not the place. Kettering was a red herring. But, Padre's inquiry may flush out the rats."

She took a sip, then said, "You still believe that Cal Norman and Delray-By-The-Sea are behind this?"

"Absolutely. I just need proof. I had it with Lexi, and you saw what happened to her."

"How did they know she was your source."

"I haven't figured that out, but I did mention to Cal that it was a former patient who knew Haley. It wouldn't have been too hard for someone at Delray-By-The-Sea to narrow it down. The question is who and how."

"Any candidates?"

"Lexi's name wasn't in the medical records that we received. All personal information related to other patients had been redacted. Dr. Westbrook and other staff like Kip Foster would have access to her complete file."

"Who is Foster?"

"He's the resident coordinator that Trey and I met with. He's also the one who spoke with Padre. Maybe you should speak to him?"

She shook her head once, which was enough. No chance in hell.

"What about getting access to Haley's entire record?" Jon asked. "Or Lexi's? How about the security tapes to get info on the black SUV? I know they have cameras outside at the main entrance."

Again, she shook her head. "You know that getting health-related information is not easy, especially regarding mental health. Or anything that could potentially compromise another patient's confidentiality. I'd have to have a lot more than I do to get a judge to go along with me on any of that."

"Can't you at least go talk to Westbrook or Foster?"

"We're working on it. But, like I told you, we have to proceed carefully."

"Any leads on Lexi's murder?"

"Not really. No witnesses, no weapons, no security cameras. She'd been tortured somewhere else and dumped at St. Peter's, but COD was the drugs. According to the tox report, she had enough drugs in her system to kill four people."

He shook his head. "No, the cause of death was Delray-By-The-Sea. And, somewhere in this area, there's a recovery home with more victims."

"We're doing everything we can, Jon. I assure you it's a priority, but we have to go by the book."

45

Stuart took Atlantic Avenue west to the Florida Turnpike, where he turned north toward Orlando.

Although traffic was heavy, as usual, the drive was boring and uneventful. When he got to the Rosen Plaza, he checked in and then went downstairs to the conference registration desk.

Although his presentation was not until the following day, he wanted to attend several sessions and the reception later this evening. He didn't care anything about the meetings but looked forward to the reception. It was an excellent opportunity to network and build business for Delray-By-The-Sea.

After the first session, he was outside the meeting rooms chatting with a talkative addiction counselor from Indianapolis. He felt his phone vibrate, which gave him a good reason to disengage. He excused himself and stepped away to check who was calling. It was Rachel.

"Hello," he said, surprised she was calling during the day.

"What a day," she said. She went on to tell him that she had driven to Fort Lauderdale to meet her girlfriends for lunch. When she took the exit ramp off I-95, the brakes failed. She ran off the ramp and into the grass before she could get the car stopped. Amazingly, she managed not to hit anything and was okay.

"Thank goodness you're okay. How did you get home?"

"The dealer gave me a loaner. They said they'd call when it was ready. So much for driving your fancy sports car."

After the call, he hurried into the next session and sat in the back. Oblivious to the presenter, all he could do was think about Rachel's call.

The evening before he left Delray Beach, she had asked him to take her Volvo instead of the Jag. She wanted to take his convertible to the luncheon with her girlfriends. He should've been the one driving. If he had, he would've been on the turnpike in heavy traffic going eighty.

The car was less than a year old, and the dealer had done all the service. No one else ever touched it other than the detailer. Then, it hit him. Ramon had referred him to the detail shop. Planning to drive the Jag, Stuart had it detailed the day before he left. The day after he'd met with Ramon.

He froze. Ramon knew he was driving to Orlando.

After the session ended and before the reception, he called the Jaguar dealer. He wanted to find out what had happened with his car.

The service manager said the master cylinder had leaked. Although modern cars had dual independent braking circuits, the master had a loose fitting, and the brake fluid had leaked out. He assured Stuart that was unheard of in his experience. They had just serviced the car a week earlier and inspected everything. In his opinion, it had been deliberately loosened sometime afterward.

After speaking with the service manager, he disconnected. His hand was shaking. He ducked into a restroom to splash some cold water on his face. At the sink, he looked into the mirror. His face was ashen, and his hands were clammy. The cold water felt good on his face.

A tall, broad-shouldered, olive-skinned man appeared in the mirror next to him. Stuart jerked around to face him.

"Sorry," the man said, holding up his hands, palms out. He took a step back. "Didn't mean to startle you. The other sink's not working."

Stuart glared at him for a second, then hurried back to the safety of the busy corridor. Glad to see other conference attendees milling about, he stepped outside to get some fresh air. Careful not to stray far from the crowd, he took several deep breaths and tried to calm his racing heart.

Ramon had sabotaged his car, probably with Cal's knowledge or even his orders. They knew he was driving to Orlando and where he was staying. He wasn't safe here. Where to go?

He contemplated what to do, then called Rachel. "Hey, I just learned that I need to stay in Orlando for a few more days. I know you've been wanting to go to Maine to see your sister. Why don't you fly up and spend a few days with her while I'm stuck here?"

Rachel was ecstatic and didn't need further convincing. She couldn't wait to hang up and book the next flight out.

Looking at his watch, he knew his assistant had already gone for the day. Perfect. He called her direct number at work and left a message, saying his schedule had changed and he had to spend an additional couple of days in Orlando.

Satisfied he'd covered his whereabouts at the office, he headed toward the reception to make an appearance. He'd be safe there, surrounded by hundreds of colleagues and it would serve as validation that he was still working. It would give him a chance to finalize his new plans.

46

As soon as Jon came into Hank's, Addie spotted him. She poured a beer and walked over to his place, setting it down as he took his seat.

"You're dressed up," she said.

He gave her an incredulous look. "No, the same outfit I always wear."

Addie cocked her head and appraised him. "No. New shirt. Clean shorts. Who is she? The nurse?"

"Aren't I entitled to any privacy around here?"

"Sure. You having dinner?"

He shook his head and pointed to his beer. "Just a beer tonight."

She grinned. "Ah, dinner with her. Where?"

"You know, you should get a job in the circus. The Amazing Addie, mind reader."

She handed him a folded scrap of paper. "If I was a mind reader, I could tell you who this is from."

Curious, he unfolded it. A telephone number was scribbled inside. Nothing else.

He cocked his head and looked at her. "Okay?"

"Guy came in here an hour ago. Sat at the bar. Ordered a beer and gave that to me folded up in a twenty. He asked me to deliver it to you and ask you to call him. I went to get his beer, looked up, and he was walking out the door. And, no, I didn't recognize him."

Before he could ask, she launched into a detailed description that only a cop or a bartender would notice.

Middle age, medium height, and build. Glasses, a ratty blue Columbia fishing shirt, and a weathered Salt Life ball cap pulled low over his face. Kind of grungy looking, but he had a shiny Rolex on his left wrist, and the hands didn't belong to someone who made a living with them. Nervous as a cat in a room full of rocking chairs.

Finished, she stood there, arms folded, waiting on his response.

The description could've matched half the people in South Florida. He looked down at the number. It didn't look familiar. Then, he noticed it was a 404 area code. Atlanta.

He stroked his chin as he thought. He didn't know anyone in Atlanta. His only connection there was when Haley was a patient in Atlanta Recovery Haven. That'd been two years ago.

These days, area codes were unreliable indicators of where the caller was. His immediate reaction was to dismiss the entire thing as a prank or scam. But why would someone go to such an elaborate ruse to contact him?

Addie watched as he punched in the number and then held the phone to his ear.

"Who is this?" a male voice answered, one Jon didn't recognize.

"Jon Cruz. Who is this?"

"I need proof you're who you say you are."

This cloak-and-dagger routine was beginning to piss Jon off.

"How the hell can I give you proof on a phone? You waltz into Hank's anonymously, leaving me a number to call. I called, didn't I? And I'm about to hang up."

Addie walked away, not wanting to eavesdrop.

"Don't hang up. Please. This is Stuart Westbrook. I need to talk to you, but not on the phone."

Jon almost fell off his bar stool. *What the fuck?*

Still thinking it might be a scam, he lowered his voice and said, "Talk to me about what? And how do I know you're who *you* say you are?"

"Megan was my patient in Atlanta."

He wasn't expecting that punch in the gut. For a moment, he didn't know how to respond.

Westbrook filled the gap. "I've got answers you're looking for, but not on the phone. People are looking for me. No one has this number but you. I'm trusting you not to tell anyone. Think of somewhere we can meet." The call disconnected.

Addie returned, this time with a beer.

"You look like you've seen a ghost," she said as she slid the beer toward him.

He took a long drink before he answered.

"I think I just talked to one."

* * *

On his way to Nora's, all Jon could think about was Stuart Westbrook's call. He wondered what Dr. Westbrook wanted to talk to him about. Westbrook sounded frightened and pleading. Far from a harassment call.

He parked and took the elevator up to Nora's condo. This was his first visit to her place. He'd asked her out for dinner, and she offered to cook at home.

He rang the buzzer. When she opened the door, he was glad he'd put on a fresh shirt and shorts. She was stunning in a sheer tropical print dress with a slit up the side up to her thigh.

"Wow," he said as he stood staring. "Nice."

"Thank you. Welcome to Casa Nora." She kissed him, then led him to the bar separating the kitchen from the dining area. There was a small table for four adjoining a comfortable-looking living area. He presumed the hallway to the right led to bedrooms and baths. Sliding glass doors led to an outdoor balcony.

"Nice," he said. It was simple. Modern, but not extreme, and tastefully decorated. The place seemed to fit her well.

"That's the second time you've said that."

"I'm a man of few words."

She laughed. "If you get the wine and glasses, we'll go out on the patio. I'll bring the hors d'oeuvres."

He picked up the wine, noticing it was a Sancerre, and the glasses. She grabbed the tray and escorted him to the patio overlooking the ocean.

"Nice," he said.

Laughing, she said, "Is that all you can say tonight?"

He glanced down at her exposed leg. "I'll say anything you want," he said, smiling. He opened the wine and poured them each a glass as they stood together at the railing.

"I like to come out in the morning with my coffee and watch the sunrise. You'll see." She snuggled up next to him.

He liked her directness and put his arm around her waist. They stood that way for a few minutes enjoying the solitude and the view and each other's company.

"You seem preoccupied," she said. "Or was it my invitation inviting you here?"

He squeezed her and smiled. "I like your invitation. That's not the problem. Before I left Hank's, I got a strange phone call. I'm not sure what to make of it."

"I'm a good listener if you want to talk about it."

"Maybe later," he said with a grin. "It's a long story, but we've got all night."

She leaned her head into him. "Yes, we do."

47

Jon had dozed off when his phone buzzed. Nora's head was resting on his chest. He disentangled himself and reached over to the nightstand for his phone.

It was the 404 number. "Cruz," he said when he answered in a low voice.

"Did you come up with a place to meet?"

He looked at the time. It was ten minutes after one in the morning. "Now?"

"It's urgent. No one knows where I am, but that won't last."

Obviously, Westbrook was in Delray Beach, but Jon was still not convinced about his intentions. Why would the man threatening a restraining order suddenly want to meet with him? Yet, he was curious. "You said you had answers. Why should I believe you?"

There was a pause, then Westbrook said, "People are trying to kill me."

"Sounds like you need the police, not me. I thought the Chief was your friend."

"Please. I know what you're looking for, and you're the only one I can trust."

He looked over at Nora. Her eyes were open. She wore a questioning look and nothing else, he knew. He decided he'd give Westbrook five minutes in person.

"Can you get back to Hank's without being seen or followed?"

"I think so."

"There's no place to park there that wouldn't be obvious."

"Not a problem. I won't be driving my car."

He wondered how Westbrook was getting around. "The only boat on T Dock as in tango. *Trouble No More*. A trawler. Meet me there in an hour."

"I'll be there."

He hung up, still skeptical. He wondered why the man who had plotted to cause him so much trouble had a sudden change of heart.

"Everything okay?" Nora asked.

"Sorry, I've got to go."

She reached over and put her hand under the covers below his waist. "You sure?"

He rolled his eyes. "Unfortunately, yes. I'll make it up to you. I promise."

Thirty minutes later, he was back at his boat. He'd told Westbrook an hour because he wanted to get there first. As he left Lucille, he scoped the area, looking for anything suspicious.

On board, he got his pistol and went up on the flybridge so he could see anyone approaching. He constantly scanned the marina for movement. A few minutes later, a car he didn't recognize parked by the A Dock. An older gentleman got out and confidently walked toward the dock. The man looked familiar, which was confirmed when he went to a sailboat and boarded. Lights went on in the cabin as the tenant entered.

Twenty minutes later, Jon saw someone shuffling along the main dock on the seawall toward him. He had not seen anyone drive up, so he assumed the person had come from the direction of Hank's Galley.

As he got closer, Jon thought it was a male based on size and gait. He had a ball cap pulled down low over his face, wearing a blue shirt, shorts, and tennis shoes. Although he feigned interest in the boats as he walked, he appeared to be scouting the entire marina.

When he got to the T Dock, he turned and approached the gate. He stopped and took a good look around. Either it was Westbrook or a thief.

He had forgotten to give Westbrook the code, then remembered the lock was broken. When the stranger pushed on the gate, it opened, and he walked through, still scanning the area.

Jon pulled his gun from the holster and eased down the steps to the main deck to meet him. Holding the pistol out in front, he stepped around the corner to see the man standing on the dock opposite the boarding door. When the man looked up, he recognized him as Stuart Westbrook.

He put his gun back in the holster and crossed his arms, making no attempt to invite him aboard. "What is it you want to discuss?"

Westbrook looked around nervously. "Can we talk inside? Give me five minutes. If you don't agree what I have to say is worth it, I'll leave."

Jon considered frisking him but could see he wasn't carrying. Besides, he had nowhere to conceal anything with his outfit and gave no indication of being a threat. Jon opened the boarding door, motioning for Westbrook to come aboard. He walked into the main salon, followed by the doctor. Inside, he stopped and looked at his watch. "Your five minutes just started."

"This thing has gone too far. They were just supposed to warn her. Nothing more."

"Warn who?" Jon knew he was talking about Lexi but wanted to hear Stuart to say it out loud.

"Lexi. Lexi Martin. Ramon claims he put her on a bus to Atlanta, but I don't believe him."

Jon tried to conceal his excitement. This could be the break he'd been looking for.

"Not that you care, but now, they're trying to kill me. They almost killed Rachel—my wife, thinking it was me. I sent her to her sister's where she's safe. But this has got to end."

"They?"

"Cal Norman and Ramon."

Jon shook his head. "That's an unlikely alliance. Where do you fit?"

"I originally developed the treatment plan to provide a more consistent, efficient, and affordable way of treating addiction."

That sounded like the brochure. "Your treatment plan was nothing but a scam, a way to squeeze more money out of everyone. Insurance companies, families. Money that you and Cal put in your pockets."

Westbrook lowered his head. "It didn't start out that way. As a physician, I swore an oath that the well-being of my patients comes first. I developed it to help families with limited resources. So they could at least get some help— whatever they could afford. But the insurance companies kept denying coverage, challenging paying for every day. Asking for more documentation, followed by more appeals. In the beginning, it was only about trying to get the insurance companies to pay. We figured it would be no big deal if we occasionally kept a patient an extra few days. It made up for the ones they didn't pay for. The insurance company could afford it, so no one was hurt."

He had to agree with what Westbrook was saying. He knew firsthand that *deny till you die* was the philosophy of health insurance companies. But it was still wrong. "Sounds like a way to rationalize insurance fraud."

"We were desperate to help people. When patients could no longer afford Delray-By-The-Sea, we discharged them to a local recovery home, which was cheaper. Everyone does that now."

"How convenient since they're unregulated. But since you are, you still must document it. So, you start encouraging patients to discharge themselves. That way, you don't have to document anything."

"Corporate set up the whole arrangement with Delray Serenity House and insisted we send people there. They replicated this model at all Moren facilities. I thought it was an arms-length business agreement and a legitimate recovery home. It wasn't until recently that I began to suspect Cal and Ramon were in business together. It was a way to recycle patients. Send them there until the families could come up with more money to put them back in rehab. Now I know it for sure."

He was losing patience with Westbrook's defense of his actions. "Would it have made any difference?"

"Look, I'm not making excuses. But that's how this kind of thing starts. One little step at a time. But I swear, I never intended for innocent people to die."

Jon's face flushed as his anger rose. "What you did was worse. You sent innocent people to Ramon's place, where God knows what happened to them. Get them back on drugs, then back to your treatment center where you could bill the big bucks. Rinse and repeat."

"I see that now. I want to make amends—atonement for my part in this sordid alliance. That's why I wanted to come to you. I'll give you enough to put them away for a long time."

He wondered if the doctor understood he'd have to implicate himself in this disclosure. It was one thing to tell Jon but another to testify under oath. "You know you'll have to repeat this to the authorities. And you're willing to do that?"

Westbrook nodded. "I know that. But I can't live with this anymore. I want to make things right."

We'll see, Jon thought. "You can start by telling me where Ramon's recovery home is. What'd you call it—Delray Serenity House?"

"I don't know where it is. The address isn't listed."

Jon clenched his jaw, grinding his teeth. He'd heard enough. "Get the hell off my boat. Now." He took a step toward Westbrook, ready to throw him overboard. Stuart held his hands up and retreated a step.

"Nobody at Delray-By-The-Sea knows. It changes. Ramon moves it around, which makes it harder to find. It may be more than one, for all I know. He's never told us. He has one of his people pick them up. Exactly where he takes them, we. Don't. Know."

He had assumed it was one location, someplace they could send in the cavalry and save innocent people. But it was not going to be that simple. *Clever,* Jon thought. This way, only Ramon's inner circle knew. And it minimized the possibility of leaks or an informant infiltrating his organization. D'Lo was right-Ramon ran a tight ship.

"Does Cal know?" Jon asked.

Stuart shrugged. "Not sure. Like I said, I didn't know until recently that Cal and Ramon worked together. I'd been led to believe that I was the go-between. Obviously, I was wrong. I think it's safe to assume that Cal knows everything Ramon does."

"How do you pay him?"

"He gives us an invoice, and we send a check to a P.O. box."

Damn, this was more complicated than he thought. It would require a forensic audit to unravel, which would take valuable time—time the other victims didn't have.

"Who knows you're back in Delray Beach?"

"Nobody. Everyone thinks I'm still at a conference in Orlando. I didn't even check out of the hotel there. Rachel's car is still in their parking garage."

"How did you get back here?"

"I bought a burner phone and paid cash for everything. I picked up these clothes from Goodwill, then took the bus from Orlando. I came to Hank's to leave that note. Since I arrived, I've been hanging out in the bus station here, waiting on you. I took an Uber here. That's why I was certain no one was following me."

Jon almost chuckled at the thought of the eminent Dr. Westbrook riding a bus. He wished he could've witnessed that. "When are you expected back?"

Stuart shrugged. "The conference ends Friday, so nobody expects me at work until Monday. Rachel's not planning on coming back till the end of next week. As long as I phone her, she'll be fine."

Today was Wednesday, so he had four days. Where to hide Westbrook? He knew Addie had a room in the back of Hank's Galley where she sometimes stayed. But he didn't want to involve anyone else at this point, especially Addie. He had to stash him somewhere safe until he could get to Beth.

He wasn't going to take a chance on losing Westbrook. He would have to stay on the boat.

48

At daylight, Jon rolled out of bed. He didn't sleep last night. He kept thinking about what Stuart had said about the recovery homes. *They picked up the patients and took them away. No one at Delray-By-The-Sea knew where they went.*

He went into the galley and made coffee, trying to keep quiet and not disturb his guest. After the coffee was made, Stuart emerged from the forward berth.

"You sleep okay?" Jon asked.

"Yes, thanks. Sorry to disturb your evening."

He shrugged. "Okay." He poured them each a cup of coffee. "You told me that no one at Delray-By-The-Sea knew where Ramon's recovery home was. You said he picks them up and takes them away."

"That's right. We—Kip Foster, the resident counselor—calls and tells them he's got a new patient."

"Could you find out when the next one is?"

"I suppose. I could call Kip and say I'm just checking in to see what's going on. Why?"

"That's how I'll find out where he takes them."

Stuart glanced at the clock. "It's seven-thirty now. He's usually in by eight. I'll call then."

"I'm going topside. That's what I do every morning. Sorry you can't join me, but everything needs to look routine and you need to stay out of sight." He refilled his cup, picked up his phone, and walked out.

On the flybridge, he took in everything as he sipped his coffee. With his new guest, he was more conscious than usual of his surroundings. Nothing seemed out of place, but that didn't make him feel better.

If Stuart could find out when the next pickup was, Jon intended to be there. But he needed another car. His was too recognizable. Addie had an older silver Ford Edge that would be perfect. There must be a million of them just in this area. As soon as Stuart talked to Kip, he'd check with her.

While he waited, he called Trey to check on him.

Reece answered. "Hi, Jon. Trey's still asleep. He didn't sleep well last night, and I didn't want to disturb him."

"That makes two of us. How's he doing?"

"Not good. He's getting weaker, I'm afraid. How are you?"

He wanted to tell her he had good news but didn't want to get their hopes up. "Making some progress, slower than I would like."

"Thank you for all you've done."

He wanted to say, *it's not enough.* "Tell him I'll call back later. Take care."

When he entered the main cabin below, Stuart was on the phone. He poured himself another cup, then walked over and refilled Stuart's just as he ended the call.

"You're in luck," Stuart said. "One transfer today. The only one until next week."

"What time?"

"I didn't ask. It's usually mid-morning, though."

He hurriedly got dressed and went to Hank's. Inside, he didn't bother to sit. As soon as Addie stepped over, he said, "I need breakfast to go. Whatever's quick. Coffee. And your car." He set his Yeti cup on the counter.

"And good morning to you, too. I'll get you an egg biscuit." She grabbed his Yeti and went back into the kitchen. A few minutes later, she came back with her car keys, breakfast, and his Yeti full of coffee.

He took her keys and laid Lucille's keys on the bar.

"I doubt I'll need her for anything," she said. A grin crossed her face. "Then again, maybe a little road trip to Key West. Lucille would like the Overseas Highway."

"Go for it," he said as he turned and walked out.

As he drove to Delray-By-The-Sea, he tried to remember the surrounding area. He thought there might be a spot he could park just down the street where he would have a good view of the driveway entrance. Stuart had told him that was the only way in and out.

The problem with that is that far away he'd have to guess. As Ramon and Beth had said, there are a lot of black SUVs in South Florida. If he wasn't careful, he could end up chasing the wrong one.

Even though it violated the trespass warning, he decided the parking lot would be better. Besides, he wasn't planning on anyone recognizing him. Maybe he could park where he could watch the entrance using the rearview mirror.

It was only eight o'clock when he got to Delray-By-The-Sea. He entered the main parking lot and spotted the ideal place in the front corner. He pulled into the spot facing the entrance where he had an unobstructed view. Being this close was risky, but no one could park and block his view. Perfect. Here, he could see every vehicle driving up to the entrance and didn't have to watch the mirror.

He reclined the seat back, pulled his cap lower, and slumped down, settling in for the duration. He pulled his phone out and queued *The Definitive Albert King on Stax* to keep him company for the next few hours.

The movies always made stakeouts look so glamorous. In reality, they were mind-numbing and tedious. The hardest part was staying alert. He watched as vehicles entered the parking lot and continued to the back. He assumed that was where the employees parked and observed them going to a back entrance.

Slowly the parking lot started to fill with vehicles. The driver would park, then the occupants would walk to the main entrance. Occasionally, someone would give him a second glance, but most paid no attention.

After two hours, he'd seen three black Escalades—none Ramon. Bringing coffee wasn't such a good idea. Coffee was like beer—you just rented it. Fortunately, he'd brought along an empty plastic bottle for that purpose.

Although women would have no sympathy, unzipping shorts and peeing in a bottle while sitting in the driver's seat was not as easy as it sounded. As he fumbled to relieve himself, a black Escalade drove up to the entrance.

Hell. Now he comes. Jon finished his business and zipped his shorts. The driver got out and walked around to the passenger side. He scanned the area, and then his gaze settled on Jon's car just as Jon was about to open the door and empty the contents onto the pavement.

It would have to wait. He put the cap on the bottle and set it in the console. Discreetly, he held his phone up, zoomed in as tight as possible, and started recording video.

The driver opened the passenger door, and a smartly-dressed woman got out. She walked through the door and inside. The driver took a small suitcase from the back seat and followed her.

Jon shook his head and stopped recording. It was a check-in, of no interest to him. He emptied the contents of the bottle, and decided it was time for a little snack. He took out the biscuit Addie had packed for him and broke it in two, eating half. He watched as the driver of the Escalade returned to the vehicle and left, minus his passenger.

Jon scrolled through his music, this time going with Eva Cassidy's *Nightbird*. One of his favorites, this album was a collection of songs recorded live at the Blues Alley Club in Washington in 1996. It was released nineteen years after her death.

Still slumped down in his seat, he resisted the temptation to close his eyes as he listened. Maybe he should've put on some classic rock-and-roll to keep him alert.

When the album ended, he looked at the time. Eleven-thirty. He was beginning to wonder if Stuart had gotten the correct information or if the discharge had been canceled.

He rested his hand on the door handle, wishing he could get out and stretch his legs. Too risky. Someone might recognize him. He adjusted his position in the seat as best as he could and tapped his fingers on the console. Then, a black Escalade wheeled up to the entrance.

He stopped the drumming and focused on the SUV. It stopped under the overhang, but no one got out and the brake lights remained lit. Once again, he started recording a video on his phone. Then, Kip Foster walked out the front door of Delray-By-The-Sea, escorting a young woman.

"Bingo," Jon said as he started Addie's car.

Kip opened the rear passenger door, and she got in. Kip closed the door, and it started to move.

Jon followed the vehicle at a discreet distance. The SUV wound its way through parts of Delray Beach he'd never seen, finally arriving at a respectable-looking house in a decidedly middle-class neighborhood. It parked in front of the closed two-car garage.

He held up his phone to record the action. He was surprised to see a well-dressed young man emerge from the driver's seat. He didn't resemble Ramon. The man wore a golf shirt and slacks, with leather shoes, as if he'd come from casual day at the office. He walked around to the passenger side and opened the door for the woman he'd picked up at Delray-By-The-Sea. Together, they walked up to the front door of the house and went inside.

He shook his head. He'd expected some rundown crack house in a poor section of town. Instead, this looked like a young professional suburban couple coming home for lunch.

Hiding in plain sight.

49

Now, Jon had the location of Ramon's recovery home, and he needed to talk to Beth. He couldn't meet her at Hank's Galley—that was too close to his boat, and she might want to come over. He wasn't ready to turn Stuart over to her. Yet.

On his way home, he called her, and surprisingly, she answered. "Uh, hi. I didn't expect you to answer."

She laughed. "Well, now that I did . . ."

"I was craving Italian. Thought maybe you'd let me buy you dinner."

There was a pause on the line. "Okay, what have you done, now?"

"I'm offended. I can't take you out to dinner?"

"Well, you get big points for Mediterraneo, as always. I've got to finish some paperwork first. Want me to pick you up around seven?"

"Why don't I just meet you there," he said, hoping he didn't appear too anxious about not meeting at the marina.

"Okay. See you there at seven."

He returned to the boat to find Stuart sitting at the table on his computer.

"Did you see them pick up the patient?" Stuart asked.

He nodded. "I think so. I followed them to an ordinary looking house and took a few pics. I'm not sure about it. I want to do a little further research." He still wasn't sure he could trust Stuart and didn't want to divulge any more about the recovery house at this point.

"We need to discuss our next steps," he said, "but I'm having dinner with a friend. I should be back in a few hours. We can talk then. Why don't you start writing down what you told me this morning? Fill in as much detail as you can."

Stuart nodded toward his computer. "That's what I was working on. Give me your Wi-Fi password and email address. I'll send what I've got and continue working while you're gone."

He was pleased that Stuart had started documenting everything. It would help him make his case to Beth when reading her in. He gave Stuart the Wi-Fi information and said, "There's plenty of food in the galley. Help yourself."

He took a quick shower and dressed. Beth called on his way to Mediterraneo.

"They're closed for a private party," she said. "Why don't you give me a raincheck, and I'll meet you at Hank's?"

No, no, no. No can do. "I'm already halfway there," he said as he frantically tried to think of somewhere near Mediterraneo. "Why don't we go to Dial?" It was the first place that popped into his head, and he regretted it the instant he said it.

"Dial? Whoa. You either really screwed up or want something big. Can't wait to hear which. I'll meet you there in fifteen minutes."

He couldn't back out now. When he drove up to Dial ten minutes later, he could see the valet licking his chops. Lucille's sedate appearance didn't fool this kid. Jon hated giving him the keys but had no choice. The only parking within half a mile was here and valet only.

Leaving Lucille running, he stepped out and handed the young guy a twenty and the keys. "Only you, and don't take the long way to the parking lot. When I finish dinner, again, only you. Nobody else. If she looks *exactly* like she does now, and the odometer is right, there'll be another twenty. If not . . ." Jon hardened his stare. "You don't want to know. Comprende?"

He didn't know if the guy understood Spanish, but he seemed to get the drift. The valet gulped and nodded. He accepted the key as if it were a hand grenade, and Jon had pulled the pin. He stood there so the valet could see him in the rearview mirror as he gingerly drove away.

Beth was waiting inside at the maître d's station. Jon shook his head and exhaled. It was the same man as the night he accosted Stuart and his party.

When he looked up and saw Jon, he immediately shook his head. "I thought I made it clear. You are not welcome here."

Beth looked at Jon and smiled, shaking her head. She leaned over to the maître d' and subtly showed him her badge. Softly, she said, "He's in my custody, and I take full responsibility. I assure you that at the least sign of non-compliance, I will cuff him and personally remove him."

The maître d' looked at her, then at Jon. "Only because you are with her. Otherwise, no." Satisfied he'd made his point, he grabbed two menus and led them to a small, out-of-the-way table next to the kitchen entrance.

After he walked away, Beth said, "I just can't take you anywhere."

He snorted. "This is the best you can do? Cal Norman had a nice table over by the window. With a view."

"Don't worry." She flashed him a coy smile. "I'll make up for it with the wine."

Shaking his head, wondering what the tab was going to be, he said, "Don't get carried away, at least with me footing the bill. Remember, I'm retired and only have a part-time job." He leaned forward, anxious to get down to business.

He was glad their table was somewhat isolated. "But it is a special occasion."

She sat back in her chair. "Really? Why is that?"

He grinned. "I know the location of Ramon's recovery home. The one that Delray-By-The-Sea uses. Where they sent Lexi and Haley."

"What? How do you know all of this?"

"I followed Ramon's guy in a black Escalade. He picked up a patient from Delray-By-The-Sea and took them to a house in Delray Beach. I've got a tag number. And a video."

She scowled and folded her arms across her chest. "You're not supposed to be on their property."

He showed her the video on his phone he had taken this morning. "Play it, then run the number."

She watched the video, then shook her head. "You took this on their premises. In violation of the criminal trespass order."

"Goddammit, Beth. I was only in the parking lot. In Addie's car, not mine. Nobody knew I was there."

Still frowning, she picked up her phone and called dispatch, explaining that she wasn't in her car and needed to run a plate. He rewound the video so she could read the license plate number on the Escalade to the person on the other end. After she did, she nodded, then said, "Thanks. Would you send it to my computer, please?" She disconnected and set her phone down. "Registered to Ramon Grant. How did you know this?"

"I can't say."

"If you have knowledge of criminal—"

"Stop. As we speak, I have reason to believe innocent young people are being held captive in this house. Somebody, including Ramon, is taking advantage of them and their families. Plus, who knows what else is going on there. But he uses different locations. You've got to investigate before he moves it again."

She cocked her head. "And exactly how do you know all of this?"

He shook his head. "I've got ironclad proof. I can't share it just yet, but soon. In the meantime, you've got to check on this house ASAP. I promise you I'll give you everything I've got as soon as possible."

"Like you did before?"

That hurt. And he couldn't blame her for being skeptical. But this time, the proof was on his boat. And this time, no one knew it but him. "You've got to trust me on this."

She eyed him suspiciously. "Send me the video. I'll take it to my lieutenant. But if you're—"

He pointed to his phone. "You've got what you need to convince him. And I promise there's a lot more where this came from."

"There damn well better be."

50

Having breakfast with Stuart, Jon was surprised to get a call from Cal Norman.

"By any chance, you haven't heard from Stu, have you?" Cal asked.

Jon looked across the table and held his forefinger up to his lips. "Dr. Westbrook? No. Why?"

"Just having trouble getting in touch with him. He's supposed to be in Orlando at a conference, but he's not answering his cell phone."

Dammit, Jon said under his breath. "The last conversation I had with him was at the restaurant where you were present. That's it."

"Thanks." Cal disconnected.

He looked over at Stuart. "Cal wanted to know if I'd heard from you. He said you weren't answering your cell phone."

"Why would he call you?"

Good question. Why would he? "You need to call your assistant," he said. "Call the main number, not the direct one. Tell her you dropped your phone in the toilet and had to get a new one. You lost all your numbers. Nobody knows telephone numbers anymore with smartphones. Ask her for Cal's cell number."

"Shouldn't I just call him?"

He shook his head. "Not yet. Tell her to let him know what happened. You've got to get back into your meeting, but you'll call him this evening before dinner. That'll buy you some time." He wrinkled his brow. "You called me on a burner. What did you do with your company phone?"

"I have it, but it's turned off."

"Have you used it since you left Orlando?"

Stuart shook his head, then stopped. "I was charging the burner last night while you were at dinner. I turned on my company phone to call Rachel. We just talked for a few minutes, and I turned it off as soon as we hung up."

"That's the only time?"

Stuart nodded. "Yes. Other than that one time, I've only used the burner since leaving Orlando."

"You haven't been outside? Nobody's seen you?"

"No.

"Get me your company phone."

Stuart went to his cabin, came back, and handed him an iPhone.

He went to a drawer and pulled out a small hammer. "Stay inside," he said. He walked out on the dock, set the phone down, and smashed it several times. Then, he picked up the battered phone and flung it as far as possible toward the channel. He watched as it splashed into the salt water of the Intracoastal and disappeared.

Stuart had been watching from the window. When Jon came back inside, he said, "You don't think—"

"I don't know, but I'm not taking any chances. We're going to have to talk to the police. Soon. I can't hide you here forever."

"I know. I told Rachel that. I emailed you more documentation last night. I'll try to finish it up today."

"I need to go make some calls." He went up to the flybridge and called Nora.

"I was beginning to think you were ghosting me," she said when she answered.

"No, just been very busy."

"Everything okay?"

"I think. I'll know more this afternoon. I'll give you a call later."

He was itching to know if Beth had talked her lieutenant into raiding Ramon's place. He called her number. "Well?" he asked when she answered.

"I can't say anything. I'll call you later."

He hung up smiling, interpreting her remarks as confirmation that something was going down today.

Back down in the main cabin, Stuart reported that he'd talked to his assistant as instructed, and she'd bought the story about his phone.

Later that afternoon, Jon was in Hank's as usual when Beth stopped by. She did not look happy, and she didn't sit. Sensing a storm, Addie kept her distance.

"How'd it go?" Jon asked.

"How'd it go? I'll tell you how it went. The house was fucking empty." Beth practically spat the words out.

"What? That couldn't—"

"The only reason I still have a job is that it appeared to have been hastily abandoned within the past twenty-four hours. So they didn't have time to clean thoroughly. Forensics is still processing everything, but that's going to take time. Neighbors also reported a lot of activity last night, including a rental truck."

He slammed his hand on the bar. "Ramon moved it. But how did he know? Where is he?"

"I don't know where he is. But I know where you'll be first thing in the morning. With whoever and whatever you have. If you're not at the station by eight A.M., I'll be here to pick you up. And I'll have a warrant to search your boat."

She paused to catch her breath before continuing. "You're lucky I don't haul you in tonight. No more games, Jon."

51

Jon brought dinner back to *Trouble No More* for Stuart.

"Did they bust Ramon today?" Stuart asked.

He shook his head. "He moved it before they got there. The only good thing is they left enough behind to prove they'd been there, so it's a start. Any visitors today?"

"Nope. All quiet. I finished emailing you everything I had."

"Good. You can walk me through it tomorrow." He didn't tell Stuart that they would be doing that at the police station. Stuart was nervous enough, and he didn't want to take a chance on him bailing.

He opened the safe and took out his pistol. He fastened it inside the holster, then looked for his phone. It was nowhere to be found. Then he realized he'd left it on the bar at Hank's. No big deal. Addie would hold it for him. He'd pick it up when he finished his sweep of the marina.

"Stay inside," he told Stuart. "I've got to make rounds. I'll be back in an hour or so."

Outside, he stopped and looked around. A nice warm breeze was coming from the south, signaling fair weather. Things were quiet. Tonight, he decided to start at A dock, the furthermost point in the marina from him. That way, he could finish up closer to home.

He tried to mix up his patrol to avoid being predictable. Different routes, different times, careful not to fall into a routine. Sometimes, he'd go out on one of the finger docks and sit for a while, observing his surroundings. He called it his meditation, a chance to clear his mind.

As he walked over to the A dock, he pulled out his list of new arrivals. Another of the many hats he wore at Hank's. Every evening, Addie would give him an updated listing so he could verify that all the transient boats in the marina had checked in. The liveaboards didn't change that often, so that was easy. Besides, he knew all of them.

Tonight, there were a couple of new boats on A dock. An Island Packet 38, *Island Time,* registered in the BVI. Although no longer in production, it was still one of his favorite sailboats.

He could tell as he approached that the boat was immaculate and expertly secured. An older couple was sitting out under the Bimini, having a cocktail. Jon waved, and they returned the gesture. These were serious sailors.

Two slips further down was a Hatteras 39 convertible, *Fishkey,* from Key West. A light was on, but he didn't see anyone. It was also in good shape and properly secured.

He was always amazed at some of the expensive boats he saw tied up at the dock with slipshod knots, too few lines, and insufficient fenders. He took his time, going down each dock, checking to make sure everything was as it should be. As he finished, he started toward home. As he passed Hank's Galley, he remembered he'd left his phone inside.

He entered and walked over to the bar, not taking his seat. Addie walked over with his cell phone in her hand. "I figured you'd stop by to pick it up when you were done," she said. As he stood, her expression changed. "Everything okay? Are you feeling alright?"

He nodded. She was curious because he didn't sit and have his usual beer. "I've got to get home." He looked around the crowded bar. "From the looks of things, I don't think you'll miss me tonight."

"Hmm," she said, grinning. "Must have another hot date with the nurse."

He blushed, wondering how she knew he was seeing Nora. Addie didn't miss anything.

He shook his head. "See you tomorrow." Stuffing his phone in a pocket, he turned and walked out. As he passed a large Sea Ray powerboat tied up on the K dock, he noticed the dock lines were sloppily tied. The excess line was lying next to the piling in a tangled mess.

As he got closer, he saw that the instruments on the dashboard were uncovered, exposing them to the elements. At the waterline, he could see barnacles forming.

Sad. At one time, this had been a nice boat. It angered him that people wouldn't take care of their property. He retied the lines with a cleat hitch, forming a Flemish coil with the excess. It was the least he could do. He stood and admired his work, even though the owner probably wouldn't even notice.

Back on the main dock, he turned toward his boat. As he did, he saw a man walking away from it at a brisk clip. His first thought was Stuart. "Hey," he yelled. "You. Stop."

Hearing Jon, the man glanced at him, then ran, crashing through the gate. On shore, he disappeared into the parking lot behind a row of vehicles. Under the lights, Jon could see it wasn't Stuart. This person was taller and thinner.

He looked back at *Trouble No More,* two docks away. The main salon had a light on, but he didn't see any sign of Stuart. Everything looked normal.

Then, the world erupted in front of him. A blinding flash lit up the night sky where his boat used to be, the deafening sound reaching him before he could react. The shock wave from the powerful explosion knocked him into the water.

52

Jon surfaced, gasping for breath. The intense heat washed over him even at this distance. He turned to see the skeleton of his boat consumed by flames.

Getting his bearings, he swam toward the Sea Ray he'd just secured. He held onto the swim platform to catch his breath before climbing aboard.

Water dripping down his face, he looked over at his home. It was burning to the waterline, flames devouring the trawler. Sirens were getting closer. He hoped Stuart had gotten out before it blew because no one could've possibly survived that.

He shook his head from side to side, flinging water like a wet dog. Someone tried to kill Stuart or him or both. He shuddered as he realized he would've been onboard had he not stopped to adjust the lines on the boat—the boat he now sat on. He patted his shorts, and miraculously, his phone was still in his pocket. Then, he moved his hand up to his waist, relieved that his gun was still in its holster.

His gaze returned to the conflagration nearby at what was, until a few minutes ago, his boat—*Trouble No More*. He shook his head at the bitter irony of the name. Maybe it was bad luck to rename a boat.

It dawned on him that almost everything he owned was gone with her. His computer, personal effects, clothes—

everything. He had an off-site storage unit with a few things, but nothing he used daily. The wet outfit he wore, his SIG, and his phone—that was all he had left.

He stepped up through the transom and made his way over to the dock, his one wet deck shoe squishing with every other step. He was amazed that one had managed to stay on his foot when the explosion knocked him into the water.

A small crowd had gathered outside in front of Hank's, watching the commotion. No one paid any attention to the drenched figure walking up to the back door next to the kitchen.

At the door, thinking he would call to alert whoever was inside, he pulled his phone out and held it up. Water dripped out of the charging port. Afraid to risk further damage, he stuck it back into his pocket.

He banged on the door. Several minutes later, Ray, the cook, opened it. Wearing his apron, the Jamaican looked as if he'd seen a ghost.

"What the . . . thank Jesus you're alive. Come in, come in."

Ray closed the door behind Jon and handed him a towel. "Addie's out front with everyone else. We heard the explosion and ran out. That's when we saw it was your boat. I came back in and called 911. I've got to go tell her."

Jon grabbed his arm. "No. Don't say anything about me. Just tell her she needs to come back to the bar. Now. Bring her to me."

Ray was confused. "But—"

"Not a word."

Ray nodded, then walked out.

Jon heard more sirens as he dried off. He cracked the door open and peeked out.

Two fire trucks were at the dock, along with several police cars, county cars, ambulances, and fire rescue vehicles. Two marine patrol boats were in the Intracoastal, blue lights flashing. It looked like every first responder in the area had turned out for the spectacle.

As he looked at the inferno where his boat once sat, he again thought of Stuart. He had told him to stay inside. If he did, there was no way he could have survived that blast. He prayed that Stuart got out in time, but his gut told him *no.*

He thought about Felix, hoping the cat hadn't returned. He would have wisely spent one of his nine lives if he escaped this.

He wondered if Lucille had suffered any damage from the blast. Maybe he at least still had a car. Addie had a key. Hopefully, she could move her when things settled down.

In a few minutes, he heard Addie fussing at Ray. They were coming toward the kitchen.

"My God, I don't know what is so damn important for me to be here," she said. "I need to be out there. I told the firefighters that Jon was on board."

As soon as Ray opened the kitchen door, Addie looked up and saw him. Her jaw dropped as she ran over and threw her arms around him, even though he was soaking wet.

"Oh, my God, I thought—"

"Shh," he whispered. She pulled back and he put his forefinger to his lips.

"You and Ray can't say a word to anyone," he said. They looked at him as if he were crazy.

"There was someone on board. A friend was staying on the boat for a few days."

Ray and Addie gasped as they realized no one could have survived that. "Who . . ." they said in unison.

He shook his head. He knew they thought Nora was on the boat. "Not who you think. It was an informant I was protecting. Nobody knew they were there."

As soon as he said it, he realized it wasn't true. Someone knew Stuart was there. Or did they? Maybe they were just out to kill Jon? Or maybe they wanted to kill them both?

Addie turned to Ray. "You need to go back out front. People will start drifting back in. I'll be out in a minute."

"What are you going to do?" she asked him after Ray left.

He shook his head. "I don't know. Everything I owned was on that boat." He pulled out his phone and gun and laid them on the small table beside him. "Well, almost everything." He realized he didn't even have a change of clothes.

"You can stay here till you figure it out," she said. She disappeared, then returned with a stack of towels and a new Hank's Galley T-shirt. "Get a shower and wash the salt off. Put this on. At least this much will be dry for now. I'll run to Walmart and get you some clothes. Give me your phone."

He handed it to her and said, "You need to put it in a bowl of rice."

She looked at him as if he'd just stepped off a spaceship, then slowly shook her head. "Just give me the damn phone."

He handed it to her, watching her turn it off and carefully dry it with a towel. Then, she opened the SIM card compartment, removed the SIM card, and dried it. She left the tiny drawer open and set the phone upright in a bowl.

"Don't touch it for at least a day, maybe two," she said. "It needs to dry out completely. This time, thirteen is your lucky number."

"Huh?" He wondered what she meant.

"You're lucky you've got an iPhone 13. They're waterproof—down to twenty feet for thirty minutes. I hope that also applies to salt water. I'm assuming you weren't in the drink for that long or that deep."

He shook his head. "Have you seen Beth?"

"Not yet, but we both know she'll be here sooner or later. What do you want me to tell her?"

He looked at her with new affection. She was willing to tell the police whatever he wanted.

"Make sure no one overhears you and let her know I'm okay and want to stay out of sight for now. But tell her there was someone else onboard. After the dust settles, get her alone and bring her here."

Addie returned an hour later with several Walmart sacks and a shoe box. She handed the shoe box and two bags to him. He was wearing his new Hank's Galley T-shirt and a towel wrapped around his waist.

"I didn't know if you were a boxer boy or tighty-whities, but you're tighty-whities now," she said.

He looked at her with amusement. "You could've skipped that."

She put her hands over her ears. "TMI. You can go commando if you want, but I don't need to know."

He pulled out the contents. She had bought him underwear, two pairs of shorts, a couple of T-shirts, and new boat shoes. A complete South Florida wardrobe.

From the sack she kept, she pulled out two smaller bags. She opened one and dumped the contents into the bowl containing his phone. They were identical to the packets stuffed in the new shoes.

"Desiccant," she said.

"What—"

"Silica gel. Absorbs moisture."

Not only did he not know what desiccant was, he wondered where you would get it.

"Walmart," she said, holding up the unopened bag. "A pack of twenty for ten bucks. Way more effective than rice. And doesn't damage the phone like rice."

He knew Addie was no fool, but he had no inkling she was also a tech wiz. He could tell she was enjoying his bewilderment.

"When you've lived on the water all your life, you learn stuff like this," she said. "Get into some dry clothes. I'm going to see if things have calmed down enough to sneak Beth in here."

53

Beth stood there with her arms folded. Addie had brought her into the kitchen where Jon sat in the corner, still wearing his Hank's T-shirt but sporting new, dry shorts, and new deck shoes.

"I don't know whether to hug you, strangle you, or arrest you," she said, shaking her head. Then she walked over, put her arms around his neck, and held him tight. "Damn you. They found a body, and I was afraid it was you."

He put his arms around her and squeezed back. He felt her tears on his shoulder. "I'm glad you picked door number one."

When she finally let him go, she said, "This doesn't mean I've eliminated the other two options. I'll decide after you tell me what the hell happened."

"On that note," Addie said. She turned and walked out.

"What else have you found—" he asked Beth.

"Oh, no. I'm not saying another word until you tell me everything, and I mean everything. Now."

Seeing her determined look, he knew better than to argue.

They sat, and she pulled out her notebook. He told her about Stuart Westbrook, starting with the phone call on

Tuesday. She stopped him when he got to the part about Stuart coming to his boat early Wednesday morning.

"That's how you knew everything you told me at dinner. So, was Dr. Westbrook on your boat while we were at Dials?" Her eyes bore into his, daring him to misstep with his answer.

He held his hand up. "He was but let me finish. Ramon and Cal were trying to kill him, so he snuck back to Delray Beach to talk to me. No one knew he was here. He was risking his life and had nowhere to stay, so I had him stay with me. I told him he would have to talk to you, and he agreed. We were coming in to see you this morning."

"Why did he come to you?"

He had given this considerable thought since Stuart showed up Wednesday morning. He'd come to believe the doctor was, at heart, a good man who started with good intentions.

Cal had tickled his greed gland, causing Stuart to turn a blind eye to reality. There was nothing to gain by disparaging the doctor. If there were a hereafter, Stuart Westbrook would have to answer to a higher power. Let the dead rest in peace.

"The murders of Haley Stevens and Lexi Martin opened his eyes. I think he felt guilty for his part in an evil conspiracy and wanted to atone for his involvement."

She cocked her head, regarding him with suspicion, unsure whether to buy his story. "Why did he think they were trying to kill him?"

He told her about someone tampering with Stuart's car. Only the fact that he changed cars at the last minute saved him but inadvertently put his wife, Rachel, in danger. Stuart was so shaken he sent Rachel to her sister's in Maine.

"It was a new Jaguar convertible," he said, "and Stuart was obsessive about it. As a car nut, I get that. Nobody but the dealer touched it. Except for the detail shop, which

Ramon had recommended. They detailed his car the day before Westbrook was to drive to Orlando, which Ramon also knew.

"Ramon and Cal are in this together. They tried to kill Stuart and maybe me as well. The only reason I'm still here is that after I left Hank's, I stopped on my way home to secure another boat in the marina. That's when I saw someone running away from my boat."

"Any description?"

He shook his head. "Not really. I was a couple of docks away, so I didn't get a good look. Tall, over six feet. Slender, I'm guessing less than 200 pounds. Shorts, T-shirt, ball cap, non-white, but I couldn't call his ethnicity. I yelled and started running toward him. He disappeared past the parking lot. Then—boom. Next thing I knew, I was in the water."

Digesting the information, she spoke. "The fire chief suspects the propane system based on the magnitude of the explosion. The boat's a total loss. He's called in the Florida Bureau of Fire, Arson, & Explosives Investigations. Their district office is in Ft. Myers, and they're on their way over."

"He thinks it was arson?"

She nodded. "He does, which is why he called Tallahassee. Also . . . they found a body, which based on what you just told me, is presumably Dr. Stuart Westbrook."

She stared at him. "You said earlier that no one knew he was here. Somebody knew. How?"

He shook his head. "I don't know. But I intend to find out. Are you going to talk to Ramon? And Cal?"

She stood. "I've gotta talk to my lieutenant first. He'll probably want to talk to you. Meanwhile, stay put. I don't want you to be dead for real."

After Beth left, Addie came back in with breakfast.

"I figured you might be hungry," she said, setting the food in front of him. "By the way, Lucille's fine. I moved her to a safer spot."

"Thanks." He was hungry and started eating.

"You're a popular guy," she said.

Between bites, he said, "Yeah, that's why someone tried to kill me."

She chuckled, then turned serious as she realized he wasn't joking. "Ricky's called, as well as the priest, R.D., and your girlfriend."

She looked over at his phone, still drying. "They've been calling your number, but it goes to voice mail. I haven't talked to any of them—Ray took the calls—but they're worried about you."

"Nora isn't my 'girlfriend.' She's simply a good friend that happens to be a woman."

"Whatever. It was all over the news, including finding a body. Your friends will show up here if you don't surface soon."

The phone in her apron rang. "What?" she answered, then said, "Send her back."

She looked at him. "Sooner than I thought. Your girl friend is here," she said, distinctly separating the two syllables.

When Addie opened the door, Nora, clad in scrubs, ran into his arms.

"I saw it on the news at work, and I've been trying to call. They said they found a body."

"Not mine." He pointed to his phone sitting in the bowl. "But we went for a swim."

"Jesus, you scared the crap out of me." She pushed him away and looked at him up and down from head to toe.

"I'm fine," he said. "Addie, this is Nora. Nora, this is Addie—my boss. She owns the place."

They acknowledged each other, then Nora asked, "What happened?"

He shrugged. "They don't know yet but suspect the propane system."

"I'll leave you two alone," Addie said, starting toward the door.

"No, you're fine. I have to get back to the hospital," Nora said. "I just wanted to make sure you were alright. You'll be here when I get off later?"

He nodded. "Nowhere else to go."

"I'll be back," she said, kissing him on the cheek. Turning to Addie, she said, "Nice to meet you."

Addie couldn't hide the grin after Nora left.

"Don't say a word," he said.

54

Before lunch, Ricky, Padre, and R.D. stopped by Hank's at different times to check on him. As soon as R.D. left, Jon insisted on going down to the dock to inspect the damage. He wanted to see the aftermath in the light of day.

It was worse than he imagined. A few charred remains of pilings were all that was left of the T dock. He could make out his boat's burned hulk just beneath the water's surface. The main dock along the seawall on each side of the T dock was also severely damaged. Yellow DO NOT CROSS tape surrounded the entire area.

There wasn't a lot left to see. Somebody had wanted to make damn sure that the boat occupants weren't going to survive. Stuart never had a chance.

On his way back to Hank's, he stopped by to check on Lucille, hoping it would cheer him up. Addie had parked her behind Hank's, next to her car. He was happy to see that, other than dust and ash, Lucille looked intact. Nothing that a good washing wouldn't fix.

D'Lo was waiting for him when he walked into the bar. "Glad to see you're still amongst the living," D'Lo said. "You didn't answer your phone, so I had to come to see for myself."

"Thanks. My phone and I got dunked, but I'm fine." He looked at his friend, then shook his head. "Actually, I'm not fine. If you've got time for lunch, I'll bring you up to speed."

Sitting at a table in the corner of Hank's Galley, he filled D'Lo in on the last two days.

"You think they were after you, too?" D'Lo asked.

He shrugged. "I think so. If I hadn't made an unexpected stop between here and my boat, they would've found two bodies."

"How'd they know your guy was here?"

"Haven't figured that out yet, but somehow they knew. What do you think?"

"I think you better be careful until you find the answer to that question."

After D'Lo left, he called his insurance company to report the claim. They said they'd send an adjuster out this afternoon and wanted copies of any official reports. He hung up, unsure of whether he wanted another boat. Addie had told him he was welcome to stay here as long as he wished, but he was anxious to reboot his life. Once again.

He needed to call Trey, even though he doubted his friend had heard anything in Cincinnati about what happened. When he called, Reece answered.

"Hi, Jon. He's taking a nap. I can see if he's still asleep."

"No, don't disturb him. How's he doing?"

"Not well. Hospice is keeping him comfortable. But he's getting weaker." Her voice caught, and she paused. "How are you?"

He shook his head. He'd been feeling sorry for himself, losing all his material things. Now, his situation suddenly felt insignificant compared to theirs. He had his health and was in one piece. "Things are fine here. Tell him I'll call later."

Later that afternoon, Nora stopped by. "How was your day," she asked.

"I don't really know. Still trying to get grounded. You?"

She shrugged. "Thankfully, things were pretty slow at work. Just before I left, I got a call from my cousin in Michigan. Dot, my favorite aunt who lives in Traverse City, is dying. They're not expecting her to make it another week. I need to go up there tomorrow."

"Go. While you can. I'm thinking about flying to Cincinnati for a few days. I called a little while ago. Trey's going downhill fast."

She looked around the small, sparsely furnished efficiency in the rear of Hank's. "You're welcome to stay at my place until you get resettled," she said.

"Thanks. For the next few days, I'll probably just stay here. Got to get started on repairing the docks and meet with the insurance adjuster. I need to figure out what I'm going to do."

"Why don't you come over tonight? It would do you good to get away. I'll fix dinner."

He nodded. "That'd be nice. Beth's coming back over later, but after she leaves?"

"Call me when you're done so I know when to expect you. I need to go shower, book some flights, and start packing."

That afternoon, Beth stopped in. Addie brought them beer and a burger and fries for Beth.

"You're not eating?" Beth asked.

"Dinner plans later."

"Oh. I see," she said, giving him a knowing look.

"I called Trey this afternoon," he said. "He was asleep, but I talked to Reece. He's not doing well. I'm thinking about going up to see him. Nothing I can do around here."

She talked as she ate. "We're waiting on the final report from The Bureau of Fire, Arson & Explosives

Investigations, but the preliminary finding is arson—involving the propane system. The body's been identified as Dr. Stuart Westbrook, though we're keeping a lid on that until we can notify his wife. This is what we've announced so far."

She handed him a copy of the press release.

MARINA EXPLOSION RESULTS IN CASUALTY

Late last night, an explosion at Hank's Marina in Delray Beach completely destroyed *Trouble No More,* a 42-foot trawler, and resulted in at least one casualty. No other injuries or damages were reported. Police are withholding the release of the victim's name pending notification of the next of kin. The cause is under investigation but is believed to have been the result of a propane leak.

He read it and handed it back to her. "Have you talked to Ramon or Cal?"

"I interviewed Cal this afternoon. In fact, he'd called the chief yesterday. Dr. Westbrook was supposed to be in a meeting in Orlando, but he'd been unable to reach him by cell phone."

"Yeah. I told you Cal had called me yesterday looking for him."

She nodded. "You did. And by the way, he has an ironclad alibi for last night. We checked. I told him that Dr. Westbrook was killed in the explosion."

"And?"

"He wanted to know why Westbrook was at the marina since he didn't own a boat. He wanted to know who owned the boat mentioned in the news. I told him the owner was a local resident—Jon Cruz."

"Why did you—"

She held up her hand. "It's public information, Jon. He wanted to know if the doctor was on the boat."

"You're beating around the bush, Beth. Why?"

"That's when the interview took a turn. He told me that Dr. Westbrook had come to see him less than a week ago. Westbrook had told him he was frightened of you."

"Are you kidding me?"

She exhaled, choosing her words carefully. "Calm down. No one knew Westbrook was in town. He was on your boat. Your car is here, but you're unaccounted for. Plus, you and Dr. Westbrook have a history of bad blood."

"Bad blood? I'd call it a healthy, mutual dislike. But I blow up my own fucking boat to kill Stuart Westbrook? Really? What do I gain from that? He's not a threat—wasn't a threat—to me in any way. Nor was I a threat to him."

"You're on record as throwing a chair through his office window in Atlanta. You accosted him at Dial and were escorted out and told not to come back. The maître d' said that you two had words in raised voices—confirmed by Cal. Cal also said that Stuart told him he was 'concerned' that you held a grudge, which is why Dr. Westbrook asked for a criminal trespass warning and was considering filing a restraining order."

"Jesus Christ, Beth. Do you really believe I would—"

She held up her hand to interrupt. "No, I don't. But you have to realize how it looks. That's what we were told and we have to pursue every lead. We would be negligent if we didn't."

She hesitated before continuing. "It's going to come out that you are a 'person of interest.' And we will need to interview you formally."

"Interview? Person of interest? Why does that sound like doublespeak for a suspect? Cal's trying to throw me under the bus. What about Ramon? Have you 'interviewed' him? Why isn't he a 'person of interest?'"

"No, we haven't interviewed him yet, but we're trying to find him. And, yes, he is also a person of interest."

"Does this mean I can't go to Cincinnati to see Trey?"

She shook her head. "No, just don't try to leave the country."

He glared at her as she cracked a thin smile.

"That was a joke," she said.

"Not funny."

55

After Beth left, Addie brought him another beer and collected the dishes.

"You know, I could get used to this," he said.

She curled her lip and gave him the finger.

"Seriously, thank you. I do appreciate everything you're doing for me. I'm thinking about going to Cincinnati. I need to check on Trey, and it'd get me out of town."

He looked at his phone still in the bowl with the desiccant. "But, I need a phone."

She put the dirty dishes down and checked his phone. Then, after turning it on and pressing different functions, she called hers to test it. When her phone rang, she answered it and handed his phone to him.

"Seems to be working," she said into the phone.

"Loud and clear," he answered on his.

She turned and left. "There's a charger on the desk."

He looked closely at his phone and noticed he had six voicemails and numerous text messages.

There were three voicemails from Nora. The earliest was from the night of the explosion. She'd heard about it, was worried, and wanted to know that he was okay. The other two were similar.

One voicemail was from Ricky, again from the night of the explosion, wanting to know if he was okay and to call him.

He also had a couple of voicemails from Padre, the most recent telling him that he was in his prayers and to please call.

Then, he clicked on messages and was surprised that four were from Stuart's burner number, a 404 area code. How could that be? When he looked at the time stamp, he realized they were from the night of the explosion before the boat blew.

He clicked on Stuart's name. The first message was stamped an hour before the boat exploded.

Called Cal. Told him I was still in Orlando be back Monday. He's going to Bahamas Saturday.

The second message was fifty minutes later, ten minutes before the boat exploded. The tone was totally different.

Where r u? Heard someone on dock. I turned off lights. Im in vberth. Somebodys on the boat.

It was eerie, like a message from the grave. He clicked on the third message. Best he could recall, this had to be within minutes of the blast.

Its Ramon I hrd him talking. I smell gas. Now what?

The desperation in the text was heartbreaking. He could imagine his phone pinging away in a noisy Hank's. If only he'd had his phone with him.

He clicked on the last text message from Stuart Westbrook. It was a voice text. He recognized Stuart's voice.

Stuart: "Ramon. What are you doing?"

Ramon: "How much have you told Cruz?"

Stuart: "Everything. You're too late."

Ramon: "I don't think so. His car's still here."

Sound of a phone ringing.

Ramon answers: "Yeah? Good, get the hell out. I'm right behind you."

Ramon: Your buddy is on his way back here. Cal was right. You two have become a liability."

Stuart: "Are you going to shoot me?"

Ramon: "Only if you try to follow me. I'm leaving, but we'll be watching. If you step outside before Cruz gets back, you're both dead."

That was the end of the message. Underneath, it read THE MESSAGE DELETES IN 2 MINUTES. KEEP? Jon pressed KEEP, not knowing how long it would be saved.

Taking his phone, he went out to the bar to find Addie.

"How long does my phone keep messages and texts?" he asked.

"It depends. Why?"

"I've got stuff that came in the night the boat blew. I want to make sure it doesn't get deleted."

She asked for his phone. He gave it to her and watched as she manipulated it. After a few minutes, she handed it back to him.

"Done. But they are only stored on your device. If you lose your phone or it gets damaged . . ."

"They're gone," he said.

"Your ISP typically stores your emails, but you should check to make sure."

"ISP?"

"Internet Service Provider."

He hadn't thought to check his emails. He clicked on the mail icon on his phone. He scrolled through the emails and saw two from Stuart, dated Thursday, the day the boat blew up.

"Can I borrow your computer?" he asked.

"Sure. On my desk in the office. Printer on the credenza." She wrote down a code and handed it to him. "Login password. When I get a break, I'll come back to check on you."

By the time she returned, he had printed all the emails and read them twice. "Do I have to do anything to save these emails?" he asked, holding up the pages.

"Like I said, your ISP saves them. Plus, they're on your phone as well."

He called Beth and left her a message. He noticed the time and remembered that he'd promised Nora he'd call as soon as he was done with the detective.

Cursing under his breath, he called Nora. "Hey, sorry. I'm leaving now," he said when she answered.

"You're phone's working."

"It is. And I've got some interesting messages. That's why I'm so late. I got it working after Beth left."

"You'll have to fill me in. I was beginning to wonder where you were. No problem—dinner won't take long. Wine's waiting."

As he started out the door, he grabbed his pistol and Lucille's key that Addie had left him. Nora's condo was only fifteen minutes from the marina. Pulling out of the marina, he noticed another vehicle flicked on their lights and pulled out behind him at a respectable distance.

In a hurry to get to Nora's, he didn't think anything about it. He made his first turn and happened to glance at the rearview mirror. The vehicle had its turn signal on and followed.

That jolted him back to reality. Ramon had blown up his boat, killing Stuart. The voice text from Stuart implied he was a target as well. By now, Ramon and Cal had to know that Jon was still alive. And here he was heading over to Nora's, possibly putting her into danger?

He picked up his phone to call and cancel, then thought better of it, concerned it may be compromised. But he had to warn her. If she was leaving town for Michigan tomorrow, she'd be safe then.

He looked again in the mirror. Was someone following? Or was it a coincidence? One way to find out. At the next intersection, he made a sudden right turn with no signal, leading away from Nora's. He slowed and pulled over to get a look at the vehicle behind him. He slid the pistol out of its holster.

It was a large black SUV. He couldn't make out the model, but it continued, not turning. He took a deep breath, vowing to be more careful. Carefully watching his mirrors, he made a series of random turns, some without a signal, and each deliberately not on the route to Nora's. It took an extra fifteen minutes, but by the time he arrived, he was confident no one had followed.

At the gate to her garage, he entered the code she'd given him and pulled inside, waiting for the gate to close before he parked. On his way to the elevator, he kept his hand on his gun, surveying the parking deck for anything suspicious. Nothing. He saw no one else.

Deliberately, he went to the wrong floor and exited the elevator. He waited for a few minutes to see if anyone else got off on that floor. Again, nothing, so he got back on the other elevator and went to Nora's floor.

She met him at the door wearing nothing but his shirt.

"Now you're really making me regret I'm late," he said, eyeing her from head to toe.

She smiled, pleased with his appraisal. When she put her arms around his waist, she felt his gun and backed away.

He stepped inside after looking each way in the corridor. "I've been keeping it close since the explosion." As he closed and locked the door behind him, he told her that the explosion at the marina was arson.

Her mouth fell open. "Arson? The news said it was a propane leak."

"It was. But it had been tampered with. It wasn't an accident. I'll tell you over dinner."

She blushed. "Yes, dinner. I'm sorry." She kissed him with a promise of more to come. "Dessert," she said as she led him out to the balcony.

She'd set the small table for two. An open bottle of chianti was in the middle of the table, along with a lit candle.

"You didn't need to go to this much trouble."

"I didn't. I had some lasagna in the freezer along with the bread and threw together a salad. The lasagna's in the oven, so let's have a glass of wine first. It'll be ready by the time we finish."

As she poured the wine, she asked, "How was your meeting with the detective?"

He exhaled. "Surprising and frustrating. That's how I found out it was arson."

"They also said they found a body. That's what scared me. I thought it was you."

"But for an unexpected stroke of luck, it would've been. The body was that of Dr. Stuart Westbrook, the CEO of Delray-By-The-Sea."

"Oh my God. Somebody blew up your boat. And Dr. Westbrook was on board?" She cocked her head. "Why?"

"It's complicated. I think I'm being set up. You might as well know I'm considered a person of interest."

"Because of your history with him?"

"Yep. Which leads me to the messages I discovered." He told her about the messages from Westbrook.

"Ramon was on the boat," Jon said. "And I've got proof."

Her eyes widened. "Have you told Beth?"

He shook his head. "I called and left a message but haven't heard back yet."

During dinner, Nora's phone rang. She looked at the screen, then excused herself. "Probably about my aunt," she said as she left the table and went inside to take the call.

She came out shortly, a worried look on her face. "Now it's my turn to apologize. She's taken a turn for the worse. I need to catch the first flight out in the morning, so I need to pack. Delta's got one at six A.M."

Jon's heart dropped. He understood but had been looking forward to spending the night with her. Plus, he would feel better taking her to the airport himself. "I can take you to the airport."

She shook her head. "Not necessary. I've already got a car to pick me up. Same driver I always use." Appearing to read his face, she added, "I'll text you when I'm leaving."

She reached out for his hand. "But we still have time for a quick dessert."

56

Jon was up early the next morning after his visit with Nora last night was cut short. She had texted him from the airport saying her flight was on time. On his second cup of coffee, he called Trey.

"Hey," Trey said. His voice was slurred and sounded weak.

"Hey, brother. How're you feeling?"

"Okay."

It was a lie, and Jon knew it. He needed to go to Cincinnati. Soon.

"Tell me some good news," Trey said.

"I know what happened. And I've got proof." He gave him a condensed version of the rehab mill responsible for Haley's demise.

"I wish . . . I would be here . . . long enough to see justice," Trey said, taking wheezing breaths in between the words.

Jon choked up. "Hang in there. We're close. I'm coming to Cincinnati to see you."

"No," Trey said.

What? It was emphatic. Maybe Trey didn't understand him. This time, Jon spoke slowly and more deliberately. "I want to fly up today. To see you."

"No," Trey repeated. "Stop them. Don't let them get away."

A tear slid down Jon's cheek as he realized what his friend was saying. He could tell by Trey's voice the end was near, but coming to Cincinnati accomplished nothing. Trey wanted him to focus on justice for Haley.

"Five by five," Jon said as he disconnected. He sat there, wishing he'd been able to see Trey once more before he passed. But that would always be his wish. Once more was never enough.

He pushed those thoughts away and turned his attention back to the problem at hand. He re-read the texts and emails from Stuart.

Jon put himself in Cal's shoes. Cal somehow found out Westbrook was staying with Jon. *How* wasn't relevant at the moment. But Cal had to know Westbrook had the opportunity to share damaging information with Jon. By implicating Jon, Cal had bought a little time. But he was too smart to wait for things to come crashing down.

Cal had to have an escape strategy. The more Jon thought about it, the more he believed Cal's escape plan started with a seemingly innocent trip to the Bahamas. Once he got there, he could take a private jet and go anywhere. Two days after Ramon had blown up his boat, Cal was going to the Bahamas? *Coincidence?* Jon was skeptical and willing to bet that Ramon was with Cal. He had to stop Cal from getting there.

He called Beth again. Once more, it went to voice mail. Where the hell was she? He didn't bother leaving a message. He called Cal's assistant.

"This is Becky."

"Hi, Becky. Jon Cruz. I hate to bother you on a Sunday, but I need to speak with Cal. Every time I call his cell, it goes straight to voice mail."

"He's probably not in cell phone range. And I'm not sure when he'll be reachable."

Jon thought for a moment, then decided to take a chance. "Is he fishing again in the Bahamas?" he said, laughing as if it were an inside joke, hoping Becky would go along. It was worth a shot.

She giggled. "Don't tell him I told you. He had me meet him at the office an hour ago to sign some papers before he left. He's probably on his way over there by now."

"Our secret," he said in a conspiratorial voice. "I'll try again later. If you talk to him, don't tell him I called. I've got some good news for him, and I want it to be a surprise."

Dammit, Jon thought as he disconnected. Cal could make it to his house in West End, Bahamas in a couple of hours. He called Ricky. "I need a go-fast boat. Like in an hour."

"An hour? Uh, for what?"

"I'm not sure. Maybe a quick run to the Bahamas. I'm willing to pay, but I need it gassed and ready to go by the time I get to you. Oh, and I need you, too. To drive."

"Whoa. Let me think about it."

"Think fast. I'm on the way. See you in forty-five minutes."

Forty minutes later, Jon wheeled into the marina parking lot and parked Lucille. He would've been ten minutes earlier if he hadn't stopped by his storage unit to pick up something. He retrieved a bag from the trunk and spotted Ricky on the dock beside a sleek center console boat.

"This it?" he asked as he walked out to Ricky. Jon eyed the three huge black Mercury outboards hung on the back. The boat looked fast just sitting there.

Ricky nodded. "Max's boat. Fountain 38 Center Console. Trip Merc 400s. When I told him what you wanted, he handed me the keys. Said he'd put it on your tab. What's in the bag?"

Jon ignored the question for now. "Ready?"

"I just finished filling her up. Let's go."

As they headed south on the Intracoastal, Ricky asked, "Where to?"

Jon gave him the directions to Cal's neighborhood.

A few minutes later, Ricky turned into the canal leading to Cal's house. "High-rent area," he said.

When they got there, *WesTex* was gone. Nothing was docked along the seawall. For a second, he wondered if he had the right place. Upon closer inspection, he recognized the pool in the back of the house. It was the same pool the housekeeper had led him past on the way to meet with Cal.

"He's not here," Jon said. "His boat's gone. Set a course to West End, Bahamas. Can we catch him?"

Ricky cocked his head. "Depends on what we're trying to catch."

"A seventy-plus foot yacht named *WesTex*."

"*WesTex?* Cal Norman's boat?"

Surprised, he looked at Ricky. "You know it?"

"Yeah. We do all the maintenance on it. A 72' Horizon. Cruises at twenty knots. We can do three times that. What are we going to do once we catch him?"

"I don't have a fucking clue."

He looked down at the bag he'd brought. Inside was a hard case containing a Barrett M107, a civilian version of the same 50 cal. semi-automatic sniper rifle he used in Force RECON. The Barrett was one of the most powerful shoulder-fired rifles ever produced, capable of penetrating body armor or even an engine block. He was amazed that it was legal in most states to purchase one. Shaking his head, he tried to remember the last time he'd shot it. It had to have been at least two years ago.

Headlines glamourize how far a sniper can accurately shoot, with recorded kill shots in the thousands of yards. But a boat-to-boat shot on open seas is one of the most difficult. Two moving vessels on the fluctuating surface of the ocean present a challenge because of the variables, not the distance. Most people don't realize the celebrated shots to free Captain Richard Phillips after the hijacking of the *Maersk Alabama* were made at a distance of less than thirty yards.

Jon doubted they could get anywhere near that close. Besides, he wasn't going to be shooting anyone, he just wanted to disable the yacht. As much as he despised Cal and Ramon, he was not willing to execute them in cold blood.

He assumed Ramon was armed and would be shooting at them. Another reason for not getting too close. But there may be others on board. How many? What weapons did they have? Where on the boat were they positioned?

Jon looked over at his young friend. Ricky had followed his instructions without question. But driving the Fountain, Ricky would be exposed and a target. Way more variables and unknowns than Jon was comfortable managing on such short notice.

It would have been far easier just to call the Coast Guard and let them handle it. But, by the time they'd cleared the necessary bureaucracy, Cal would be in the Bahamas or, worse, even farther away.

As they approached the last bridge to the open ocean, Jon tried to reach Beth one last time.

"Beth, where are you?" he asked when she answered. "Hold a minute." He pressed mute.

He looked at Ricky and made a circle with his index finger. "Hold tight for a few minutes while I take this." Ricky nodded, then pulled the throttles back to idle, making a lazy eight in the mouth of the Intracoastal.

Jon unmuted his phone. "Sorry. I'm outside," he told her. "I've been trying to reach you. I've got the goods on

Cal Norman and Ramon Grant." He proceeded to tell her about the messages and emails from Westbrook.

"Can you bring it to the station? I want my lieutenant to hear this."

He swore under his breath. "I can be there in an hour, but we have a more pressing problem. Cal is on his boat heading to the Bahamas. I'm guessing Ramon is with him."

"How do you know where Cal is going?"

"His assistant told me. He's on his way as we speak. We've got to stop him."

She snorted. "What do you expect me to do? Call the Coast Guard and have them pick him up based on your phone call? You know it doesn't work that way. Besides, we have an extradition agreement with the Bahamas."

"Goddammit, Beth. He'll be there in a couple of hours. That's not his final destination. Once he gets there, he can take a private jet to who-knows-where. You'll never get him back."

"You know it's not that simple."

He looked at his watch. If they were going to stop Cal, they had to leave. Now. It was decision time, that point where there was no turning back.

"I've gotta go. I'll call you later." He disconnected, switched the phone off, and put it in his pocket. He donned his headset and gave the other to Ricky. At the speeds they would soon be going, it would be impossible to communicate otherwise over the noise of the powerful outboards and the wind.

As soon as they were outside protected waters, he braced himself and said to Ricky, "Let's go."

Nodding to confirm, Ricky opened the throttles as he turned east northeast toward West End, Bahamas. The outboards roared as they were unleashed, and the boat quickly picked up speed, bouncing across the water. Jon glanced at the speedometer to see they had passed sixty knots and were still accelerating.

At this speed, they'd overtake the much slower *WesTex* soon. Jon scanned the horizon ahead, looking for her. Clouds were building to the west. In a rush, he'd neglected to check the weather. Was a storm brewing? Crossing the Gulf Stream in lousy weather was foolish. Besides, he didn't know for sure Cal was heading to the Bahamas. What if he was going in the opposite direction and had left breadcrumbs to lead followers astray?

Jon shook his head. More holes in his hastily-conceived plan. He knew from experience that rushing without checking and double-checking could result in fatal mistakes.

He glanced over at the GPS, showing their track and position. If Cal was going to West End, he should soon be within sight.

He raised the binoculars and scanned the horizon ahead. A boat the size of *WesTex* should be visible ten miles away. He was beginning to get discouraged when he spotted a large boat in the distance at eleven o'clock. He tapped Ricky's shoulder and pointed. Ricky nodded and adjusted their course.

Jon kept his eyes on the boat as they drew closer, and it grew larger. Although he couldn't read the name, it was the profile of Cal's yacht. Now what?

The priority had to be to stop or disable the yacht before it got to the Bahamas. Once in the Bahamas, a waiting private jet could quickly whisk him away to anywhere in the world. Cal's kind of money could buy a lot of options.

Having Bahamian citizenship meant Cal and *WesTex* wouldn't have to clear customs to enter Bahamian waters. *WesTex* was probably also registered with the Royal Bahamas Defence Force (RBDF), unlike the Fountain that they were on. If he and Ricky were spotted, the RBDF was likely to stop and question them.

"Can you paint me a ten-by-ten target of where their engine room is?" Jon asked.

Ricky gave him a thumbs up and described the location of the twin diesel engines. He told Jon from the side exterior the engine room was vertically framed between the main deck and the waterline. Horizontally, it was between the rear window and the midship window.

"Go over to his port side," Jon said. He wanted an unimpeded view of the target from his seat in the Fountain. "Maintain one thousand yards separation and match his speed."

A thousand-yard shot on land under normal conditions with a spotter would be a slam dunk. Out here on a rolling sea with both vessels moving was the stuff of Hollywood, not the real world. But this distance would allow him to safely scope out the boat as he figured out what to do.

As they got closer, Jon could make out Ramon on the deck, watching them. He had what appeared to be a short-barrel AK-47 slung over his shoulder. A great choice for a drive-by but not for a long-distance shot. Score one for the good guys. But he had no idea of Ramon's skill with a firearm. Regardless, the AK-47 would pose a serious problem if they got too close.

Also, Jon didn't know if others were on the boat with better skills and more capable weapons. His gut was churning. His comfort factor was too low with this many unknowns.

"Does Cal have a captain?" he asked over the headset.

"He likes to play captain, but only in fair weather and for short trips like this."

That meant Cal was probably at the helm. Suddenly, a woman emerged from the main salon onto the rear deck. Jon refocused the binoculars to sharpen his view.

She was an attractive young brunette wearing a skimpy bikini. She carried a tray with a single drink, indicating she was serving only one person—a good sign. He watched as she walked around to the foredeck and out of sight.

His first thought was a steward, but something didn't make sense. He'd been on a few crewed boats, and the staff had always been smartly dressed, not wearing a scanty swimsuit.

He turned the binoculars to the helm. The darkly tinted windows prevented him from identifying the person steering. Was it Cal? If not, then who? Assuming Cal was at the helm, that meant at least four people were on board *WesTex*.

He swore under his breath, starting to panic. He had to calm down and focus on what he did know.

Although a ten-by-ten target seemed big, Jon figured he would have to get within at least two hundred yards to hit the engine room. That was uncomfortably close to Ramon and the AK-47. It could hit Jon and Ricky at that distance, even with untrained hands. With a skilled shooter, they would be easy targets.

He looked inside the bag and found two ten-round magazines. One was empty, and he tossed it back in the bag. The other contained three cartridges. Three tries to hit a target he couldn't see and do enough damage to disable the boat. He should've checked the ammunition when he picked up the rifle from his storage unit.

There was also the possibility he could hit something else, causing an explosion or fire, killing everyone on board. He wasn't too worried about Cal or Ramon, but the thought of killing innocent people like the steward disturbed him.

He looked at the GPS. Soon, they would be in Bahamian waters. Suppose they got stopped with the Barrett by the

RDBF. In that case, he and Ricky faced a certain sentence in the Bahamas' notorious Fox Hill prison.

"Goddammit, Jon, stop it." He recalled the phrase that the Marines had drilled into him: Improvise, adapt, overcome. *You gotta play the cards you're dealt.*

Jon opened the hard case and assembled the rifle, skipping the suppressor. He didn't need it out here.

"Holy fuck," Ricky said when he saw what Jon was doing. "What is that?"

"A Barrett 50 caliber." Jon rechecked his work and adjusted the scope for two hundred yards.

"Maintain your speed and close to two hundred yards," Jon said.

As they closed the gap, Jon continued watching Ramon. When they got to within three hundred yards, Ramon swung the AK-47 toward them.

Shit. He was getting ready to fire. Jon put his hand on Ricky's shoulder. "Close enough."

Jon rocked in the magazine and pulled the charging handle back, chambering the first round. He wedged himself in the best position he could, setting the bipod on the gunwale and clicking the safety to Fire.

Snipers were trained to shoot solo but usually had a spotter in the field to call wind, distance, and other factors to assist the shooter in compensating. No spotter here, so he'd guessed at the adjustments.

Jon slowed his breathing, concentrating on his task. When satisfied with the picture through the scope, he exhaled and gently squeezed the trigger. Just as he did, the Fountain dropped several feet from a wave, and he heard the boom from the rifle.

"Jesus," Ricky said, "That sounded like a cannon."

Jon watched through the scope to see where it hit, knowing the sudden movement had screwed up his shot. He kicked the side of the boat. It was worse than he'd thought. He'd missed the entire boat. How could he miss a seventy-two foot yacht?

"Where'd it hit?" Ricky asked.

Jon shook his head. "Nothing. That wave hit right before I fired. You've got to keep us steady."

"Steady? We're in the Gulf Stream on the Atlantic Ocean with one-to-three-foot seas. This is as flat as it gets out here."

Then, Ramon fired a short burst at them, causing Jon and Ricky to duck. A spray and pray. Lucky for them, it was more for show at that distance.

But next time, Ramon might get lucky.

57

Jon put the rifle down and slammed his fist on the seat. Ricky was right. It doesn't get any better than one-to-three-foot seas out here.

Plus, he was out of practice with no spotter and only two more shots. He wasn't sure he could hit it at a hundred yards, which was way closer than he wanted to get to someone firing an AK-47 at them. But three hundred yards was too far.

He cut his eyes over to Ricky, who stared at him. His eyes mainly expressed trust and hope but were now tinged with doubt. Jon knew he was close to falling short with his young friend, just as he had with Trey and Haley and Lexi and Stuart. He had to focus. Cal was getting away. If he did, it would mean their lives had been in vain. Jon refused to let that happen. They deserved justice.

He shook his head. They had to get closer, but how close? He weighed what he remembered about an AK-47's range against the minimum distance he needed to make the shot. A hundred yards were where they needed to be, but that close, exposed, on the open water, he and Ricky would be easy pickings. Ramon would shoot them both before Jon could squeeze the trigger.

"Close to two hundred yards," he said to Ricky over the headset. "The second I fire, get out of his range as soon as possible."

As Jon set the bipod back on the gunwale, Ramon fired another burst in their direction. Jon flinched as a bullet hit the metal frame of the console above his head.

He composed himself, slowing his heart rate. He exhaled and squeezed the trigger. As he did, he heard another shot hit the boat as Ricky shoved the throttles forward and turned the Fountain away from *WesTex*. Within seconds they were another two hundred yards away, safely out of Ramon's range.

"Damn, that was close," Ricky said. He cut the throttles back to idle so Jon could see where his shot landed.

Jon already had the binoculars up. He saw where the shot penetrated the hull, but there was no indication that it did any real damage. "Upper left quadrant," he said, handing the binoculars to Ricky.

"I see the hole," Ricky said. "Engines are two feet to the right, three feet lower."

Jon shook his head. He didn't doubt Ricky's assessment. What he doubted was his ability to adjust with that precision under the circumstances.

He took another look at *WesTex*. Ramon was still standing in the same spot. The steward approached him, cowering. Ramon gesticulated with both hands, then pointed back to the main cabin. She wasted no time in leaving.

Then, it hit him. She was one of Ramon's "girls," just like Haley and Lexi. An indentured servant at his beck and call, bound with drugs and enabled by Cal Norman.

Jon flushed with rage. He set the binoculars down and picked up the Barrett. This was his last round. He wished he had more so he could put this one in Ramon's head.

He took a deep breath and looked over at Ricky. "I've got to get closer." He hesitated, not wanting to put Ricky in greater danger. Those last two shots from Ramon were too close for comfort.

Ricky stared at him, awaiting further instructions.

"This is my fight, not yours," Jon said. "I can't ask you to—"

"I'm in. You were there for me. I'm here for you. Just tell me what you want."

Jon smiled, then nodded. "Get as close as you dare. Call it when it's flat. Soon as I fire, get the hell out."

Ricky eased the throttles forward, turned, and headed straight toward *WesTex*.

Jon shouldered the rifle and flicked the safety to Fire. As they got closer, he looked through the scope, getting his bearings. He kept waiting for Ricky to cut the throttles and turn broadside. Four hundred yards, then three hundred. Jon ignored Ramon, focusing on the target area.

Two hundred yards, and Ricky was still closing. Jon heard the chatter of the AK-47, then a bullet ping off the metal frame above the console. He fought to keep the scope steady and ignore the incoming fire.

Suddenly, Ricky cut the throttles and turned broadside.

Time seemed to slow as Jon loosened his shoulders and calmed his breathing, waiting for Ricky's mark. He refused to be distracted when he heard a thud as a shot from the AK-47 slammed into the hull of the Fountain. He steadied the rifle, focusing on the sight picture and waiting on Ricky.

"Now," Ricky said.

His finger on the trigger, Jon exhaled, then squeezed. He felt the recoil against his shoulder and heard the boom as the supersonic round left the barrel. The boat rocketed forward and turned as Ricky shoved the throttles of the powerful outboards wide open.

Jon put the rifle down and grabbed the binoculars. He could see the hole in the lower right corner of the target area on the big boat's hull, within a foot of where he imagined the engines were.

For a few seconds, there was nothing. Then, black smoke emerged from the rear of *WesTex*. The yacht suddenly stopped, the wake overtaking it. *WesTex* was bobbing like a cork on the water, no longer underway. Jon heard what sounded like an explosion, then the cloud of smoke intensified. His last round had found its mark.

Ramon hurried down to the lower deck, no longer firing at them, and disappeared into the cloud of smoke. Ricky throttled the Fountain back to an idle.

Jon glanced toward the west. The clouds were getting closer. And darker. A storm was coming toward them.

He picked up the Barrett and studied it with an emotion bordering on affection. A supremely made killing machine, it had served its purpose well. Without ammunition, it was no more than a costly anchor. But it was still dangerous. It had the potential to imprison Ricky if he was caught with it onboard.

After a moment's hesitation, he pitched it into the deep waters of the Atlantic. He turned to Ricky. "Close to within one hundred yards. Careful."

Jon removed the overboard bag from underneath his seat and dug out the flare pistol. A bandolier with three shells was attached. He loaded a shell, then shoved the flare pistol into his pocket. He pulled the SIG out of his holster and handed it to Ricky.

"Can you get me to the swim platform?" Jon asked.

Ricky turned the boat toward *WesTex* as Jon continued watching the yacht. There was no activity on the deck. He guessed Cal was at the helm while Ramon was down in the engine room fighting the fire.

As Ricky eased closer to the big boat, Jon saw smoke pouring out of the open walk-through hatch in the middle of the swim platform. Ricky had told him this was the only entrance to the crew quarters and engine room. Jon hoped no one else was in there. Steps on either side of the platform led up to the main deck.

"Soon as I get off, fall back a hundred yards on their port side. Don't come closer unless you see my signal."

He could read the unspoken question on Ricky's mind. "If I don't show, go home. Call the Coast Guard on your way back."

As soon as Ricky was next to the platform, Jon jumped over to the larger boat, trying to stay as far away from the hatch as possible. He stumbled, almost losing his balance and falling into the water. He sat back against the hull and gave Ricky a thumbs-up. As quietly as possible, Ricky maneuvered away.

Jon took the flare pistol out of his pocket, then looked around, waiting to see if anyone had emerged through the hatch. He knew the entrance to the engine room was opposite the exterior hatch. Ramon was in there somewhere, armed with the AK-47.

He was contemplating his next move when suddenly, Ramon materialized from the smoke-filled hatch, coughing, the AK-47 still slung around his neck. He turned, surprised to see Jon sitting there. He pulled up the AK, but Jon was quicker. He pointed the flare pistol at Ramon and pulled the trigger.

The 12-gauge phosphorus flare exploded into Ramon's chest, knocking him off the platform into the ocean, steam coming up from the surface.

Ramon was dead before he hit the water. Jon carefully reloaded the flare pistol, sat back, and waited a few minutes to see if anyone else emerged from the hatch.

No one appeared. With the flare gun ready, he inched up the steps to the main deck, where he peeked around the side into the galley.

The brunette, her back to him, poured a glass of wine. She placed the glass on a tray and exited through the side door to the foredeck.

Curious about who she was serving, he crept into the galley and stared out the front window. An attractive redhead lie on her back on a foredeck lounge. She was topless, and he couldn't see her face from where he stood. He furrowed his brow. Something about the picture before him prodded his memory, but he couldn't place it.

When the steward approached the woman, she sat up and turned to take the proffered drink.

What the fuck? It was Nora Jenkins.

He stared, recognizing the now-familiar body that had so pleased him. His first thought was that she was a prisoner like the steward.

As Nora casually took the wine, he shook his head, realizing how naive that sounded. She was no prisoner. She was a guest. Jon had shared his bed and his innermost feelings with Cal's paramour.

"It is a nice view, isn't it?" The familiar voice came from behind.

58

Jon had been so preoccupied watching Nora that he hadn't noticed Cal behind him coming down the steps from the helm.

Before Jon could react, Cal added, "I've got a fully loaded 9mm Glock pointed at your back, so don't even think about using that flare pistol. You won't make it. Slowly set it on the counter next to you. The slightest misstep and you'll have three bullets in you before you can turn around."

Jon swore under his breath, angry that he'd let Cal get the drop on him. He gently laid the flare pistol on the counter to his right as he tried to think of another way out of his predicament.

"Good. Now, put your hands in the air. Turn toward your left and face me. Slowly."

Jon gritted his teeth. Turning to the left made it impossible for him to grab the flare gun. He turned to face a grinning Cal, pointing a semi-automatic pistol at him. At this close range, even a poor shot wouldn't miss.

The cocky bastard wore shorts, a tropical-print shirt, and deck shoes. Jon clenched his fist, repulsed at the thought of Nora screwing this asshole when she wasn't in bed with him. He was angry with Cal but furious with Nora and more furious with himself. He'd trusted her, shared with her, and made love to her. What a fool he was.

He heard the door behind him shut.

"Marie, go back out front and keep Ms. Jenkins company. Mr. Cruz and I have a little business to discuss."

Jon heard the door open and shut behind him. He wondered if Nora would intervene, then dismissed that thought as more folly. He was on his own.

Cal took two steps to his left and motioned the gun toward the rear deck. "Why don't we go out back to chat. Since you know the way, you lead."

He took a quick step, then Cal said, "Slowly. Don't even think of trying anything. I won't hesitate to shoot an intruder on my boat."

An intruder. Jon could guess where Cal was going with this. He would maintain that pirates had disabled his boat and shot his partner. Cal intended to kill him, shove the body overboard, and claim self-defense.

He walked slowly through the open sliding glass door, stalling for time. He was convinced that Cal intended to take him down to the swim platform to shoot him. Probably didn't want blood on his immaculate yacht. Jon almost chuckled at the macabre thought.

Strange sounds radiated from the bowels of the yacht. Smoke continued to billow out the rear hatch to the crew quarters. He wondered if Marie slept there or if Ramon forced her to keep his bed warm.

At the back edge of the main deck, Jon stopped and turned as he subtly scanned the horizon hoping to spot Ricky. Nothing. He could only hope his young friend was watching through the binoculars. Maybe Ricky could get close enough to distract Cal. Nora and Marie were standing on the foredeck, talking. Whatever, Jon had to buy time.

"Is Marie one of Ramon's girls?" he asked. "Another Delray-By-The-Sea former patient?"

"One of the perks of our business relationship. Of course, I had Nora, too." Cal smirked.

Jon had to restrain himself. Unarmed, he was no match for a loaded Glock pointed at him. *Stall,* he said to himself.

"Quite a racket you and Ramon had going," he said. "Bleed the victim's parents dry, then turn them over to Ramon to get them back on drugs. By that time, the family has raised more money. Rinse and repeat. The recovery home was a nice touch."

Cal shrugged. "They go back on drugs anyway. You know that firsthand, don't you?" Another smirk. "Might as well get them from us."

Jon felt his face flush at the reference to Megan. He bit his lower lip, wanting to feel the pain and taste the blood. His rage grew as he thought about how Marie, Haley, Lexi, and others had been abused. Somehow, someway, he was going to kill Cal Norman. Even if it meant losing his life.

"Was Stuart part of this?" Jon asked.

Cal chuckled. "I was the one who saw the genius of his treatment plan and how to turn it into millions. Keep tweaking it to match whatever funds the family can raise. Keep recycling patients through the system. Amazing how creative the families can get. Which, by the way, Stu also benefited handsomely. He turned a blind eye and did what I told him to do. Up until you came along and tickled his conscience."

Jon thought about Stuart Westbrook. He was far from blameless but a saint compared to Cal and Ramon. And he was trying to make amends when they murdered him. "So, you had Ramon blow up my boat?"

"You were supposed to be on it, too."

"You won't get away with this."

"Oh, but I will." He waved the gun toward the steps. "Enough chitchat. Let's go down to the swim platform."

As Jon made his way down the steps, the boat was listing to starboard. The breeze was blowing the smoke in the other direction.

He stopped when he stepped onto the swim platform, reaching out to steady himself with the railing. Water lapped over the teak platform. *WesTex* was sinking.

"Move over toward the hatch and stop there," Cal said.

Jon took as long as possible to go the short distance. When he was opposite the hatch, he turned around.

Cal stood at the edge of the platform at the bottom of the steps, still pointing the gun at him. "You couldn't turn loose, could you?" Cal said, wearing a sick grin.

Over Cal's shoulder, Jon saw Ricky creeping closer in the Fountain. He had to keep Cal occupied.

"What are you going to do without Ramon?" Jon asked.

Cal shrugged. "Ramon's expendable. He was the brawn, not the brains. There's plenty of others like him."

"How are you going to explain killing me?" Keep Cal talking. He hoped Ricky would take a shot with the SIG when he got within range. If he got close enough soon enough.

"Pirates disabled the boat," Cal said. "One came aboard and killed my business associate. As Marie and Nora will attest, I had to shoot him in self-defense."

Jon nodded back over his shoulder as if indicating Ricky was behind him instead of behind Cal. "My partner's still out there. He's probably already called the Coast Guard."

Cal glanced over Jon's shoulder. "Good. I'll call him on the radio and tell him you're hurt. When he comes for you, I'll add that he tried to come aboard, and I had to kill him, too."

A creaking sound emerged from the hatch as a black cloud belched out. Jon could see flames deep within the smoke. The boat was definitely listing now. And the back edge of the platform was underwater. The waves were picking up and the sky was getting darker.

Cal noticed it too. "Looks like we may need your boat after all. Too bad there's not room enough for you."

As Cal raised the gun, Jon braced for the shot. He glanced again at Ricky coming toward them. He was too far away and wouldn't get there in time.

Jon was ready, as ready as anyone could be, for the end. He wondered if he would feel anything, if he would feel the pain. His mind shifted to Megan and Erika, wanting them to be his final thoughts.

A thunderous boom shattered the silence. Jon flinched, shutting his eyes.

But he didn't feel anything. Puzzled, he opened his eyes to see a flare had landed in the water behind Cal. Cal's shoulder was bleeding. How did a flare graze Cal?

A scream came from the main deck where Marie stood at the top of the stairs. She was holding the flare gun with both hands, her face grimacing.

Momentarily confused, Cal swiveled to shoot her. Jon lunged at him, knocking the gun from his hands as he slammed Cal into the railing. He pummeled Cal's face with his fists. Cal's nose spewed blood as he desperately tried to block the blows with his hands.

Cal went low and with his good arm, landed a punch into Jon's midsection, knocking him to his knees in the water on the platform. Cal kicked at him, but his boat shoes had come off in the scuffle, and besides, the kicks weren't effective. He grabbed Cal's legs and stood, flipping him over the rail and into the ocean.

Cal's blood stained the water as he thrashed about and screamed for help. Marie was standing on the platform now, her hand trembling as she leveled the flare pistol at Cal.

"No," Cal said between gulps of water. "Please. Don't." Before Jon could say anything, she pulled the trigger.

It clicked as the hammer fell on the spent shell. She hadn't loaded a new shell in the single-shot flare pistol since she'd fired it at Cal the first time, winging him.

Jon reached out and gently took the gun from her. He removed the last shell from the attached bandolier and reloaded the pistol. Marie held her hand out, her eyes pleading with him to hand her the loaded flare gun. He knew she wanted to be the one who sent Cal to the hell he deserved.

Jon knew firsthand the weight of killing another human being. She had enough baggage without having to live with that burden for the rest of her life. He shook his head, then stepped over to the rail, where he raised his arm and aimed the pistol at Cal.

"Jon. Please. I can pay." Cal begged as he desperately flailed about with his one good arm, trying to get closer to the boat. The water around him was tinged red with his blood.

That's when Jon noticed first one fin, then another behind Cal. He lowered his arm as Cal screamed. Cal spotted or felt them underneath the water, sizing up their quarry.

As a combat veteran, Jon had seen many examples of man's inhumanity to man. But never had he personally witnessed the brutal efficiency of an apex predator devouring its prey. A chill ran down his spine as he realized his feet were ankle-deep in the same water as Cal, with only a metal railing separating them.

He glanced over at Marie, wanting to shield her from the spectacle. But as he saw her staring at Cal desperately trying to fend off his attackers, he knew she needed to see it. She wanted to see Cal get his just reward.

A final primal shriek pierced the air as Cal managed to get out one last pathetic cry as the sharks roiled the water, dragging him under for the last time.

From the rail above them, Nora Jenkins screamed.

59

Ricky eased the Fountain up next to the platform, stealing nervous looks at the spot in the water ten yards away where Cal had succumbed. "What the hell?" he said as he tied a line to the rail, now only a few feet above the water.

Marie was trembling as she turned to look at Jon. A tear rolled down her cheek. Jon took off his shirt and put it over her shoulders. "It's okay. You're safe, but you have to get off this boat right now."

She glanced back at the spot where Cal had met his violent death as if to confirm he was gone. Then, she looked at Ricky, who nodded and held out his hand.

As soon as Jon helped her get on board, he turned toward the steps.

"Where the hell are you going?" Ricky said, glancing up at the sky. "This storm's almost on us."

Ignoring him, Jon raced up the steps to get Nora. Flames were beginning to lick out of the open hatch. She sat at the table on the rear main deck, staring at the horizon.

"Nora, we've got to go. Now."

She looked up at him with soulless eyes. "I'm sorry, Jon."

"We can talk about it later, but we have to leave right now." He held out his hand.

Ricky was yelling. "Jon, we've got to pull away."

She stood but didn't take Jon's hand. "I've got to get my bag," she said, her voice preternaturally calm.

He shook his head. "We don't have—"

"I'll be right back," she said as she turned and walked into the galley. He watched as she disappeared down the stairs leading to the berths below.

Gurgling and hissing sounds emanated from the bowels of the big yacht. He had to grab the railing as the back end of the yacht started slipping under the water. Waves were increasing and the wind had picked up.

"We've got to go," Ricky said, yelling above the noise.

Jon took one last look through the galley at the stairs leading below.

Nora wasn't coming back.

60

One month later

Jon walked into Hank's and headed over to his usual spot at the bar. He was tired and discouraged. All afternoon, he'd been on Addie's computer looking at boats. Since he'd returned from that fateful encounter with Cal Norman, he'd searched in vain, looking at dozens of makes and models. What he really wanted was his old boat back.

Max, at the boatyard, had come across the perfect match, a newer twin to *Trouble No More*. "Midnight" Malone, a blues musician in the Keys, had a 2001 Grand Banks 42 Classic and had approached Max about possibly finding a buyer.

Max had called Jon, and they drove down to Key Largo to see it. As soon as Jon saw it, he fell in love. He took the name—*Nightbird*—as a sign it was meant to be. But after two weeks of unanswered offers, Jon realized Malone didn't really want to part with the boat.

He couldn't blame him. It was a beautiful boat, immaculately maintained. Malone was the original owner, and the boat had become the bachelor's family over the years. Just before entering the bar, Jon called Max, who confirmed it wouldn't happen. Malone had informed him that he'd changed his mind.

Addie came over with a beer. "Your dog missing?"

"My boat is," he said after taking a drink.

"Max can't talk him into selling?"

He shook his head. "I just got off the phone with Max. Malone has officially backed out. Time to look for something else." He looked around the bar. "Where's Marie?"

"Running errands."

When they'd returned from their high-seas adventure, Marie had led Beth to Ramon's recovery home, operating under the guise of Delray Serenity House. They rescued eight victims, all former patients at Delray-By-The-Sea. They'd been given drugs, then forced into prostitution, selling for Ramon, recruiting other addicts—you name it. If their families came up with more money, they were readmitted into Delray-By-The-Sea to start the cycle all over again.

Over ten arrests had been made so far, with more to come. HHS-OIG, the FBI, and the U.S. Attorney General's office were investigating them and Moren Health with more indictments pending.

Addie had taken Marie under her wing, letting her stay at her house and giving her a job at Hank's.

"She okay?" Jon asked.

"Quit worrying. She's doing fine. Smart, and a great bartender. Likable but tough."

He chuckled. "Like someone else I know."

Addie's phone rang. She looked at it, then excused herself.

He wanted to order something to eat, but Addie was still on the phone at the other end of the bar.

A few minutes later, Ray came out of the kitchen, wearing his apron. He waved at Jon and walked over to Addie. She whispered to him, then she returned.

"Want to walk down to the T dock with me?" she asked. "It's finished, and they want a check."

T dock had been Jon's dock. For the last two weeks, a crew had been working overtime on replacing it and repairing the damage to the main dock along the seawall. With no boat on his horizon, he wasn't in the mood to see it.

"I'll look at it later," he said. "Besides, I want something to eat."

"Ray can't go back to the kitchen and cook till I return, so come on. Let's go take a look so they can get their money. Then he can fix you something."

Grumbling, Jon finished his beer and stood.

Outside, as they walked toward the T dock, he looked up. "There's a boat docked there."

"Must have come in this afternoon," Addie said.

As they got closer, he saw it was a Grand Banks 42 and stopped. Now he was in a more foul mood. The last thing he wanted to do was socialize with the owners of a boat that reminded him of *Trouble No More*. "Let them get settled," he said. "I'll check the dock out tomorrow."

"Oh, come on. The least we can do is say 'hello.'"

He shook his head. "Whatever."

As they turned to walk out the T dock, Jon heard voices and laughter coming from the rear deck of the Grand Banks. He stopped short when he saw Marie standing at the side entry door wearing a huge grin.

"What are you doing here?" he asked, surprised to see her.

Marie held out her hand. "Welcome aboard."

He looked at Addie, who shrugged and said nothing. Shaking his head, he took Marie's hand and stepped onboard.

She led him toward the rear deck. As he rounded the corner, applause broke out. Jon froze. He couldn't believe what he was seeing.

Beth, Reece, Max, Ricky, Padre, D'Lo, and R.D. Stone were standing there to greet him.

"I don't understand." He was baffled, and it was all he could manage to say.

"Don't tell me you've changed your mind," Max said. "I'm not sure I can get my deposit back."

"Deposit?" Jon said, even more confused. "What the hell are you talking about?"

"Nightbird," sung by Eva Cassidy, burst from the speakers.

"This is *Nightbird*," Max said. He held out a key. "When he heard what you'd done, Malone called me and agreed to sell her—but only to you. His only condition was that he wouldn't accept your final offer, insisting on a lower amount. So I gave him a deposit. She's yours if you still want to buy her."

Jon looked around the boat, trying to comprehend his sudden change in fortune. "This isn't a joke?"

Everyone started laughing.

"I've got the papers right here, ready for your signature," R.D. said, holding a folder in one hand and a pen in the other.

Jon looked over at Addie. "You were behind this. No wonder you were so insistent that I come out to the damn dock."

"If I had told you the real reason, you wouldn't have come."

He nodded, still in shock.

"Well?" J.D. said, holding the pen out.

Jon looked around at each of them in turn, overwhelmed with gratitude. Shaking his head, he took the pen from J.D. "Where do I sign?"

As soon as he signed the papers, Addie said, "The bar is open." Everyone cheered and rushed up to Jon to congratulate him.

Yesterday, Max and Ricky had brought her up from Key Largo, docking at the boatyard last night. This morning, Ricky cleaned and serviced the boat while Marie stocked the refrigerator. This afternoon, they brought her up the Intracoastal to her new home—the newly rebuilt T dock at Hank's Galley and Marina.

"You look quite surprised," Padre said.

"That's the understatement of the year. Shocked is more like it."

"You're a good person, Jon. You deserve it."

He looked over and noticed Ricky and Marie talking in the corner. Turning back to Padre, he asked, "How's she doing?"

Bryce had been counseling her, along with Dr. Williams, who continued to see Ricky.

"She's doing well, especially considering all she's been through. But she's strong and resilient. She's helping me out at the church twice a week, which is good for the people who come in and good for her, too."

"If she needs anything . . ."

Padre nodded. "I know—you're here. She knows that too. By the way, Moses is coming by pretty often, and I'm trying to get him to the clinic. He's progressing, but we'll see."

Jon had asked Padre to make a special effort to help the homeless man who'd helped Jon look for Haley. "Thank you for coming, Padre. The world needs more people like you." He hugged the priest, who then moved away.

D'Lo stepped up and embraced Jon in a bear hug, almost crushing the breath out of him. "I've never seen you at a loss for words."

His deep, gravelly voice made Jon smile like it always did. "I've never had a surprise quite like this one. I appreciate you coming and your help with everything."

"You've done a lot of good around here, brother. Not just for my family but others, too," he said as he waved his hand toward the crowd. "Enjoy your new home—you deserve it. I'm going to get something to eat." He stepped aside for the last person in line.

Reece Stevens, Trey's widow, was patiently waiting. Then, with Jon to herself, she hugged him affectionately.

At last, she took a step back. "Thank you for everything," she said. Looking upward, she added. "I know Trey's watching."

"I just wish I'd be able to see him one more time." Trey had passed before Jon could get up to see him after the encounter on the Atlantic.

She nodded. "I know, but you made the right choice. It was what he wanted. The last thing he told me was to make sure you knew how much he appreciated all you did for us."

He started to protest, but she put a finger on his lips.

"You're a good man, Jon. You've made the world a better place. Don't you forget it." She turned and walked away.

Out of the corner of his eye, he caught Ricky and Marie still talking in the corner. He was about to walk over when Addie blocked his path, bringing him a fresh beer.

"Stay, Fido," she said. "They're drinking soda."

He looked over her shoulder and saw them laughing, oblivious to everyone else. Then, Beth whisked them away, and they disappeared into the main cabin.

"They're both adults and good for each other," Addie said. "Don't meddle. The detective is chaperoning. Why don't you have a seat?" Addie patted the table.

As they sat, Beth, Ricky, and Marie appeared with a stack of wrapped gifts. They set them on the table as everyone gathered around.

Jon shot Addie a sideways glance. She smiled and crossed her arms, waiting for him to begin.

Reluctantly, he complied, opening them individually as Beth handed them to him. The first was a bottle of El Tesoro tequila, which he held up, laughing. Next was a blender. Although *Nightbird* was well equipped, there were various items for the boat since he'd lost everything with the sabotage of *Trouble No More*. He commented on each, thanking everyone each time.

Finally, Beth handed him the last present, the size of a book. A hush fell over the table as she gave it to him.

Curious about what it could be, he opened it to find a framed picture, face down. He looked up at the anxious group surrounding him. No one said a word or gave any indication of what to expect. He turned it over and stared.

It was the photo of him and Megan at the beach on Saint Simons Island.

The tears came, and he couldn't stop them. Tears flowed down his cheeks as he studied the picture, then looked over at Beth. "How?" was all he could manage to say.

"I am a detective, you know," Beth's voice catching as she wiped away a tear. She looked at Reece and nodded her to come over.

"Beth told me that was the only picture you had on your other boat," Reece said. "So, I reached out to Erika. I knew your ex had the picture and she had a copy made for you."

All he could do was shake his head, speechless and crying. Beth reached over and put her arm around his shoulder.

He looked at his friends gathered around the table. They were nodding in approval. There was so much he wanted to say, but he struggled to find the words. After a few minutes, he found his voice.

"Thank you all. I don't have the words to express how much I love you and how much I appreciate everything." He looked around and waved his arm. "I love *Nightbird*. She's perfect." Making an allusion to *Trouble No More,* he added with a wry grin, "And, I definitely won't change the name."

Everyone laughed and came over to give him another round of hugs. Eventually, the crowd thinned out. Addie, Marie, Ricky, and Beth helped him clean up. Ricky and Marie slipped out, leaving Addie and Beth.

"I've got a bar to run," Addie said as she prepared to leave. "Take the night off, but I expect you to be back at work tomorrow."

Jon hugged her. "Thank you. For everything."

"Don't get all mushy on me," she said, laughing. "I wouldn't know what to do." She waved goodbye as she stepped onto the dock and headed to Hank's Galley.

Beth made one more pass to make sure everything was clean. "I think you're set."

He followed her off *Nightbird* onto the dock, where she turned to face him. "So, are you ever going to tell me the truth about what happened out there?"

He knew she was asking about the confrontation on the high seas. "I told you the same thing I told the Coast Guard. Halfway to the Bahamas, we found Cal's yacht disabled and on fire. Marie was on the swim platform. We got her off, but it sank before I could look for Nora."

Beth stared at him. "I'm sure you know what Marie told the investigators."

Marie had stated that pirates stopped *WesTex* and boarded while she and Nora hid. They heard gunfire and then heard the intruders leave. When they emerged, Ramon and Cal were nowhere to be found. Smoke and flames were billowing out of the rear hatch, and the boat was sinking. Nora went below to get her valuables, then Jon and Ricky appeared.

He shrugged. "I know what she told us when we rescued her, but I wasn't on board, so I don't know what happened. All I know is what I just told you."

She shook her head. "Why were you and Ricky going after Cal? And why wouldn't Cal have radioed someone that pirates were attacking them? You didn't know Nora was on board?"

"I told you—and them. I wanted Cal to know I had the evidence and persuade him to turn himself in. Since I wasn't on board, I don't know what Cal did or didn't do. And I didn't know Nora was on the boat until Marie mentioned it."

"You and Ricky didn't see anyone leaving *WesTex?*"

"No. We saw a few other boats out and about, but none we could identify. Why don't you send divers down or salvage it?"

"It sank in over a thousand feet of water, probably not intact. Other than possibly Nora Jenkins, we don't think anyone else was on board. It's just not practical to salvage it."

"I don't know what else to tell you."

She stared at him for a few seconds, then shook her head. "We've got statements from you, Ricky, and Marie. I guess that'll have to do. So, when are you going to take me out on your new boat?"

"Whenever you want." He looked down at her. "Thank you. I know you were the one responsible for all of this."

She shook her head. "No, everyone here had a part, Jon. We all wanted to do this. Despite your cantankerous ways, you are much loved."

As they stood there, a ginger cat strolled up and rubbed against Beth's leg.

"Felix?" Jon said, incredulous. He stared at the cat, questioning his vision. Although thinner and scruffier, the cat had the same white vest and other markings. If it wasn't Felix, it was a doppelganger.

Beth reached down and petted him, scratching his chin. Jon could hear him purring.

"Where the hell have you been?" he asked.

"Maybe he's been waiting on you to come back."

Acknowledgments

A few years ago, I read a transcript of an NPR broadcast by Peter Haden on WLRN in South Florida. It grabbed me by the throat and I started writing this story. But COVID-19 as well as another book intervened, so I had to put it on the back burner. This year, I finally returned to it and finished what is now known as *Treatment Plan*. I encourage you to read the following link:

https://www.npr.org/2017/06/06/531714290/opioid-overdoses-overwhelm-south-floridas-addiction-centers

Thanks to the following generous people for taking the time to read my manuscript and offer much-appreciated advice: Otis Scarbary, Cindy Deane, Diann Schindler, Jo Gilley, Linda Whitaker, and Linda Reynolds.

A special thanks to Christian Jurs and Rich Vaughn for their patience and help with my technical questions.

I am grateful to find Michael Totten as an editor. His comments and advice were most helpful.

Thanks to Bob O'Lary, photographer extraordinaire and friend, for the author photo.

Once again, kudos to Carl Graves. He has done all my covers and continues to amaze me.

And, as always, thanks to my wife, June, for continuing to support my writing habit. I couldn't do it without you.

Any mistakes that remain are mine.

Made in United States
Orlando, FL
01 December 2023

39733715R00188